The Testimony of Bendigo Fletcher

Keira F. Jacobs

Ironcroft Publishing
P.O. Box 370 Hartland, MI 48353

First Edition 2022
ISBNs: 978-0-9771688-7-3 (paperback), 978-0-9771688-8-0 (ebook)

Cover art © 2022 by Violet Design
Editing by Robin LeeAnn
Formatting by Jeff Fenzel

For my dad. You are the reason I write.
And for my mom, for loving Bendigo as much as I do.

"I hereby testify that all parts of this journey are true."
    \-   Bendigo Fletcher

The City of Orenda: 400 years ago

No one knows where The Book of Prophecy came from. Only how it was found.

On a bitter winter night, a single librarian weathered the tundra in Orenda's empty streets. All the windows in the cobblestone city had been shut tight, blocking the pestering frost that dared to seep through the cracks. He pulled his cloak tighter around his neck and buried his chin inside its scratchy wool.

An irritating nag tapped against his temples. He had to bear the weather *twice* due to his tiring forgetfulness. He had made it all the way home only to realize that he hadn't smothered the candles in his office before leaving for the night. Now, the air seemed to nip at his nose harder, and his numb skin did little to lessen the bite.

The library door creaked as he forced its frozen hinges open and stepped inside, pausing in the dim space to listen. He knew he was the only one in this equally frigid and musty space, yet he felt that he was not alone. Which was nonsense, of course, because he was the only one who held the key to this treasured building. It was *his* library. He knew every spine on each shelf, and his eyes were always drawn to where his apprentices had misplaced a book.

Like now. He noticed a leather-bound book that had been shelved incorrectly. The shelf was obviously reserved for the dark blue spines of mathematics books, and this book did not belong.

He made his way to the book and ran his fingers down the spine. It was bumpy with vine-like engravings, and upon touching it, a strange clash of conviction and glee exploded in his chest. He yanked his hand away, his heart speeding.

Then his hands touched it again. This time, he pulled it down and threw the cover open. But nothing was there. He fanned through the pages with his thumb, examining the entire book in one sweeping scan to confirm that what he saw was true.

All the pages were blank.

No words, no pictures, and no maps. Nothing. The leather cover had promised something spectacular, but after investigating, it seemed mindless. An unfulfilled promise. Yet something about it made the librarian stuff it into his cloak.

He rushed to the library's back room, blowing out the candles he had so hastily forgotten about earlier that evening.

The frosty air stung his face once again on his second trek home through the cobblestone streets. He shuddered, listening for any sign of invasion. Magical creatures had been getting closer to the city of Orenda. The People of the World—who were fighting them off—had sent word two days ago, warning Orenda of encroaching danger.

Magic always had a place in the world of Tarsha. Until The People of the World deemed it too dangerous. Too powerful. Too untrustworthy. To keep the creatures who housed it away, The People of the World built an army founded on fear and pride. They outcasted those who were born with magic or used it. The two sides held bitter hatred toward each other for years until a war erupted. It had been three years since, and there seemed to be no end in sight.

The librarian entered his single-room dwelling, safe from the cold at last. He placed the mysterious book on his kitchen table and strode over to the fireplace. As he struggled to thaw his stiff fingers over the fresh flames, a loud, heavy thud sounded. He turned his head.

The book lay open on the floor.

He stiffened and rotated his body to see what could have caused it to fall, thinking that perhaps a winter gust had swept through an open window. Though that was not the case.

Ink now filled its once blank pages. Black words seeped out to create sentence after sentence, as if an invisible hand used a quill that never ran dry. The sentences formed stories. Stories of war and hate and triumph. Reading them, he soon found that the sentences weren't words of a story passed but words of a story to be.

In the weeks that followed, every word in the book proved to be a prophetic telling of the war. Word of this mystical tome spread fast throughout the city. Everyone wanted to see the stories of tomorrow and prepare for the battles to come.

Each night, after the moon had taken its place, the people of Orenda would light their torches, brave the cold together, and flood to the librarian's home. The librarian would stand at his second story window and recite the prophecies that had appeared that day to the masses in the streets below. Sometimes, the stories took hours, leaving the Orendans trembling and numb in the dead of winter's night.

The book gave The People of the World the upper hand in the war, and their continuous sulking and fear subsided day by day. Orendans praised the librarian, naming him the Keeper of The Book of Prophecy. Enthralled with their newfound knowledge, they were too preoccupied to notice a new evil worse than magic had crept into their world.

This new evil had descended from the spiritual realm—a place that was untouchable to any living being and only spoken of as someplace that would be a sanctuary in death. A sacred thought. A peaceful belief. It was never told through myths that evil beings resided within that treasured realm. Perhaps no one knew. But the Twilights' appearance brought that reality to life.

They came as an army of wispy, black-cloaked spirits who desired control in both life and death. They took advantage of the war and suffocated Tarsha with death and disaster. Crops died. People faded into insanity. Families turned on one another. Their powerful presence overtook The People of the World and magical creatures alike. It seemed as if nothing could prevent their reign.

It was then that The Book of Prophecy closed.

A full year had passed since the Keeper had first been in possession of it. On a frosty night, just like the previous year, a rumbling shook Orenda's city walls. A darkness came over the moon so heavily that some claimed the moon fell from the sky.

The Keeper rose from his seat by the fireplace, still holding onto The Book. He shook and heaved at the last sentence he had laid eyes on before The Book's cover slammed shut, unable to open again. He feared to tell his fellow Orendans the prophecy, knowing it would destroy them. Though keeping it a secret would not save them from the fate they all now faced.

That night, Orendans traveled as a herd with their torches lit and their cloaks drawn around their bodies to hear the new prophecy.

"The Twilight army has left us," the Keeper proclaimed from his window.

Mumbles of uncertainty rumbled through the crowd.

"Though they fought hard and gained power over us, they could not overtake our souls in this life as they had wished. But they have taken something more precious in their departure."

More mumbles, further concerned this time.

"They have stolen the afterlife from us. We now live only to face darkness upon our deaths. They may not have us here, but they will have us there."

The fear that had once gripped The People of the World

now turned into horror as they wailed through the streets, crying out to the sky as they pleaded for the Twilights to give them back hope in life after death. But no matter how desperate their cries, the evil gave them no pity.

The winter turned even harsher, the frost too invasive to keep from crawling under the doors, and the falling snow was bitter to the touch instead of the fluffy wet clumps that usually laid atop Orenda's roofs. But worse than the weather's turn was the Orendan's desperation to hear a hopeful word from The Book of Prophecy again.

Yet The Book remained closed.

For seven days, the Keeper stayed hidden in his dwelling, sleeping with The Book on his chest. He woke only to set it down by the fire and watch it lie still all day. Over and over, like a spinning wheel, the thought of darkness after death consumed him. He skipped meals, didn't wash, and didn't buy more wood for his fireplace. There was no reason to live life with purpose if the end led to nothing.

The Orendans believed the same thing. Except they grew desperate enough to take to the streets one extra bitter night. Raging flames lit their torches as they flocked to the Keeper's dwelling like they had so many times before. Only this time, they didn't mean to hear words from him. They wanted to *take* the words from him.

They bellowed and thundered through the streets with intent to rip The Book from him and pry it open themselves, forcing the pages to speak another ending.

The Keeper heard the approaching shouts, and it drew

him to his windowsill to find their angry faces marching toward his dwelling. His heart leaped to his throat when he realized the danger they brought. He then *wanted* to live, though it was for nothing.

He staggered back from the window and fell over himself to get to The Book. Without reason or clarity, he knew he had to keep it safe and away from the Orendans. Prying it open would only result in more turmoil and unrest. He knew. He had already tried. A dense fog had seeped into his dwelling where it hung for three days, watching him every second and keeping him afraid to ever try it again. The Book was more than a source of knowledge. It was power. It needed to leave Orenda.

The Orendans' angry shouts thundered closer and echoed in the frosted streets below. The Keeper grabbed the warmest cloak he owned, and he barely had it draped around his body as he and The Book made for the back stairway that led to the alley behind his dwelling. The air stung his face, and his feet clattered onto the cobblestone. His fingers shivered as he held The Book against his chest and under his cloak. He heard the mob breaking through his front door on the other side of the building, but he gave no care to the state of his possessions as his legs carried him through the frosted night.

The cobblestone eventually broke apart and gave way to brittle, stiff fields of dormant tall grass. The Keeper carried on, crunching over the weeds. Up ahead in the distance stood a barn that housed Orenda's working animals. He knew he had to have four-legged help if he wanted to depart quicker. His heart sped as he blindly collected the first horse from the front stall and mounted it. The other animals in the barn shifted and moaned at the disturbance in this ungodly hour.

The Book jostled against the Keeper's chest as he leaned down into the horse's ear and whispered, "To Whimselon."

His own directions startled him. The words had departed from his mouth without thought. He clutched The Book even tighter as the horse jolted forward, understanding the command. They galloped into the forest and left Orenda behind.

Why had the village of Whimselon been his choice of escape? Perhaps because it was the farthest west on the map. Or maybe it was because the people there held such a stature of vanity that they would be more prone to keep The Book a secret just for the sake of possessing a treasure that no one else had.

But as the horse ripped through the winter night, the Keeper felt in his deepest discernment that The Book itself had chosen Whimselon. That perhaps The Book knew of a future where Whimselon could offer an end to hopeless days.

Even if it took four hundred years.

One: Whimselon [Wim-sa-lon]

Bendigo Fletcher bent over to roll up his linen pant legs. The water in the woodland marshes had risen since the last rainfall. Even though he was on the outskirts of Whimselon where the marshes would dry up—giving way to packed, muddy ground—the swamp was unusually deep. He rolled his pants up to the bottom of his calves but decided the water was still too high, so he pulled the cloth to just below his kneecaps and chuckled at how he now looked like one of Whimselon's gardening women.

He used his hand to shove his smile down. Better not risk getting caught laughing to himself in the thick of the forest, alone. Most of Whimselon already side-eyed him when he passed by. He knew many wondered why he delighted in keeping to himself or—better yet—delighted in avoiding conversation. The fact that he laughed to himself didn't need to be reviewed on top of his withdrawn behavior.

With bare feet, Bendigo stepped onto the marsh, not sinking into the mud but resting lightly on top. Being a Whim, his bones were too light to break the muck's surface. He tilted his dark-haired head back to check the time. The sun was starting to set, casting a golden glow on the highest twigs of the tallest bald cypress trees. If he didn't hurry, he might miss his window of time. He needed to get into one of the trees to see if he could spot the abnormal shadows he had seen last night.

His stomach tightened a little, thinking about seeing strange apparitions floating on the horizon line. The first time he saw them was an accident; he had just been hiding out in one of his favorite trees, trying to get a perfect view of the coral and mango colored sky as the sun dipped low. But he saw strange shapes instead, so he had to come back for another look.

Grabbing onto a branch with gray moss hanging so low it touched the tip of the swamp, Bendigo swung his tall, lanky figure up to a perched stance. He stood and moved to the tree's trunk on the balls of his feet. With quick, fluid motions, he traveled upward from branch to branch until he webbed through the fragile twigs at the top. They bent beneath him but didn't give way, thanks to his light bones.

His head broke through the top. He gazed above the moss-covered trees that decorated the marshland. A few miles out, thousands of twinkling lanterns dotted the horizon where the Whims had created a beautiful community of treehouses. It grew every year with not only places to live but also businesses. Whimselon sold or traded the best herb medicine in all of Tarsha. Most businesses benefited from and supported the herb trade one way or the other. Like too many other Whims, the herb business was Bendigo's future.

His gaze moved to look toward the setting sun. The red glowing mass still sat above the horizon line. Silhouetted against the sun's fiery light were black, wispy shadows that moved in and out of each other. He clenched the twig that kept him steady. They appeared bigger since last night, slightly closer to Whimselon. Their shape was hard to make out from this far away, but at moments, it seemed like they took on a form similar to himself. Arms and a head but not really legs per se. Their bottom half floated out like a black cloak that faded to wisps.

Bendigo squinted, trying to gain as much focus as he could. There were a lot of them, but he still couldn't figure out what they were exactly.

Looking down at the marsh below, he shrugged away a shudder. Though he had only fallen a few times, he could slip, sail to the ground, and break his neck. It would all be over. Done. Darkness would be the only thing that awaited because that was all there was.

He knew about the afterlife that *used* to promise peace after death. While Tarsha's ancestors had fought to contain magic and suppress its power, an unknown evil had slid in undetected and conquered them both, stealing the afterlife as its own.

"Hey!" a voice sprang into Bendigo's ear.

He jumped, almost losing his grasp on the twigs that held him. The spike of startlement ceased when he saw Willy sitting below him, a grin spreading wide across her dirt-streaked face.

"Willy." He dropped down to her. "You shouldn't do that. It's not fair to whimsle a Whim." Whimsle was what the Whims called it when a Whim sneaked up on something. Mainly for hunting an animal, which made sense. Not normally on people.

"I don't care if it's fair or not." She pushed the loose sandy-colored hair back from her bun. "It's fun."

He smiled. He really wanted to be alone out here tonight, especially since today was one of his more withdrawn days, but he knew that having company usually snapped him out of his uncontrollable sadness. "What are you doing all the way out here?"

She followed him down the tree, back toward the marsh. "Looking for something fun to do."

He landed quietly on the ground. "All the way out here?" He didn't turn around to help her; he knew she wouldn't want it.

"Yeah." She landed next to him. "I finished studying hours ago."

"You finished all the botany assignments? Already?"

"You didn't? Ben, come on. This is our last year of academics. Don't you know how to weasel your way through it yet?"

"I just don't do it." He shrugged and walked away from her.

"Really? If I knew that, I would have stopped doing it years ago! Why didn't you tell me?"

"Because it's a bad idea? I'm not doing well."

Willy strode next to Bendigo as they waded through the marsh, back in the direction of the treehouses. "Do you just not care?"

"I really don't. I'm just going to work with my brother in our herb business."

She drew up her nose. "That sounds so boring though. No wonder you're sad all the time."

He felt the familiar pang of being misunderstood and put up one more brick on his internal emotional wall.

"Not in a bad way." She seemed oblivious. "You like to be sad, don't you?"

"What makes you think I *like* to be sad?"

"Well, you like to be alone."

"That's true."

But it was *because* he felt sad that he liked to be alone. He just didn't know why he was sad. The sadness would come on like a heavy wave, fogging his brain. He would withdraw, hoping to clear his head, but being alone only made him sadder, which made him want to be alone. It was a vicious cycle.

Although, it was also the reason why he didn't mind Willy bothering him all the time. She had always been around since they were young—at first uninvited and then eventually an unlikely best friend. As children, not a day went by that they weren't together, unless her parents came up with another reason to put her on house arrest. She had a knack for talking his ear off and being too pushy, but her presence usually snapped him out of his mental fog.

Though he had never told her that.

"Well, what were *you* doing out here?" She snagged a piece of long grass as she walked and whittled it between her fingers.

He glanced sideways at her. "Have you seen the shadows riding in with the sunset?"

"Shadows? No. What kind of shadows?"

"They don't really look like shadows. I just don't know what else to call them." He waved his hand, mimicking the shadows' motion. "They float like they have no legs, but sometimes when they weave in and out of each other, they look like they have arms and a head. They're still too far out to get a good look, but I feel like they're headed for Whimselon."

"It could be some sort of magic," Willy suggested.

"Yes, but coming from where? Not the Orphic Forest in the east; these are coming from the west."

Bendigo had never seen whatever was beyond the western sea. Most Whims hadn't. Their village had a small delegation that would make a five-day trip to fish and bring back game, but other than that, not one Whim had ever ventured farther out into the open waters. Bendigo had never even *set eyes* on the sea.

"I don't know, but there have been rumors about weird things happening," Willy said. "I heard yesterday that a farmer from Lhan had set his own barn on fire and danced in his field as it burned."

Bendigo cringed. He had heard rumors that towns miles

away were experiencing unusual circumstances: strange behaviors from their people, unnatural acts of nature, and mysterious disappearances. It brought out the fear that everyone in Tarsha had been trying to contain for the past four hundred years. "*Dancing* as it *burned?*"

Willy drew up her nose. "That's what I heard. It's bone-chilling, isn't it?"

"You can absolutely say that." He already felt a little less withdrawn, warming up to her presence as she jabbered on. "Has anything out of the ordinary happened in Whimselon? I haven't really noticed anything."

"No." She shrugged. "All everyone pays attention to is if The Book has opened or not."

"We would know if it opened."

"Do you think it ever will again?"

He looked around at the blue haze that fell on the marshland, which told him that they wouldn't make it back to the treehouses before dark. "What would be the point of The Book if it never opened again?"

She didn't reply.

The two slunk through the trees and back to their lighted town in silence. Well, Bendigo stayed quiet. Willy never stopped talking. As usual.

They crossed the cedar bridge under the wooden archway that had *Whimselon* carved into it with white paint filling in the letters. Little boardwalks zigged and zagged over the soft ground, connecting different sets of wooden stairs. Lanterns hung in the trees lining the wooden drawbridges that suspended every which way. They lived on opposite sides of the treehouse clan. A shame, considering how much time they spent together.

Bendigo placed his hand on his stairway's railing. "Guess I'll see you later?"

"Yeah." She glanced over her shoulder.

Bendigo followed her gaze to her treehouse: a lopsided, shingled base with a thin, pointed roof. He knew she hated going home. Her parents weren't fond of her. It had always been like that, sadly.

Whimselon really was a peaceful place. Beautiful and simple. But ideologies suffocated it beneath the surface, vanity being the worst one. He knew her parents were disappointed at how she looked. She didn't have the beautiful blond hair that most Whims had, and a few freckles dotted her face. A flaw, apparently. Bendigo carried the usual delicate features of Whims with the rigid eye frame and sharp nose, but she was different. Her eyes were rounder, and her grin took up half her face. She wasn't a frail, angelic figure.

He turned and headed up the steps. "Night, Willy. Come find me tomorrow before the academy. You can help me with the botany assignments I so intentionally forgot about."

She blew air into her falling bangs. "You wish."

He grinned, knowing she would come to his aid. "Goodnight." Turning his back, he trod up the steps.

"Why have you always been nice to me?" She sounded

softer than her normal self.

He stopped, used to her brazen remarks. He looked down the railing to find her standing still on the boardwalk in the middle of the marsh. "Why wouldn't I be?"

"Because no one else is."

He gave her a smile and tilted his chin down, giving her a stern look of disagreement. "Don't say things like that."

She looked at her feet.

"I'll see you tomorrow. *Goodnight*, Willy." He ascended the stairs and watched her make it to her house before he moved across a hanging bridge.

Bendigo came to his and his older brother's treehouse and sped up the rope ladder to the porch. He pushed open the door his mom had painted yellow years ago and stepped inside. His brother, Zachary, had a fire going in the mud molded fireplace, while he repotted and watered about twenty different herbs into red clay pots on their scuffed kitchen table.

Zachary had a sturdier, more fit shape than his brother, making Bendigo seem even thinner than he already was. But they shared the same brown hair. That was the only similarity between the boys.

Bendigo plopped down into a wooden chair tucked under the table. "Still working?"

"I got behind." Zachary glanced up. "I thought I'd have help tonight."

"Oh." He dragged a pot toward him. "You could've just asked."

"I did."

"Oh…" His voice trailed.

"This morning."

"Oh…"

Zachary brushed his hands together over a pot to get rid of the excess dirt. "What's wrong?"

"Has The Book opened?"

He frowned. "No?"

"Has the Keeper said *anything* weird is happening?"

"No. It's been the same old, same old." He pushed down on the dirt again with his fingertips. "Why are you asking? I wouldn't be the first to know anyway."

"I bet you would be." Bendigo slid a mint sprout into his pot. "Everyone here thinks of you as their leader."

He shook his head. "That's just because Dad died to save Whimselon. That's all. I wouldn't have done the same thing. Not for this vain town."

Bendigo gazed out the window at the glow of Whimselon's nightlife. He remembered that terrible night. A woodland dragon from the Orphic Forest had somehow made its way to Whimselon. They had begged their father not to fight it since he was their only parent left. But their father was a good man. As the woodland dragon killed him, he killed the dragon, saving Whimselon but leaving his two sons to fend alone. The dagger he used was pulled from the dragon's chest and given to the boys. It now sat in a glass box above the fireplace on the wooden mantle. A reminder of the night the boys were left alone.

"Why are you asking about The Book anyway?" Zachary had stopped potting again. "It's been through six Keepers in the last four hundred years, and it's *never* opened."

"Something is coming to Whimselon, and I don't think it's just a type of magic passing through." Bendigo stood. "I see it coming from the west when the sun is setting."

"What does it look like?"

"Black cloaks. Floating like they're shadows but contorting like they're alive."

Zachary's gaze hardened. "You see Twilights."

"There's no way."

"This isn't good, Bendigo."

"How can you be sure they're Twilights?"

"They're drawn in every history book and explained in horrific detail."

Bendigo's pulse quickened. "What can they do to us?"

"They can turn brother against brother and nature against man. Their return means one thing: death."

A chill pricked at his neck. "Death to who?"

"Whoever gets in their way," Zachary whispered into the pot between his hands. "They want the world as their own. They couldn't have it then, but they may have found a way now. They've had four hundred years to figure it out."

"So, what do we do? There has to be a way to stop them. Isn't there?" He rubbed his palms on his thighs, trying to rid nervous sweat.

Zachary rubbed his eyes.

"Zach?"

"Just pray they pass over Whimselon." He stood, leaving the herb job incomplete.

"What are the odds that they skip us?"

He turned away.

"Zach, we can't just *avoid* their coming. Don't you at least want to explore the thought of stopping them?"

A laugh erupted from his mocking lips. "*Stopping them?* Are you hearing yourself, Ben? They are an evil magic; we are People of the World. We're better off submitting to their reign if it comes down to it."

"And live a life that's worse than the one we already live?"

"Bendigo, what is so bad about this life? You ought to be grateful that you're even alive. If it weren't for Dad's sacrifice, we wouldn't be here."

"But what is the *point* of being here?"

Zachary spun and leaned over him. "To live life to the fullest and avoid the darkness of death for as long as you can. This life is short, and we have nothing waiting for us when our time is up, so you better not take this life for granted. That's selfish."

The threat of tears tapped on Bendigo's eyes. "We have nothing to hope for."

"You're right. But that's just how it is. Fearing death will do nothing good for you."

"But neither will living an aimless life."

Zachary waved him off. "You live with your head in the clouds."

"Better there than here."

The astonishment on Zachary's face told Bendigo that he had gone too far. "I'm done talking to you. Hopefully in the morning, you'll have collected yourself and realized how awful your words are."

"I didn't mean to—"

"Goodnight." He strode into one of their small rooms and drew the curtain closed.

The sting of his brother's words danced around in Bendigo's head. *You live with your head in the clouds.* And he did. It was the only way he could escape these hopeless days. A part of him actually *wished* something evil would come. Especially if that meant having a chance at a fruitful life. But the thought felt wrong, so he pushed it from his mind.

He strayed over to the kitchen window that overlooked the village. Was he the only one left who cared about other places besides Whimselon? No one ever ventured out. No one ever traveled. No one ever wondered. He wondered every day though. He wondered about others. If they were kind, if they were brave. Maybe others in the world felt the same way he did.

Sleep wouldn't be on his side tonight, but eventually, he climbed into his bed that was tucked in the very back room of the treehouse.

The familiar sense of loneliness swallowed him whole. No one understood him or even tried to. Ever since his father's death, Zachary had pushed and shoved and forced him to stop dreaming and to think realistically. He tried—

he really did—but he was just...sad. It was like the word had been written on his heart and couldn't be cleansed.

So, like every other night, he closed his eyes and let sorrow comfort him to sleep.

Two: The Ports of Orphic

There they were again: the whispers that had been waking Shem up in the middle of the night. He sat straight up in bed and threw his covers aside. His long braid brushed his bare back as he tried to stay relatively quiet while running to the window. He lived above a group of fishermen who had to be up before sunrise to head out from the Ports. If he woke them, they wouldn't be too happy.

Shem pushed the tiny, hinged window open and leaned his head out. The smell of the sea and the damp deck wood gusted across his face. The Ports stayed silent, as they usually were at night. The only sound came from the wooden fishing boats that occasionally tapped the decks they were tied to. He scanned the docks below, looking for the source of the whispers. He knew he wouldn't actually see anyone. He never did.

The moon sat right above the sea, where the port channel met the open water. His heart stopped when he saw movement. Black masses hovered in the moonlight, gliding across the sea's surface. Twilights. He had never seen one personally until now, but the legends were enough to make him believe that was what they were.

And he knew they meant death.

As quickly as possible, he grabbed the tan tunic he had worn yesterday and pulled it over his toned body. Pieces of his hair fell out of his braid as he leaned down to shove his boots on. He snatched his sword up from his dresser, getting a quick glimpse of himself in the mirror hanging above.

He paused. He looked older since the last time he had passed himself in the mirror. His twenty-eight-year-old face had a few more lines, and his eyes were less bright. Tired. Tired of carrying the burden of being the only fighter in the Ports of Orphic. Everyone relied on him to keep the Ports safe, and he could never let them down.

Shoving his sword into the scabbard that hung around his waist, Shem left his single-room shack and darted down the wooden stairs that led to the docks. The wind had picked up, keeping his loose hairs out of his face. The water lapped up over the wooden walkways. His boots splashed against the damp, slick wood as he jogged to the end of the docks. He kept his hand on his sword as he gazed out toward the horizon.

He no longer saw the Twilights. Gone. As fast as they had come, they had disappeared. He didn't move though. He closed his eyes as the wind continued to pick up. Something was definitely happening. The sea hadn't felt this threatening in months. The only time the channel waters had gotten as high as this was when a storm was coming, but no black clouds moved in the distance. Something *else* was happening.

Shem let out a tired breath. He eased himself down and rested against the wooden post at the end of the dock. He knew he had to stay here, make sure nothing entered the Ports that weren't supposed to. At least he'd gotten a few hours of sleep. The wind blew across his shoulders and down his shirt, chilling his core and making him wish he had grabbed his cloak.

He closed his eyes and thought about his wife. She would have had a fire going inside their shack to make sure he was warm when he returned, even though he would have told her she didn't need to. She may have even stolen a few glances out their window to make sure he was still safe. His peaceful thoughts trailed to hurtful ones of when she had demanded he stay at the Ports while she left for the city of Orenda. The cobblestone city had promised better medicine than their harbor town. She had promised to come back when she got better, but that was eight years ago now.

He always wondered if she made it to Orenda or not. Maybe she got better and decided to stay. Maybe she didn't get better at all…

Shem opened his eyes and forced the thought from his head. It didn't matter now. He couldn't let those thoughts cloud his judgment. Not when Twilights were out on the sea somewhere.

☾

"Excuse me."

Shem's eyes shot open. It was still early enough that the

morning light was more blue than white. The wind had died down, and the docks were slowly coming to life. A couple fishermen up the harbor checked their nets and untied their boats. But what had awoken him was a voice down toward the water.

A little wooden boat floated about two feet from the dock. A man sat inside of it, looking up at Shem. "I'm sorry if I woke you," he said, looking calm, relaxed.

Shem pushed himself up to his feet and grabbed his neck, trying to stretch the kinks out. "I shouldn't have been sleeping anyway. Are you a merchant wanting to pass through the Orphic Forest? You can tie your boat farther up the channel."

The man smiled slightly. "I'm not a merchant."

Shem studied him. He had olive skin that made his brown eyes seem lighter than they really were. The scruff on his face and his shoulder length hair made Shem think the man had been out at sea for weeks, but his ankle-length cloak was untarnished. Not made from quality material but clean.

"Do you have a name?" Shem reached forward to grab a rope from the man.

The man tossed it to him. "Dagon."

"A last name?" He slipped the rope around a deck post and pulled it tight, drawing the fishing boat closer to the platform.

"Just Dagon."

He anchored himself into a secure stance and reached

forward, grabbing Dagon's forearm to help him out of the boat. When they touched, a warm sensation flooded through his entire body. All his muscles relaxed, and for a moment, he felt peace.

"Thank you." Dagon shook his hand. "It feels good to be on land."

He was so taken aback by the peaceful feeling that he fought to speak clearly. "Yeah. Can I help you get to where you're going?"

Dagon gazed around the harbor. "I've just arrived."

"You mean your destination is here? The Ports of Orphic? Are you sure? People only come here when they want to continue traveling through the Orphic Forest to get to Orenda or through the Horemburg Forest to get to Lhan. No one actually *stays* here."

"Well, I'm staying here." Dagon's scruff moved with his smile. "What's your name?"

"Shem."

"Why were you sleeping out on the end of the dock? Do you not have a place to stay?"

"No, I have a place to stay. I was on watch."

Dagon tilted his head. "Asleep?"

"I wasn't supposed to fall asleep," Shem admitted.

"Was someone supposed to take over the watch this morning?"

"No. I'm the only one."

"The only one who stands watch?"

Shem studied him. "That's right."

Dagon placed a hand on Shem's shoulder. "You look tired. I'm tired. Is there anywhere we can get some of that coffee I keep hearing about?"

Shem squinted and paused. How did Dagon know that the Ports had coffee? They were the only place besides Orenda that had it, and no one knew that. It was a Port secret. Something they enjoyed quietly, so people wouldn't travel from all over to take it away from them.

"Yes, we have coffee." Shem looked up toward the day bar where one of the retired fishermen cooked breakfast every morning, even when ice storms closed everyone in. "Let's go get some. I like the sound of that."

As they entered the dingy day bar, Dagon looked around, examining the wooden interior that was lit only by the natural light that poured in through the three front windows.

The fisherman appeared behind the wooden counter. "Good morning, Shem."

"Hey, Mitch." Shem sat on a bar stool. "Did you already brew coffee?"

Mitch grabbed two metal mugs. "Already served quite a few cups. Who's your friend?"

"Dagon." He tilted his head to the side. "Just arrived this morning."

Dagon only smiled and nodded.

Mitch seemed to get caught in a stare when he made eye contact with Dagon. "Right. Well, here you go." He slid the cups toward the men. "Enjoy. Any breakfast this morning?"

"Might as well." Shem rubbed his tired eyes. "For me and Dagon. On me."

Mitch nodded and headed to the back.

"Much appreciated." Dagon looked down at his cup. "So, tell me, does this really make you feel alive?"

"In a way." Shem brought the cup to his lips. "It makes you feel awake."

Dagon tasted the black liquid, made a slight face, and then nodded. "Does this taste good to you?"

Shem tried to hide a laugh. "You just have to get used to it. In Orenda, they pour milk into it to cut the bitterness, but we use our milk sparingly here. So, we drink it black. I like it better bitter anyway."

"Then I will try to like it bitter as well," Dagon teased like they were old friends.

Shem tapped his tarnished ring against his cup. "So, if you're not a merchant, why are you here?"

Dagon drew in a deep breath. "Has a traveler been through here lately?"

"Every day. All people do is travel through here. None stay though."

"No one has asked to stay?"

"Only you."

Dagon hummed a low tone. "I must be early."

Shem's heart rate rose a little. "Is someone coming to meet you here?"

"That's what I was told."

"By who?"

Dagon brought the cup to his lips again. "Why are you the only watchman on the docks?"

Shem paused, wanting to pry the information out of Dagon, but decided it was better to let the conversation carry on. "It's just how it is. The fisherman here either go out to fish or are retired and too old to protect the harbor. It just landed on me. That's all."

"But you don't mind it," Dagon stated like he knew.

"I like doing it. I love the people here."

"It's rare for someone to do something solely out of love these days. Especially for someone as young as you."

Shem shook his head. "I'm twenty-eight. I'm not *that* young."

"I still consider myself young." Dagon lifted his mug toward Shem. "But if you say twenty-eight is emerging into elderhood, then I'm *in* elderhood."

"Come on. You can't be much older than me."

"Around thirty-two."

Shem slammed a sip of coffee down. "See? You're not much older than me. And what do you mean *around* thirty-two? You don't know your actual birthday?"

"No." Dagon didn't seem to mind the questions. "I just know the year. Roughly."

He spun his cup with his finger. Dagon was a strange one. The man blew in from the sea with no other destination and no birthday. Yet he felt like they were similar. Friends even. Normally, he wouldn't trust a stranger this fast, but he sensed no threat in Dagon's presence. If anything, it made him feel like the Ports had gained an ally.

Dagon peered over at Shem's cup. "You really drank that fast."

Shem refocused. "Yeah. I told you I like it bitter. The harder you try to like it, the more you really do like it."

Dagon chuckled. "I must need to try harder." He took a huge sip and pounded the table with his fist as he forced it down.

Shem broke out into laughter, something he hadn't done in a long time.

"How was that?" His eyes watered in pain.

"Much better." Shem slapped his back.

The two new friends ate breakfast together that morning. A ritual that would go on for the next few days. Until the traveler arrived.

Three: Whimselon

The feeling of being shaken awoke Bendigo. His bed frame knocked against the wall and scooted across the floor. He sat up, gasping for air, as books and pictures fell from his shelves. Dirt particles from the ceiling sprayed down over his face. He threw his covers to the side. The sound of pots crashing made him run into the kitchen.

Zachary emerged from his bedroom with a lantern in his hand.

"What's going on?" Bendigo looked around their house. Everything shook. The walls. The floors. The furniture.

"Get outside." Zachary shoved him toward the door. "Hurry."

He burst through the front door and slid down the rope ladder to the hanging walkways. The drawbridges rocked as if wind whipped them around like a kite. He gripped the bridge's ropes and struggled to stay upright. Everyone around him fled their treehouses, heading to the ground for safety. He followed the crowd. Anxious cries and shouts filled the air as Bendigo and Zach landed in the marsh grass, squishing together with everyone else.

"Bendigo!" Willy slid in between the crowd to get to his side.

He grabbed her arm. "You okay?"

"I'm fine. What's happening?"

All of Whimselon had gathered in the center of the marsh, looking up at their rattling treehouse town. Bendigo looked toward the highest tree, where the Keeper's tower sat peaking above the tips of the twigs. The single window cast out an orange glow. A window that was usually dark.

The quake suddenly stopped.

The bridges swung slower until they eventually suspended into silence. The treehouses didn't rattle against their host branches, and the cries of distress faded. All the Whims stood still, huddling together.

A cry arose from the crowd. "The Keeper is coming!"

Some Whims mumbled to each other. Others craned their necks in the direction of the Keeper's tower to see if he *was* in fact coming.

Bendigo couldn't get his eyes high enough over everyone's heads. "Zach, can you see?"

Willy pulled on his arm. "Is he really coming?"

"There he is!" Zach pointed. He looked down at Bendigo. "You knew. Last night, you knew."

Bendigo cast his eyes at the ground. He hadn't known; he had only wished. Now he feared. Feared that his wish may have come true. That something *bad* would turn the world inside out.

Not a word was spoken as the crowd turned to face the Keeper. His robe hung down past his feet, and his glasses sat on the end of his nose. He had been the Keeper of The

Book for the last fifty-six years, rarely ever leaving the tower. Now, he stood with The Book in front of him, the front cover in his left hand and the back cover in his right. *Open.*

Bendigo swallowed. Willy still held onto him. A breeze blew through the crowd, and everyone shifted.

Then the Keeper spoke. "My people of Whimselon."

Bendigo's heart thudded.

"The Book has opened," he whispered.

Zach rested his hand on Bendigo's shoulder.

He pushed his glasses closer to his eyes. "Words have bled onto the empty pages tonight, appearing as they did four hundred years ago. As we all know, what The Book says must occur, and I'm afraid that this time, one of you must make the occurring happen. I'm sorry."

"What's he talking about?" Willy whispered to Bendigo.

"I don't know." He patted her hand that was still on his forearm. "It's okay. Try not to worry."

"Len," Zachary projected from the back.

The Keeper looked toward him.

"Read to us what it says. It seems we have all gathered here together by fate, so we all deserve to know what is foretold."

Len sighed. "Yes. Yes…" He searched the crowd for a minute before resting his eyes back on The Book. His lips parted and he drew in a steady breath. "*Let his feet be swift. Let his heart be light. For the road ahead is eternal night. The shadows are unleashed, and the Twilights begin their reign. But now is the time to alter the end. Find the one they call Dagon. To the Ports of Orphic, he must go. The one who does the going is called Bendigo."*

Bendigo's blood turned to frost and cracked against his veins. Len looked up from The Book and made direct eye contact with him through the crowd. All of Whimselon turned to face him, their mouths hanging open. Even Willy stepped away from him to gaze.

Bendigo forced his lungs to push out words as he blankly looked at the Keeper, trying to focus through his blurry vision and wobbly knees. "Are you sure?"

Len closed his eyes and nodded. "It has been written."

He looked around at his town. They gawked at him like he was some kind of saving grace. Some sort of hero. But he wasn't. What he did know was that The Book spoke of the future, and he had no choice. "I'll go."

Zachary stepped toward him. "Ben."

"You know I have to." He forced out the courage. "You know I will."

"Bendigo." Len held The Book close to his chest. "You must go. Tonight, I'm afraid. If the rumors are true, the Twilights are already staking claim on our world. You must waste no time."

Zachary and Bendigo held a gaze. "I'll help you pack," Zach said in a hushed tone.

"Pack light," Len added as if he still heard Zach anyway. "I feel you will have help along the way."

As Zach led Bendigo away, Willy melted into the crowd, a tear escaping her eye. The people of Whimselon stayed together, talking and meandering. They seemed dumb-founded that out of all Whims, Bendigo Fletcher had been written about.

Bendigo thrust through his front door and headed straight for the kitchen table. He staggered, throwing his palms onto the surface. He hung his head, closed his eyes, and breathed shallow, letting his strong façade down.

"Ben." Zach grabbed his shoulders, making his brother face him.

"How am I supposed to do this?" Bendigo fought to straighten his panicked expression. "I'm not anybody. I'm *eighteen*. I plant herbs. I climb trees. I'm an everyday Whim."

"Listen to me." Zach held him close. "You aren't an everyday Whim. The *rest* of us are everyday Whims. Last night, I said I wouldn't die for this town, but I saw the look in your eyes. You would die for them. Not because you love them but because you know *someone* loves them. You are the *only* one who could do it."

"I'm going to leave, and you're going to be alone."

"I won't be alone. I'll lead this town. They haven't had a leader in years, and I think that needs to change now. I'll protect them, while you protect the world."

Bendigo embraced his brother.

Zach held onto him. Just like he did the night their father died. "You're going to help us." He faced him again. "This is a new beginning."

"I thought you didn't think that was possible."

"This changes things."

Bendigo drew in a breath. "Len said pack light. What should I bring?"

"Let me run across the bridge and see if I can get food donations. Fill your canteen while I'm gone."

Zach left, leaving him to stand alone in the middle of the kitchen. The lantern hanging from the ceiling sat cold. The kitchen was in complete darkness, but he didn't move to light the flame. He wanted to *feel* the darkness, *feel* the ominous caving in. He wanted to feel what his heart screamed.

Someone knocked on the window.

He jumped but then saw Willy's face hovering behind the glass. "Willy." He opened the hinged window.

"Can I please come in?" she begged, eyes wide.

"Yeah." He helped her through. "But why this way?"

She used him as leverage as she landed on the floor. "I don't want anyone to know I'm here. I want to ask if I can go with you."

"Go with me? What? No. The Book didn't say that two people went; it just said *I* went. We can't do what The Book doesn't say."

"No, we just have to do what The Book says. It says you *have* to go, but it doesn't say I *can't* go."

He thought about it as he pinched the bridge of his nose. "The answer is still no. This could be really dangerous. I'm not letting you risk your life."

"Ben, please." She followed him as he grabbed a canteen from the shelf. "Look at me."

He didn't glance up.

"Please. Just look at me."

He stopped next to a shattered clay pot near the kitchen table and lifted his eyes toward her.

"I-I don't belong here," she choked. "Look at my hair." She grabbed a few wispy strands. "What color *is* this even? It's the color of dust. Not the beautiful, blonde, silky locks that every other girl has. And have you ever seen me wear it down? I wear it in this bun every day. I never put dandelions in it on special occasions, and I never use Whimselon mud to mask my face and purify my skin. My parents *hate* that I'm not a beautiful Whim. And besides, I hate how moist everything is here. Please, Bendigo. If you leave, there will be no one left who cares about me. You're my only friend. Please don't leave me here."

Bendigo felt her honest pain in his heart. She truly believed no one cared about her, and a part of him knew that was true. He tolerated her, sure, but he never knew how much she relied on him. He couldn't just leave her here alone. "Okay."

Her voice turned airy. "What?"

"I said okay. You can come with me."

"Really?" Willy leaped forward and grabbed both of his arms. "Really? You're being serious?"

"I'm being serious." He somewhat laughed. "But keep it down. We have to keep it a secret."

"Okay." She let go and pulled herself together. "Okay. What should I pack? When are we leaving?"

"Just bring water. I got the rest. Meet me on the far east side of the marsh. Don't let anyone see you, and don't tell anyone goodbye. They'll try to stop you."

"Okay," she whispered. "Got it."

"Go before my brother gets back." He didn't want Zach to demolish their plan. "Hurry."

Willy scooted out the door only a few moments before Zach returned.

Zach handed him a pack of donated bread and cabbage. "You ready?"

"I am."

Zach turned toward the fireplace and stopped. His hand twitched at his side before he reached out and grabbed the glass box with their father's dagger. He opened it, staring at the piece for a long moment before pulling it out. "You know, Dad would have wanted you to have this."

"The dagger?" A lump caught in Bendigo's throat. "Zach, it's the last piece of Dad we have."

"No, it's not." He took Bendigo's hand and folded his fingers over the dagger's hilt. "It's the last piece of that night we have. Dad died saving Whimselon with this dagger. Now you go save Tarsha with it."

Bendigo held it close to his chest. "Thank you."

Zach breathed a few times before speaking again. "I'll walk you out to the produce track." He grabbed a folded piece of paper from his bag that sat against the bookshelf. "Take this. It's a map." Spreading it out on the table, he pointed to where the produce track sat.

The produce track started in Whimselon and ended in the harvest town of Lhan. Once a week, the farmers of Lhan hooked up a donkey to a cart full of produce that Whimselon couldn't grow, and the donkey would deliver their produce to Whimselon. The Whims would feed and give the donkey water before loading the cart with herbs and medicine to send back to Lhan.

"Follow the produce track to Lhan." Zach guided his finger over the paper. "After you pass through Lhan, head to the Horemburg Forest. It backs up to the Ports of Orphic. That's the last stop in our territory's trade route, so it should be a pretty safe venture. Should take you no more than five days. Four if you're quick."

"Got it."

"Let's go. Time is not on our side if Len is right about the Twilights."

Bendigo and Zach walked side by side through Whimselon. The entire town still stood outside under the rising sun. They watched as Bendigo headed for the bridge in silence. The brothers passed beneath the wooden Whimselon sign.

Feeling the presence of hundreds of eyes on him, Bendigo turned around to get one last look at his people. Everyone had lit their lanterns and held them in the air as a salute to him. They, for once, let their vanity seeking eyes see that maybe—just maybe—there was something else to look for in a person.

The brothers made it to the produce track as the sun

rose. They stood on the track, gazing at how far the path went as it faded from their view. White light filtered through the trees, making the moss on the track look greener and the forest more welcoming. It seemed like even nature knew today was different.

"So, just follow it?" Bendigo asked, stalling.

"Follow it." Zach's shoulders tensed. "And keep The Book a secret. No one must know we have it."

"I will," Bendigo said softly.

Zach rested his elbow on his shoulder.

"Hey." He nudged his brother. "I'm going to be back."

Zach blinked and forced a laugh. "You better be."

"I promise." He hugged him.

"And listen," Zach whispered into his ear, "your voice is never too far away. If you need help, call and I will come."

He took a step down the track. "I will. Once I find Dagon, I'll relay the message to him and come back home."

Zach raised his hand. "I'll see you soon then, brother."

Four

The sun shined like a comforting presence on Bendigo's face. The trees swayed, as if to salute him as he trekked down the wooden tracks. He smiled, a mix of angst and peace swirling inside him. He had always dreamed about leaving Whimselon but not under such circumstances. In his wildest thoughts, he never imagined himself as some sort of ranger to seek out a mystery man. Normally, the unknown rattled his brain, sending him down fearful rabbit holes. This time though, his mind loosened up its prison gates.

For once, he didn't feel trapped.

"Pssst." Willy peeked out from behind a tree. "Is the cost clear?"

"Yeah." He waved her over. "Come on. We're alone now."

She ran out and leaped onto the track. "I can't believe we're *doing* this! When do you think they'll notice I'm gone?"

"Who cares? It'll be too late by the time they notice." He grinned.

"So, what's the plan?" she asked, excitement riding on her breath.

"We follow this track all the way to Lhan and then pass through Horemburg Forest to the Ports of Orphic."

Willy pointed up the way. "You know this track is really, really long."

He adjusted his small leather backpack. "You know this requires a lot of walking, right?"

"Of course, I know that. But do you want to speed it up for a minute?"

"What do you mean?"

"Let's race. First one to that redberry tree wins."

Bendigo found the redberry tree poking out of a cluster of live oaks up the way. He stopped and turned to her. "Okay."

She giggled. "I was kind of joking."

"I'm not." He tucked his backpack straps behind him. "We make the rules now. Let's race!"

The two stood side by side—in a ready stance—looking at each other out of their peripherals.

"On three." He held his hands slightly out in front of him.

She casually examined him. "Got it."

"One. Two. Three!"

Their feet pounded into the wood as they tore down the track. Neck and neck, they shouted at each other, willing the other to lose. He pulled into first and let out a whoop as he approached the finish line. A few inches short of the tree, his cloak yanked back. He struggled to keep his body upright, and his ankles gave way as he tumbled onto the track. She collapsed behind him, still gripping his cloak. He lay on his side with her folded awkwardly over him.

"You filthy cheater!" He shoved her off, a smile spreading across his face. He was only mildly surprised at her drastic attempt to win.

She rolled over onto her back and looked up at the sky, wiping away a laughing tear. "I couldn't help myself."

"You're unbelievable." He rolled next to her. "I won."

"Barely."

The two lay on their backs, watching the clouds float above the trees.

Bendigo looked over at her, glad she was with him. Her recklessness and all. "We should get going," he said, regretful for pulling reality back into focus.

She sat up. "You're right. When do you think we'll reach Lhan?"

"Nightfall." He stood and reached down to help her up. "Long trek ahead."

Three hours in, Bendigo realized the extent of travel they would be doing. His ankles ached with every step. The familiar soft, wet terrain he grew up in was cushiony to his hollow bones. This ground was dry, packed and stiff. Very few marshes lay about the woods. Once, they passed a single pond that was so large, they dreamed up a make-believe village that they could build over it, laughing at the grand blueprints they bounced off each other. After that, they saw not one single puddle of water.

When the sun began to set, the two had chatted about

everything they could think of and took to traveling in silence. Even Willy kept her mouth closed. Silver moonlight streaks replaced the setting sun's amber shades and became the only guiding light for the Whims. The woods gradually thinned and ended at a wheat field that basked in the lunar blue's easy haze. The produce track kept going into Lhan, where in the distance, lanterns glowed in cabin windows, softening the night. The Whims stepped off the track and took to the wheat field.

Bendigo dragged his feet, glancing behind him to make sure Willy was still with him. "You still there?"

She crashed through the trees, staggering a bit. Anything but graceful. "I'm starting to regret this decision. I think my feet are going to fall off."

"If they fall off, I'll carry you."

She put her hands on her hips and glanced up at the sky.

His tease must not have been funny enough to deserve a laugh. "Just come on," he said. "Let's get out of this field. Maybe we can sneak into one of those barns and get a few hours of sleep before we keep going."

The wheat field spread out for quite an expanse between the Whims and the village, but the looming barns and tiny cabins in the near distance promised rest. Maybe.

Willy ran her hand along the top of the wheat. "Who do you think Dagon is anyway?"

"I've been thinking the same since we left. He must be fairly important if I'm supposed to travel all this way to find him."

"*Fairly* important? I'd guess he is powerful. Maybe a little intimidating. It's been four hundred years since The Book opened. I don't think anyone it mentions is *fairly* important. Including you."

He looked sideways at her. He had been trying to bury his brief waves of fear, but the more she talked, the more he struggled to keep it down. "I could just be a little piece of the plan. Once we find Dagon, we might just…turn around and head back home."

"I don't know." She pulled on a piece of wheat. "I think—" Her voice cut short. "Ben!"

He spun around and found a wheat plant wrapped around each of her wrists, imprisoning her. "What's happening?" He reached for her flailing arms.

"It's got my wrist!"

He gripped the wheat and yanked, trying to break her free. It tightened around her more with every tug he gave, like it was alive. Like it wanted to keep her captive. He dug his fingernails into the straw, clawing at it to rip it apart.

She grabbed at his shoulder as the plant curled around her ankle and pulled her down. "Bendigo, help!" She breathed hard, hyperventilating.

He reached inside his jacket and drew his father's dagger. He then clung to her outstretched fingers and struck the plant with the blade, cutting it in two. The straw around her wrist shriveled up and fell to the ground, squirming like it felt pain. He repeated the same motion for her other wrist, and the wheat plant drew back, releasing her ankle.

She fell forward, toward him, and he pulled her away from the plant that still thrashed around.

He felt around her wrists. "Are you okay?"

Willy glanced back at the plant. Her hands shook in his. "What was that? Magic? Does Lhan have magic?"

"That wasn't magic," he said. "That was evil. Nature is turning."

"Against us?"

He nodded. He ran his blade along the tops of the wheat plants, daring one of them to make another move.

She pulled at him. "Let's just get out of the field."

"You're right. I'm sorry, Willy. I'm so sorry. I shouldn't have said you could come."

"What?" She walked next to him at a fast pace. "You're regretting that I came?"

Bendigo thrashed at the wheat with his arms as he plowed through. "It's not that I don't want you here. I just don't want anything bad happening to you."

"I'm going to be fine," she mumbled. "Don't worry so much."

"Don't worry?" He stopped and pulled her back. "Willy, this isn't a game. Sure, it's fun to be out of Whimselon, but didn't you hear what The Book said? The Twilights are beginning their reign. That means death. At any moment."

A piece of her hair floated across her forehead. "Where are they then?"

"They don't have to *be* anywhere. Just their spiritual presence can affect nature, affect mankind."

"How do you know so much about Twilights?"

He let his arms drop to his sides. "I-I don't know. I just started talking, and it came out. Zachary told me a few things about them but not that much."

A silent breeze blew between the two. The crickets and frogs had stopped their happy songs. Even the moon hid behind the clouds.

Willy paused, seeming to notice the change in nature's song. "We need to get you to the Ports."

But he had stopped listening. Behind her, a figure approached with a lantern swinging from their hand, pushing aside the wheat as it moved.

"You!" the figure shouted. "Show yourselves."

Willy spun around and scooted back against Bendigo.

The figure held the lantern up, revealing the face of an older woman. Strands of gray hair hung loose from a bun, and she wore a nightgown with a robe draped over her strong body. "Who are you? Step into my light!"

Bendigo and Willy didn't budge.

"Now, you thieves!"

"We aren't thieves." He stepped in front of Willy. "Just passing through."

The woman inched closer. The lantern's flickering fire lit up her face in an unproportionate dance. "You're a Whim."

"Yes, yes we both are."

"Why have you come to Lhan? No Whim ever comes to Lhan. No Whim ever leaves Whimselon."

"I know." Bendigo searched her eyes, trying to read if

she was fearful or hateful. "But we were sent here. Just to travel through."

The woman shook her lantern forward, almost touching his face. "Travel? What kind of travel?"

The heat from the lantern tightened his skin. He swallowed.

"The Book." Her eyes grew dim. "Did it open?"

Willy crept up beside him. "What book?"

"*The* Book." The woman moved her lantern to Willy's eyes. "The one that everyone tells stories about. I know Whimselon has it."

"We don't have a book." She crossed her arms. "Bendigo and I left Whimselon because some of our people are sick. We're heading to the Ports of Orphic to get medicine and bring it back."

The woman's wrinkly face tensed. "But you're the ones who make medicine."

"Not the kind we need," she said bravely. "We need something different. Something we can't create."

The woman looked to Bendigo for clarification. He nodded, eyes wide. He had almost forgotten that they had to keep The Book's whereabouts a secret.

She lowered her lantern, and her eyes brightened a tad. "Where are you staying for the night?"

He cleared his throat. "Um…we weren't…we didn't have a plan."

She studied the two and then sighed. "Follow me. You can stay in my barn. The hay should make it somewhat comfortable, and I'll bring down some blankets from the house."

She walked up toward a barn that leaned crooked in the distance, as if no negotiation was needed. Bendigo and Willy shared a flicker of eye contact before jogging after her.

The barn she took them to was tall, peaking into the sky with a lantern on the arch like a beacon. She yanked the big wooden door open and led them inside, down rows of stables where cows sleepily lifted their heads to watch the newcomers.

"I would let you stay in the house"—the woman opened an empty stall—"but you're strangers, and I have three grandchildren who live with me. You understand, don't you?"

"Of course." Willy stepped into the stall. "Thank you for doing this, Ms…"

"Just call me Lila."

"Thank you, Lila."

Lila pointed to the straw on the ground. "It's fresh straw. A new horse is arriving tomorrow. It's not a bed, but at least you have a roof."

"Yes, thank you." Bendigo looked up at the ceiling that stretched so high that it practically disappeared in the dark. "We appreciate your kindness."

She moved toward the door. "There is something to say about Whims who travel away from home for the fortune of someone other than themselves." She stopped walking. "I'll be back with blankets."

The groan of the barn door shutting behind her echoed inside Bendigo and Willy's stall.

She plopped down in the hay. "Well, this is strange, isn't it?"

"The Keeper said I would have help along the way." He sat beside her, leaned forward, and yanked his shoes off, rubbing the soles of his feet. "Do Whims really have such a bad reputation?"

"What do you think?"

"Yes?"

"Yes. We are full of pride."

"But not every Whim is like that."

She shrugged. "Doesn't matter. We all take the fall for it."

"Why do you think that is?"

"Because no one takes the time to know Whims like us," she said as if to mock a fake celebrity status.

He snorted. "Yeah. Like we would change their minds."

"One day we could."

He gave a teensy smile. "Good lie by the way."

"Thanks." She grinned. "I thought you were going to give us away."

"I almost *did*."

She lay with her hands behind her head. "Don't worry. You do the saving; I'll do the lying. That's how we survived day one."

"That we did."

Sighing, she shut her eyes. Her breathing drifted into a

shallow rhythm, and her shoulders fell limp. Asleep before the blankets arrived. He was exhausted too, but he watched her for a second. Why had danger seemed more enticing than Whimselon to her? He feared she would soon regret her decision to leave home. But she slept soundly, as if in her own bed. Afterall, home isn't always the roof over your head.

Five

Lila didn't let Bendigo and Willy leave on an empty stomach the next morning. She refilled their canteens and sent them off with an orange and a muffin each, waving goodbye from a distance as they walked toward Horemburg Forest at the first light of day. Fog lingered above the dew-covered town, and the chill of the morning was wet, but the Whims were dry, wrapped in their cloaks that were still warm from their barn slumber.

Bendigo stood at the edge of the forest, staring back at Lila. "She terrified me at first."

"Me too." Willy shuddered. "I wonder what made her want to help us in the end."

He walked into the woodland and stepped over a limb covered in soggy moss. "Trust. She trusted our story and had sympathy for us. The worst part is that we were actually lying."

She walked behind him. "But for good reason. We couldn't tell her about The Book."

"I just hate to lie." He let his voice drop as a cringe seeped into his heart.

"Why do you think so deeply?"

He smiled, examining the woods around them. No matter how deep into the trees they went, fresh sunlight still cascaded through the branches to light the ground and make the leaves look silvery. "I don't really have a choice. My mind does it all on its own. Even when I don't want it to."

"That must be kind of annoying." Willy swiped at a spiderweb that danced into the light in front of her face.

He shrugged. "Sometimes it is. Sometimes it's not."

A quick rustle and shifting of leaves made the two dart their eyes in the sound's direction. A doe and her fawn took off, away from them. The fawn's spots flashed in the sun before disappearing.

Bendigo's shoulders relaxed, and he moved his hand away from the hilt of his dagger. "Just deer." He let out a slight laugh. "We can't let every noise frighten us. We'd be terrified all the time. Pretend we're in Whimselon. We don't get alarmed there."

"That's because we *know* what lives in the marshland." Willy stayed close to his side. "This forest could have woodland dragons."

At the mention of a dragon, his mind fought to stay out of a dark place. "There aren't any woodland dragons in the Horemburg Forest. They would be in the Orphic Forest. That's where all the magic is."

"Not *all* the magic. We have The Book in Whimselon, and Whimselon has seen a woodland dragon."

"Yeah, I know," he snapped.

She looked down, slightly moving away from him.

"Sorry," he mumbled, pulling ahead and quickening his pace.

The faster they got to the Ports of Orphic, the sooner this would all be over. Fear rose in his chest. Her words made him overthink the mission. That maybe their travel wouldn't be as safe as he had thought. That maybe he was the one being too naïve.

The first two nights in the Horemburg Forest were generally uneventful. Lying on dirt and twigs in unknown territory unsettled them, especially with the sounds of the night. They made it a point to talk in the dark until exhaustion took over and carried them into a slumber.

On the third day, the humidity made a dramatic entrance and sucked away all the mustered-up strength from the Whim's bodies. They weren't making decent time, and occasionally, they second-guessed if they were even going the right way. The sun and stars kept them on track, but their minds fogged, and their weariness slowed their steps. Even so, the two traveled all day into midafternoon. The forest provided enough shade to ease the suffocating humidity that increased the closer they got to the Ports, but sweat still fell down the back of Bendigo's neck like rain sliding down his treehouse's roof: slow and constant.

"Make sure you're drinking water, Willy." He twisted his canteen open and let the liquid fill his mouth.

When they were children, he often had to remind her to drink water during the hot summer days. She used to get so lost in playing and running through the marsh that her face would turn beet red, and she would feel sick.

"What happens when I run out?" She shook her canteen. "I'm almost empty."

"Already?" He wiped sweat from his forehead. "We refilled just this morning."

She cringed. "I guess I thought we would reach the Ports by nightfall."

"It's okay. Don't worry." He patted the ground. "This is river grass. There is freshwater around her somewhere. We can fill up."

A voice, as smooth as water over a flat stone, floated in behind them. "There is a creek about half a mile south."

Bendigo turned to see a short, thin man dressed in ragged clothes that were far too big for his body. Not one piece of his curly hair was out of place. Bendigo was unaware of any village or dwelling that may lie within the Horemburg Forest, and the man's sudden emergence brought about severe discernment.

Bendigo stepped in front of Willy. "Who are you?"

The man slowly tilted his head to the side. "You are Bendigo Fletcher and Willy Hemmingway, yes?"

He paused, wondering if this was a moment to lie or not.

The man held his hands up, showing sickly white palms. "I'm just a messenger. I was sent to find you."

"Sent from where?"

"The Whims sent word to Lhan, and I left Lhan shortly after you two to find you. I'm supposed to tell you that the mission has been called off. Nothing waits for you at the Ports of Orphic. You need to turn around and go back to Whimselon."

A plague of nausea hit Bendigo's stomach. The messenger's pupils seemed to expand, his eyes turning into black dots.

"Why would it be called off?" Bendigo challenged. "What The Book says has to occur."

The messenger rolled his neck. "I'm just telling you what I was told to relay. If you go to the Ports of Orphic, you won't leave alive."

Something inside his stomach made him look down. When his eyes reached where the messenger's raggedy clothes met the ground, it appeared that he *had* no feet. This man floated above the ground, his clothes hiding his missing limbs.

Bendigo reached back and touched Willy, who had remained still. "Willy. He's not real."

"That's not logical, Mr. Fletcher." The messenger grinned. "Of course, I'm real. What else would I be?"

"You're a Twilight," he whispered. "Willy, run!"

She didn't think twice.

He leaped over a rotted tree trunk, landing on the other side in a sprint. His backpack shook up and down, back and forth. Twigs poked and stabbed his feet. He kept his eyes on Willy ahead. The forest whizzed past him.

To his right, a black cloak with no face flew through the trees. The Twilight twisted around the tree trunks, slipped through the branches, and stayed close. It wove toward him, screeching.

Bendigo grabbed for his dagger. He gripped the hilt and slung it out. The Twilight reeled and then plaited in toward him again, reaching for his throat. He slashed the dagger, and the blade grazed the spirit's wrist. The Twilight squealed, drawing back.

Willy spun around. "Ben!"

"Keep going!" He prepared for another attack.

The Twilight flew over his head. Its black cloak dragged across his hair. He reached up with the dagger and slashed. No contact. It didn't come back for more. Instead, it headed toward Willy.

"Willy, get down!" he shouted, trying to move faster.

The Twilight zipped over her head and dropped down, covering her body.

"*No!*" He ripped his arms through the air, forcing his body to get to her despite the excruciating pain in his lungs.

The Twilight wrapped around her, muffing her screams as it dragged her to the ground.

He took a running leap and yanked the Twilight's head backward. It still clawed at her even as he rolled to the side, taking the cloaked evil with him. He dug his nails into the being, and with one hand, he speared the dagger right through its core.

Their tussling ceased.

The Twilight made an airy hissing noise. Its wispy mass drooped. Then it faded. Willy and Bendigo lay on their sides, gasping for breath as they watched it become dimmer and dimmer.

It disappeared.

Her eyes met his. Fear, panic, disbelief, confusion. Loose hair clung to her cheeks and forehead, plastered by sweat.

He pushed himself up and crawled over to her, barely able to move his limbs. He got a hold of her body and pulled her close, brushing the hair out of her face. "Are you all right?"

Her body shook, but she nodded, looking into his eyes.

"I'm so sorry." He hugged her, feeling her heartbeat against his chest.

She drew back to look at him. "Sorry for what? You saved me."

"I'm sorry I let you come."

"Bendigo." She grew stern. "I'm not sorry I came. I will never be sorry I came. Stop thinking you are the one who put me here. I don't want to hear you say I'm sorry anymore."

He looked down. "Okay."

She sighed and leaned over him, grabbing the dagger that laid on the forest floor where the Twilight had faded to nothing. "Here. You're gonna need this again."

He took the dagger and slid it back into the sheath beneath his shirt. He stared at where the Twilight had been. "I didn't know you could kill them like that. They're spirits. Shouldn't that make them safe from material harm?"

She gazed at the ground. "It makes a little sense that it can die, doesn't it?"

"How so?"

"We have spirits, and sometimes, our spirits can die. Like we can lose our fighting spirit, our spirit of happiness, our spirit of freedom… It sort of makes sense. A little bit."

"A little." He struggled to stand. "But one thing is for sure."

She joined him. "What's that?"

"Something important waits for us at the Ports of Orphic, otherwise it wouldn't have tried to make us turn back."

"How far out are we?" She found the sun to pinpoint their direction again.

"By the humidity and the increasing breeze"—he tightened his backpack straps—"I'd say we may be there a little after dark. We at least should try to be. I don't want to know how many other Twilights are out here, and I don't want to find out."

Six: The Ports of Orphic

The full moon tried to break through the smothering clouds as Bendigo and Willy sat on the hilltop, gazing upon the harbor town below.

He rested his chin on his knees, slightly dismayed. "So, this is it." The stuffy air suppressed his skin. "The Ports of Orphic. I thought it would be...grander."

The Ports of Orphic looked tiny, insignificant, lonely. Isolated. Firelight from inside the rundown buildings lined the channel that emptied into the sea, which was far vaster than he had ever imagined. The town—if it could even qualify as that—was protected by nothing. The Horemburg Forest towered above it from a hill on one side, and the Orphic Forest loomed in the distance on the other. The port itself rested in a valley between the two, vulnerable to nature from all angles.

Willy waved her hand toward the wind and waves. "Are you even seeing this? Look at the *sea*. Did you imagine it would be that big? That *alive*? It moves over and over again. In the same pattern."

"The sea is incredible." He watched the waves form and disappear. Its greatness took his breath away. "But it's so powerful. It could swallow up the harbor if it tried."

"Exactly." She rose to her feet and put her hands on her hips. The breeze made her linen shirt ripple. "But people decided to live here, knowing it's a vulnerable location. That's courage to me. That's strength."

Bendigo watched as Willy stepped closer to the hill's edge and looked down at the terrain leading to the harbor. She was right. More than right. Strength. These people had to have it.

"Thank you, Willy."

She turned to him and furrowed her brow. "For what?"

He strode over to her. "For realizing what I don't."

The instant the two set their feet on the docks, the sound of singing, from a nearby building, floated into the air. The building's windows flickered with firelight, and the front door was propped open, casting a rectangle of yellow light out onto the harbor. The singing sounded like all men. Some clapped, and some cheered when they would reach a part in the song that struck a relatable chord.

"They sound like fun." She nudged him. "You think Dagon is in there?"

His eyes traveled up and down the harbor. "It seems like the whole town is in there. All the other buildings look dark."

"Not *everyone*." A set of hands grabbed both Whims' shoulders. They belonged to a man who stood nearly two feet taller than them with a scraggly beard that hadn't been tended to in months. "Who are *you* two?"

Bendigo yanked his shoulder out of the man's grasp and

then swiped the man's other hand off Willy. "Lay off. We're traveling through."

The man grinned, showing yellow teeth. "No one travels through the Ports at this time of night." His face shined with filth in the singing building's light.

Bendigo stepped in front of Willy.

"Oh, don't worry." Yellow Teeth stepped closer to her. "I'm not gonna hurt her. Unless she has coins." He reached past Bendigo and grabbed the front of her shirt, pulling her close to his face.

She threw her hands out and tried to push free. "Let go, you *disgusting* reptile."

Yellow Teeth laughed at her spitfire.

"She said let *go*." Bendigo drew his dagger and spun it underneath the man's chin.

The man retracted his knobby fingers from her shirt and stepped back, his grin fading.

"Hey!" a voice boomed from up the dock. Another man had emerged from the singing building. Built and intimidating. The opposite of everything Bendigo was. "Leave them alone, Donovan."

Yellow Teeth, or Donovan apparently, stepped back some more, glaring.

The new man placed himself between Bendigo and Donovan. "Go home," the stranger said. "You've had too much to drink."

Donovan spat on the ground and bumped into the hero's shoulder as he limped up the dock.

The stranger faced the Whims, his long braid resting over his right shoulder. "You two all right?"

"Yeah." Bendigo hesitated before putting his dagger away. "Thanks."

"Sorry about that. Donovan always goes above his limit. I knew he must have been up to no good when I couldn't find him. I'm Shem by the way." He held his hand out.

Bendigo shook it. "Bendigo. This is Willy."

"Hi." She waved shyly.

"Welcome to the Ports of Orphic," he said. "I wasn't expecting any more sailors to arrive tonight. It's rare to navigate the dark waters. How did you fair that? And only the two of you."

"We didn't come from the sea." Bendigo shifted. "We're travelers by foot. From Whimselon."

He drew his brows in. "Travelers."

The sudden change in his voice struck Bendigo's core. "Yeah. We're here to find someone."

"Dagon," Shem spoke in a hushed tone.

Bendigo's heart lifted. "Yes."

He stood straight. "Follow me."

Bendigo and Willy followed Shem into the singing building, which he realized was the pub. Must and heat rose from the sailors and dock workers crowded in the small space. He scrunched his nose. Willy held onto his arm as Shem weaved his way through the lively, out of tune men. Some women too. A few bodies jostled Bendigo but they merely apologized and raised their glasses toward him.

Shem broke through the crowd to the back of the pub where one man sat at a round table. The man sat back in his chair, watching the singing sailors and smiling. He himself had no drink of his own, but his hand tapped along to the song's beat on his thigh.

Bendigo paused. A glow of comfort washed over his mind. As if sensing his presence, the man brought his eyes up to meet his. The two held a gaze. The music faded from Bendigo's ears, and all other sensations became nonexistent. He couldn't even feel the air around him. Everyone in the pub moved in slow motion, and all he could focus on were Dagon's eyes. He knew it was Dagon, and he knew Dagon knew he was Bendigo.

The pub's noises slowly seeped back into his ears, and the singers around him moved again. Willy had let go of his arm at some point and stood beside him.

Shem caught the stare shared between the two and lowered his voice. "Looks like you already know, but Dagon, this is—"

"Bendigo Fletcher." Dagon stood.

"Yeah." Bendigo's heart boomed. "I am."

The four stared at each other for a moment.

Bendigo dropped his hands to his sides. "Sir, why am I here?"

Dagon let a hint of a smile twitch in his eyes and turned to Shem. "I think it's time we go somewhere private."

Shem led the group out of the bar. They slipped through the night, up a flight of wooden stairs, and into a home. A makeshift bed of blankets, a pillow, and a few cloaks rested on the floor. Bendigo and Willy stood together awkwardly near the front door, while Shem and Dagon lit lanterns to give the place a glow.

"Coffee?" Shem's sturdy figure seemed squished in the all-wood kitchen area.

Willy's eyes widened. "You have coffee?"

Dagon sat at the kitchen table that had been made from a retired fishing boat. "Don't get *too* excited. It leaves a bitter film in the back of your throat." He pulled a chair out next to him. "Come sit."

Bendigo nodded at Willy, and she crept forward to take a seat next to Dagon. He slowly lowered himself into his own chair, watching Dagon the whole time.

"The coffee will be a few minutes." Shem pulled tin cups down from an open shelf. "Water?"

"Please," Bendigo and Willy answered at the same time, having drunk their last sips of water from their canteens hours ago.

Shem worked a lever to pump up two cups of water and slid them onto the table. "Sorry for your brutal welcome from Donovan. He needs an extra eye on him."

"He does," Willy agreed. "I'm just glad he didn't turn out to be Dagon."

Dagon laughed in a quiet kind of way. "Willy, right?"

Her jaw dropped.

He seemed unfazed. "Short for what?"

"Short for Willy. That's all."

He nodded. "Well, I like the name Willy. Suits you. Bendigo? You seem uneasy."

Bendigo stiffened. He *was* uneasy. There had been no introductions, yet somehow they knew each other. "How did you know I was coming to find you? I was prepared to explain myself, but…you already know…"

Shem shifted his eyes to Dagon like he too didn't know the whole story. It struck Bendigo as odd that Dagon was obviously bunking with Shem, yet Shem seemed just as in the dark.

"Yes." Dagon rubbed his thumb and pointer finger over his facial scruff. "I do know. I know that The Book, which resides in Whimselon, opened and ordered you, Bendigo, to set out for the Ports of Orphic to find me. A simple task but one that required a leap of faith. I arrived a few days ago, and Shem let me stay with him. My stay has been enjoyable, but your arrival gives me even greater joy."

Bendigo shrugged. "Why?"

Dagon leaned onto the table. "Your appearance means the revival has begun."

Seven

Lantern light inside Shem's home danced on the walls and on the four faces sitting at the kitchen table. Bendigo cast a side glance at Shem, wondering if he knew of the plan already, but his face was tight and stern, just as lost as the rest.

Bendigo leaned forward. "What's the revival?"

"Do you have a map?" Dagon reached his hand out to him.

He nodded and fumbled around inside his backpack to pull out the map that Zachary had given him.

Dagon unfolded the paper and spread it out across the table. He dropped his finger over the Ports of Orphic. "Here we are. The Orphic Forest begins up the valley to the east. It covers the distance between the Ports and Orenda."

"Orenda." Willy perked up. "That's where The Book originally was."

He nodded. "It was, and some believe The Book is still there. When we enter Orenda, we must be careful. Nature has always been skeptical of Orenda since the first Keeper tried to open The Book himself. The fog still creeps in sometimes, searching for the one who knows where The Book is."

Bendigo's throat tightened. "We're going to Orenda?"

Shem shifted, sitting up taller and leaning in.

Dagon looked up from the map. "You didn't think the journey ended here, did you?"

"Dagon, I know nothing about why I'm here." Bendigo grew irritated, brought on by how fatigued he was. "I thought once I found you, my part was over."

"I'm afraid not." He tapped the map again. "The whole picture is right here." He dragged his finger to the end of the map where the Isle of Kalon sat.

Kalon was well-known for its magnificent bluff with an empty castle perched in ruin. At least the stories say it was empty. But the castle wasn't talked about as much as the mystical falls. On top of the bluff was a waterfall that cascaded down to feed every river in the world. The Source of Life was what the people of Tarsha referred to it as. If the waterfall ever dried up, there would be no rivers, no fresh water to run about.

Only the story was often dismissed as a myth. No one could prove the waterfall was real because no one ever made it to the Isle of Kalon. Even if they did, they never returned to tell about it.

Kalon was cursed. Those who went never came back.

"The Isle of Kalon?" Shem crossed his arms. "That place holds no answers, only mysteries."

"No." Dagon shook his head. "That's where the Twilights are gathering."

All the flames in the surrounding lanterns blew to a near

fade. The atmosphere dimmed to an unsettling hue. The four shared glances with each other. Then just as mysteriously as the change occurred, Shem's home rewinded, bringing back the haze and flicker of normal flames.

Bendigo trailed his line of vision around the cramped home, spooked. He thought about the moment the Twilight consumed Willy and relived the fear that he was going to watch his friend die. "Tell me about the Twilights. What do they want?"

"The Twilights have decided that it's time to return and take the world as their own." Dagon's eyes held heavy sorrow. "In time, they have built up penetrating greed. Reigning over our souls in death has become nothing to them. They want more power. Power over our lives."

"Aren't Twilights strong spirits?" He tried to remember the bits and pieces he had learned about them through stories, myths, and history. "Couldn't they just force us under their control without having to form an army?"

Dagon shook his head. "They're strong spirits, but so is the spirit within mankind. To have a war between flesh and blood, there must first be a war between spirit and spirit. Mankind must forsake their good conscience and submit to the Twilight's authority in order for the Twilights to control them. Some people will turn, some will not. When enough people have joined the Twilight's side, that war will begin."

Bendigo ran his hands through his hair. "That's why towns are reporting strange behaviors in their people. The Twilights are getting to them, aren't they."

"Every town the Twilights pass through, they leave with people who they have enchanted and recruited to be a part of their army. People have started disappearing from their homes." Dagon closed his eyes. "I wish it weren't so, but that is the truth. And even so, the people aren't enough for the Twilights. They need more. More authority. More persuasion."

"So, they're turning nature." Shem stood and ambled over to where the boiling water had finished dripping over the coffee grounds. "I've noticed the change. In the wind. In the waves. If nature is against us, we barely stand a chance."

Willy looked toward Dagon's brown eyes. "Why the Isle of Kalon?"

"Kalon is the one place where people don't go," Dagon said. "If they do, nature doesn't let them return." He sighed. "Nature protects the Isle of Kalon. No one can see the Source of Life and leave to tell others about it, otherwise Kalon would be invaded. People could destroy Kalon and its life-giving waterfall in their greed for power, and the whole world would go down for it. The Twilights know this, so they feel they can find sanctuary there for now."

"So, why can the Twilights form their army there without a hitch?" Bendigo grabbed a crooked coffee mug from Shem. "I mean, if nature is so hostile to anyone who goes to Kalon, why not to the Twilights too?"

"Because the Twilights have turned nature to their side. They're manipulative. Intelligent. The Twilights have a couple thousand men and women, nature, *and* the Isle of Kalon to work with. Once they reach the strength that they think they need, they will invade. Every forest, every town, every city, and every port. Anyone who stands in their way will face immediate death. Death without an afterlife." Dagon raised a finger. "But if you choose to fight *for* the Twilights, you will get to live on Tarsha as a servant. You will still be breathing, but your life will not be your own."

Willy's eyes enlarged.

Dagon softly touched her arm. "Don't be afraid. We are all going to bring the afterlife back."

"We are?" Shem and Bendigo blurted out together.

She pointed at Dagon. "I thought *you* were. That's what The Book said."

He waved his hands over the three in front of him. "Don't you see the divine gathering that has occurred? The Book picked Bendigo because of his faith. His faith is not absent of love, which is why he allowed Willy to follow. I showed up at the Ports of Orphic, thinking I was only going to find Bendigo but instead, I befriended Shem. Shem is a fighter and a protector. A good one too. I need to get to the Isle of Kalon, but I can't do it alone. I need an army, and it's only by divine coincidence that the four of us have come together."

Shem cleared his throat. "So, what you're proposing is that the four of us are going to the Isle of Kalon to take on *thousands* of beings?"

Dagon's eyes rested on him. "It must be done. If you

don't want to go, I will be deeply saddened, but in the end, it is your choice. Though I'm afraid Bendigo doesn't have the luxury of choosing. He must go."

"Me?" Bendigo grabbed his chest. "I don't even know what this all *means*. What do I have to offer?"

He leaned forward and put his hand on Bendigo's heart. "Faith."

Bendigo's heart rapped against Dagon's touch. "Faith in what?"

"The revival of Tarsha." He didn't move his hand. "You had faith to leave Whimselon, and it's your faith that will see us through to the end. What we must do at the Isle of Kalon is dangerous and frightening. Some of us may want to turn back, but you are going to be the one to follow through. That's why you were chosen, Bendigo." He pulled his hand away.

Bendigo sucked in a breath, still feeling the shadow of Dagon's hand on his chest. "Why would *you* turn back? Can't *you* go without me?"

Dagon's eyes fell. "Even I may think about retreating."

Willy played with her untouched coffee cup. "How do you know all this stuff anyway?"

"The same way Bendigo knows things about the Twilights." He looked at him. "Revelation. Helpful, isn't it?"

Shem dropped his fist onto the table, making Bendigo jump. "Dagon, I don't wish to stay behind. I'm on board. I'm meant to protect. And I can't sit idly by while knowing someone is putting their life on the line for the world."

"I'm in." Willy nodded. "I've made it this far. Giving up now would be like carrying a basket of raspberries to the bottom of my treehouse steps and leaving them on the ground for someone else to do the hardest part."

Bendigo locked eyes with Dagon. He knew that if he broke the gaze, the comforting sensation would fade.

Dagon's lips turned up into a gentle arc. He didn't blink. "Do you trust me?"

Bendigo swallowed. "For some reason I do."

"We need your faith." His words pierced Bendigo's heart.

"Okay. I'm in."

He let his teeth show behind his scruff as he reached out and squeezed Bendigo's shoulder. "It is your faith that has brought us together. In the morning, we leave."

"Better not drink that entire mug if you want to get some rest tonight." Shem cocked his head. "You haven't even touched it."

"I'm a tad skeptical." Bendigo looked into the dark liquid. "Why is it black?"

"Let's try it. Come on," Willy encouraged. "We'll do it together."

He held the mug in front of his lips. Since they were kids, she had always been the one forcing him to do silly things. He had gotten used to following her suggestions and suffering the consequences. This time seemed no different, but he couldn't let her brag about how she had tasted the famous drink called coffee and he hadn't.

"Fine," he huffed. "On three. One. Two. Three." He took a big gulp and gagged as it slid down his throat. He slammed the mug onto the table. "That's *terrible*."

"What's so terrible about it?" She took another sip.

Dagon widened his eyes and turned to her. "You are a strong one, my friend."

Shem snickered. "You're the first person who has liked it on the first try. I'm impressed."

Her face grew red, and she tried to hide it by looking down into her mug.

The four sat around the table, talking and bantering, until they couldn't hold their eyes open anymore. Bendigo wished it could have lasted forever. He had never felt a connection to others like this before. When they settled down for the night, he couldn't help but lie awake in anticipation. Nervousness filled him. But he felt confident in his new friends.

His new army.

Eight

Thunder woke Bendigo from his restless sleep on the now moist wooden floor. Rainwater seeped through the windowpane above as the storm drove sideways into the glass. The frame wasn't strong enough to keep the water from soaking into the wall and creeping down into the floor, dampening the withering blanket that he had wrapped around his body.

He sat up and looked around. Willy still lay under her cloak a few feet from him, but her eyes were open, looking up at the ceiling. Dagon pulled an oversized garment over his head, while Shem hustled about in the kitchen, throwing bread and vegetables into cloth wraps.

"What time is it?" Bendigo's voice was drowned out by the splitting sound of thunder.

Shem cut a piece of twine off a spool and tied it around one of his cloth sacks. "Five minutes till full sunrise. Not much of a sun to see this morning." His voice sounded taught.

"Are we going out in this?" Willy sat up, her hair bent and matted.

Dagon walked to the window. Lightning flashed across his face, illuminating the curiosity in his eyes. "We are.

Nature doesn't want us leaving the Ports of Orphic. It's trying to stop us, which is why we must do the opposite."

A crackling roar shook the building as Shem glanced up at Bendigo. Bendigo could read his eyes. Shem agreed with Dagon, but there was a sense of wary doubt.

"Don't be worried." Dagon turned back around. "Nature can't rage forever. It will have to let up when it realizes we aren't going to submit to its terror."

A boom exploded in the sky, as if it had just heard what he said.

"The sooner we leave, the better." He waved Bendigo and Willy up from the floor. "This rain could flood the Ports. If we leave, the storm will follow."

"How safe are my fishermen?" Shem threw a pack of food to Dagon.

Dagon caught it and passed it to Bendigo. "I wouldn't leave them if I knew they were in danger. Leaving is the best thing we can do."

Bendigo underhanded his canteen to Shem. "Let's get moving then. I don't want your people to be in six feet of water because of me."

Shem grabbed the canteen and pitched a full one back to Willy. "From now on, it isn't just because of you, it's because of all of us. Don't ever put blame on yourself, kid."

Willy hung her canteen around her neck and then slid Bendigo's dagger toward him with her foot. "Don't forget this."

"What's that?" Dagon peered over his shoulder.

"Oh." Bendigo swiped it up from the ground. "Just a blade. Something my brother gave me. It used to be my father's. Foolish. Small." He winced at how he had just insulted his father's dagger. But how could his dagger be taken seriously when a sword hung defiantly from Shem's hip?

"Foolish?" Dagon reached to touch the blade. "What makes this weapon of little value? The bearer of the weapon is what carries the worth. Was your father imprudent?"

Shem screwed on the canteen's lid slowly as if to eavesdrop.

"No, sir," Bendigo rasped.

"Are you reckless?" Dagon asked.

"Hardly."

"Then your weapon isn't as insignificant as you think." He curled Bendigo's fingers around the dagger's hilt. "Have faith."

The four huddled together through the Ports as the rain pounded on their backs, punishing them for defying nature's warning. The channel had risen so much that the docks were flooded; some fishing boats had even ridden the waves up to the walkways, now sitting ducks.

Dagon led the way out to the steep embankment of rock and dirt-turned-mud that rose to the Orphic Forest's tree line. Bendigo followed close behind, trying to keep a visual on Dagon's back through the sheets of rain. He reached behind him to make sure Willy was still with him. Her hand wrapped around his, and he squeezed her fingers, struggling to keep his grasp from slipping. He knew Shem was in the rear, but he couldn't see him through the storm.

Dagon stopped at the foot of the ridge. "The climb is going to be slick!" he shouted over the relentless falling roar. "Use both your hands and your feet."

Lightning ignited the sky, revealing the steepness of the muddy cliff above. Bendigo blew water from his nose and pulled Willy's ear close to his mouth. "You go first. If you slip, I got you." He shoved her in front of him.

Dagon had already begun his climb, reaching down to help her onto the embankment.

Bendigo dug his hands into the mud and pivoted his foot to get a good stance before pushing himself up. To his right, a chunk of dirt broke away from the mound and avalanched down. He tried to quicken his pace, but the rain made it difficult to get any sort of grip. Yes, he was a Whim, and Whims could climb, but they climbed trees, not muddy mountains.

He focused on his hand placement and willed himself to keep going. He dragged himself upward on all fours, keeping his chin down to keep the rain from smacking his eyes. When he glanced back to make sure Shem was still behind him, he shuddered. Though the climb was slow, they were already fairly high up. Heights weren't a fear of his but falling was.

Dagon's voice faintly pierced through the storm. "Mudslide!"

His heart threw itself against his chest. He searched, frantic to find where the mudslide was coming from and where it was headed. Willy's back was barely noticeable in the downpour, so how was he supposed to spot a *mudslide?*

Then he saw it.

A river of nature flooded toward him, just missing Dagon's ankles. Dagon had pulled Willy into his arms and out of the way of it. Bendigo wouldn't be so lucky. He didn't have time to move or someone to hold onto.

"Bendigo, brace!" Shem shouted from behind.

The mud river grew louder, and Bendigo dug his fingers into the dirt. He shut his eyes as the mudslide contacted his knees. Its force bent his body sideways, and he struggled to keep his footing. The once sturdy muck beneath him gave way, and he collapsed onto his stomach, the muddy avalanche consuming him. He clawed at the ground, trying to regain control, but he wasn't a fair match for nature.

In a desperate reach, a firm hand wrapped around his wrist.

"Hang on." Shem's muscles bulged against the mud's force as it tried to pull Bendigo down.

Bendigo threw his other arm toward Shem. Shem managed a successful grasp, pulling up. The mudslide continued downward, breaking off another piece of land but leaving Bendigo behind in Shem's hands.

Shem set Bendigo onto his feet and propped an arm around his waist, letting him regain his balance. "Steady?"

Bendigo threw an arm over his shoulder. "Thank you."

His legs shook, and he tried to stabilize himself away from Shem's grip. The rain had let up, falling only as gentle pitter patters. It was easier to hear now, easier to see Dagon and Willy peering down from above. Bendigo felt like he had gotten a point across to nature, like his escape from the mudslide was a discouraging blow that forced the storm to retreat and rethink its tactics.

Shem and Bendigo climbed side by side the rest of the way, thankful when they took hold of Dagon's and Willy's hands as they pulled the boys up and over the final ridge.

"Geez, Bendigo." Her eyes were extra round. "That was too close."

He let out a relieved laugh. "You can't expect a hollow-boned Whim to stand a chance against a mudslide."

☾

Shem shook water from his hands and turned to face the sea. The Ports sat far below, quiet, damp, and vulnerable.

Dagon came up from behind him and put a hand on his shoulder. "Well done."

He only nodded.

Dagon's eyebrows frowned. "You're worried about your people."

"I am." He didn't pull his gaze away from the horizon. "How am I supposed to know they will be all right?"

Dagon blew a breath through tight lips. "They aren't the

main threat to the Twilight army right now. We are. The Twilights will come for us before they come for the Ports of Orphic. Leaving the Ports will buy them time. Trust me."

Shem adjusted the sword at his hip. "Do you think I'll ever come back? Truly." He lowered his voice. "Do you know what lies ahead?"

The wind blew through Dagon's shaggy hair as he stared out at the sea, which had calmed. "I want to tell you that I know you'll come back, but the whole picture is not before me."

He turned a sly eye toward the mysterious man. "What about half of the picture?"

Dagon chuckled. "I don't believe that's how it works."

He rotated and watched Bendigo and Willy sitting in the dirt, chatting and pointing to the Orphic Forest. "It's a strange lineup. Us four."

"Better together."

"What?"

"We are better together." Dagon turned and headed toward the Orphic Forest's tree line.

☾

Bendigo lifted his head as Dagon approached.

"Everyone recovered?" Dagon rubbed his hands together. "The sun will be hot soon, and I want to be deep within the forest where we'll have shade. Nothing makes travel worse than burning skin or an empty stomach.

Wouldn't you agree?"

"Or those two combined." Willy stepped into stride with him.

"That's the truth." Shem looked at her. "Let's not get to that point. We don't want to turn on each other."

Bendigo tried to hide a smile as her face visibly turned rosy. She only got shy around people she was afraid of or attracted to, and he knew she wasn't afraid of Shem.

She just smiled back at Shem, a loss for words plaguing her tongue.

The four stopped at the edge of the Orphic Forest. The black tree trunks twisted like two pieces of rope. Their branches, full of olive leaves, held a tint of silver when the wind blew and turned them up. With any other forest, the depths beyond the tree line would be visible but not with the Orphic Forest. Everything past the tree line was dark, as if the night sky itself clashed with the twisted trunks and consumed the space on the other side. It looked like there *was* no forest.

"It looks more threatening than it is," Dagon said, "but there are a few things you should know. The Orphic Forest is the dwelling of nearly all magic. Nothing about this forest is grounded in logic, but it doesn't mean that it's all bad. Some of it is quite beautiful, and then some of it is undeniably dangerous. Use your senses."

Bendigo wiped his moist palms on the side of his pants. "What about woodland dragons?"

Dagon took a step toward the trees. "Yes. They are

here."

Willy glanced at Bendigo, then fixated on Dagon. "What happens if we run into one?"

"They don't have any known weaknesses. Probably not what you wanted to hear, but if we run into one, be prepared to get creative." He waved his arms. "All right. Step up to the tree line."

Bendigo wasn't quite over Dagon's blunt reply, but what could he do? Turn back and go home? At this point, that was definitely not an option. So, he shifted forward, and a strange pressure pushed against his forehead.

"There is a visibility shield around the forest," Dagon explained. "See how it looks dark past these outside trees? It's just an illusion. Once we step through the visibility wall, we can see the forest, and outsiders won't be able to see us."

Bendigo reached forward, feeling the pressure increase. "Why is it like that?"

"It's to protect the magic. You'll know what I mean when we get through."

Willy hugged herself. "Is it gonna hurt?"

"It shouldn't. You may feel heavy or hard pressure but no pain. Shem?"

Shem glanced up.

"I'm going to go first," he informed. "Bendigo and Willy will follow, and I want you to go last. We can't go more than one at a time, or the forest will think we're invading, and it will throw us back out."

A nod was all Shem gave.

Bendigo studied their protector. A man of a few words.

Dagon inched toward the invisible force. "See you on the other side." As silent as a ghost would pass through a solid wall, he melted into the visibility shield and disappeared.

Bendigo's jaw dropped. He had never seen magic like this. He had dreamed about it in his self-isolation, but that was to escape to someplace more fun. Now, with real magic standing in front of him, his nerves grew. He couldn't control this magic. It had the ability to hurt him. Yet it also had the ability to awake his mind to what he had been imagining all his life.

"I'll go next." Willy took an apprehensive step. She then closed her eyes and moved forward. Her body too disappeared.

Bendigo noticed how Shem's shoulders rose. "She's stronger than you may think."

"Hm?" Shem drew his eyebrows down.

"Willy. She's a really strong person. You don't have to worry about her."

Shem seemed caught in a lie. "I'm not worried. Just cautious. About all of you. I want nothing more than to return to the Ports of Orphic and be back with my people, and I'm sure you two feel the same. I just want you both to be able to go back to Whimselon."

Bendigo gave him an honest downcast look. "It's not at the top of either of our priorities."

"It isn't? Why?"

"That's a conversation for another time, which I'm sure we'll have enough of. I'll be sure to enlighten you somewhere along the way of our travels."

He waved Bendigo forward. "All right. You should go. They'll start wondering where we are."

Bendigo stepped forward and felt the pressure increase yet again. He stopped and turned to Shem one last time. "Oh. Willy finds you attractive, by the way."

Shem straightened. "She what?"

He smiled and stepped through the trees.

Nine

The invisible shield around Bendigo pressed for only a second, like a dry wave, and then he emerged into a scene that took the air from his lungs. Dagon and Willy stood in the middle of a small grass clearing that was so vibrant that he wasn't sure if it was actually glowing or not. The trees around them had trunks that twisted like a braid and eventually met with leaves toward the top that fanned out in ovals as big as Bendigo himself. Little red shrooms, as he had seen in books, covered the forest floor, but what he had *never* seen was the sparkly blue flowers that sprang out from the tops of the mushrooms. The farther he looked into the forest, the more specks of red and blue decorated the ground.

It was like he could see his imagination. He saw the colors that his wandering mind had made up and the atmospheres that he used to wish were real.

"It's so beautiful," he whispered.

Shem appeared behind him and came forward to say something but stopped short when he laid eyes on the forest. His bottom lip dropped, and he lifted his chin up to the trees. "Whoa."

"You've never been in here?" Willy stooped to touch a

mushroom. "You live right down the valley."

Shem brought his chin down to her. "The Orphic Forest is dangerous. Our ancestors banished magic to here in fear of its power. We don't reserve the right to come and go as we please. Only to travel through, and even then, danger lurks."

"Shem is right," Dagon warned. "Don't let its beauty deceive you. Magic is not something you should handle lightly. With magic comes power, and power can lead to corruption. We must look out for each other."

Bendigo tried to get a sense of direction. "How far is Orenda from here?"

"A seven-day journey." Dagon moved forward.

"Wait. Did you say seven?" He jogged up next to him.

Dagon turned his head slightly. "The Orphic Forest is vast. This is no two-day stroll, which is why I said we must all be on guard. The longer you stay here, the easier it is to want to stay forever."

"Why forever?" He had felt a strong attraction to the forest as soon as he laid eyes on what it had to offer, but he couldn't imagine never wanting to leave.

"I said it already." Dagon let out a sigh. "Magic is power, and power is attractive. Right, Shem?"

Bendigo twisted toward Shem, who had stopped following the others. He faced the other way, staring at the forest as if yearning for something to appear or maybe hoping he could look long enough to capture the image for good.

"Shem." Bendigo strode to him, reaching out to grab his

elbow. "Hey."

He blinked and stepped back with the force of Bendigo's grasp. "Yes. What?"

"Stay with the group," Bendigo spoke low. "I think I see what Dagon means."

Shem nodded, looking like he was trying to sort out what had just happened to his mind. "Right. Thank you."

Dagon's expression was none other than concern, but he tried to conceal it when Willy looked his way. "Let's get moving," he said with urgency. "No need to linger when we have seven days ahead of us."

Bendigo tugged on his backpack straps and stayed next to Shem, while Willy paced a few feet ahead, talking Dagon's ear off. He had already lost track of which way they had come in, and as they headed deeper into the trees, the growth became denser. Thick green plants suffocated every open space.

Shem quieted his voice. "What you said before we entered the forest…"

"Don't think too much about it," Bendigo teased. "It's just a mere crush."

"She's young."

Bendigo shrugged. "I don't mean harm by mentioning it. I said it just so you know why she acts shy around you. She might also think you're going to be rude to her."

Shem's mouth turned down. "Why? Have I done something?"

"No, not at all, but most men in Whimselon are harsh

toward women who don't look the part of the usually gorgeous Whim."

"What does a gorgeous Whim look like?"

"Shiny blond hair, rosy soft skin, no blemishes, and thin framed."

They looked at Willy's dusty colored hair and toned arms. She continued to explain some sort of story to Dagon, her freckles dancing on her nose.

Shem frowned. "I don't see anything wrong with the way she looks."

"That's because you're not a Whim." Bendigo chuckled. "You're surrounded by fishermen."

He seemed to shake a memory from his head. "Yeah, I suppose I don't have beauty in the front of my mind when it comes to befriending people."

"Have you ever been in a relationship?"

He stiffened. "With a woman, you mean?"

"Yeah. You're older than I am. I would just guess that maybe you have, at least once, met someone in your lifetime."

"I meet people all the time. Men, women… They all travel through the Ports. None of them stay though, as I'm sure you've gathered."

"Not one?"

Shem rolled his shoulders back and looked forward. "Maybe there was one, but what does it matter?"

"How long did you know each other?"

"We've been married for ten years."

"You're *married*? And you just left the Ports without saying goodbye? Shem, I—"

"She isn't there." His voice was tight, like someone had a hand around his throat.

Bendigo looked down as his feet moved over an unknown species of aqua moss. "Where is she?"

"She left for Orenda eight years ago when she fell ill with a sickness we couldn't cure." He cleared his throat. "I begged to go with her, but she wouldn't allow it. I'm the only protector of the Ports now, and I was the only protector then too. If I had gone with her, all the fishermen would be left to fend for themselves, and half of them are barely strong enough to continue sailing or rowing. The ones physically able consume themselves in enough liquor to sleep for two days straight. Great people, not great protectors. My wife talked me into staying. She said she would return when she got better, but it's been eight years. I wake up every day regretting that I didn't leave with her."

Bendigo nodded. He originally was skeptical of why Shem had agreed to go with them without a thought, but he now saw the full picture. "Do you think she's still in Orenda?"

"There is a chance."

His soul grew heavy. Eight years? There was *barely* a chance, but he didn't have the heart to break that to Shem. "Well, when we get there, let's look for her."

Shem seemed surprised by his remark. "That would be...great. Thank you."

They walked in silence, lingering even farther behind Dagon and Willy.

Shem nodded his chin toward the chatter box. "And what about you?"

"Willy and I?" Bendigo let a quiet hoot escape. "We grew up together. Annoying little thing, she is. I appreciate her though. She's the closest thing I have to a real friend."

"But you'd rather be with a blonde-haired Whim?"

"No. I guess if I were to end up with a Whim, it'd be someone like her, sure."

The corners of Shem's mouth twitched up.

Bendigo caught Shem's look. "But it's not like that."

"I won't tell anyone." He went to nudge Bendigo, but Bendigo blocked it with his forearm.

"Tell anyone what?"

Dagon turned around. "Tousling already?" A teasing light lit up the corners of his eyes.

"Just getting to know each other," Shem said, covering for them.

Willy gave the boys an eye roll before turning back around.

"What about Dagon?" Bendigo whispered. "What do you think his story is?"

"The only thing I know about him is his age, and he doesn't even seem to be too sure about that. There's something about him though, isn't there?"

He remembered how the bustling pub faded in the background the first time he saw Dagon. "You feel it too?"

Shem brushed a low hanging branch out of the way. "Entirely."

"Quicken the pace, fellows," Dagon called from ahead, "or Willy and I might beat you to Orenda."

The four traveled across the forest floor well into the evening. Waves of hot air stayed tame behind the shelter of the treetops, and the sun had a hard time penetrating through to illuminate their surroundings. No one complained about the darkness since it meant shade, but even with the shade, sweat soaked their necks and dripped from their eyebrows.

Dagon held a hand up, halting the exhausted travelers.

Bendigo nearly ran into Willy, grabbing onto her to stop himself. "What's wrong?"

A muscle in Dagon's finger twitched. "I'm getting a feeling."

Shem slowly moved his hand toward his sword. Bendigo followed suit and got a hold of his dagger.

"Backs together," Dagon ordered. "Now."

Bendigo threw his back against Willy's as Shem and Dagon pressed on both sides, forming a tight circle that faced all directions. Willy breathed in and out in anxious beats, and her ribs expanded and retracted against his back. The dagger was difficult to hold onto with his suddenly sweaty palms. Every noise—even a cricket hopping to another blade of grass—made him jump. It felt like endless minutes passed as they stood. Bendigo was sure Dagon was about to call it off.

Then the Twilights appeared.

They rocketed out from behind the trees. Four of them. Their cloaks zipped through the air, circling the travelers. Their long, needle-like fingers reached for their enemies. They dove in, hissing, screaming, and swirling.

Shem drew his sword and sliced one in midair as it dove for Dagon's head. It fell to the ground and squirmed before fading away. The other three swarmed him, trying to consume him. He thrashed his sword around, stumbling left and right in the spirits' tormenting tornado.

"Willy, get out of here!" Bendigo threw her to the side. He lifted his dagger and plunged it into the back of one of the Twilights. It arched backward and let out a cry, shocking him with fear.

"Down!" Dagon shouted.

Bendigo dropped to the ground. Dagon launched over him and slung his arm around Shem, taking Shem and the Twilights down in a tousle of flesh, bone, and spirit.

"Hey!" Bendigo shouted. "Over here!"

One of the Twilights floated up from the brawl and faced him. Its empty hood turned to the side as if registering who he was.

The dagger in Bendigo's hand hung at his side. His arms shook. He saw Willy crouching behind a tree to his far left. She had no weapon. Shem was down. Dagon was down. He had to lead the Twilight away. So, he darted.

Branches whacked his face, chest, and arms, but he desperately carried himself forward. The Twilight lurched after him, grabbing for his tunic and hissing every time it missed.

A thick branch hung down ahead of him. He pumped his arms, leaped, and grabbed the bark. His feet hung above the ground, and the Twilight zoomed under him. He pulled himself up onto the branch and ran across it to the tree's trunk. Gliding like a woodland creature, he maneuvered up the tree into the safety of its greenery.

The Twilight must've realized that it lost its target. It circled back around toward the branch Bendigo used to escape.

Standing on his tiptoes and pressed up against the tree trunk, Bendigo held his breath. He watched the Twilight spin around the branch, as if looking for some sort of clue. It reached its hand out and touched the tree trunk, shivering. What was it feeling for? A presence? Warmth? Could they even detect that kind of thing? He wasn't sure, but he knew if he breathed, it would hear him, so he squeezed his lips together.

His lungs burned, his head grew dizzy, and his stomach clenched. He shut his eyes and realized he would have to breathe sooner or later if he wanted to live. Slowly, he let out his breath and opened his eyes. The much-needed breath of new air caught in his throat when he looked down and saw that the Twilight was gone.

"Where are you?" he whispered.

A Twilight's wail exploded in his right ear. He slipped as the spirit filled his vision. His feet no longer stood on the branch. He was free falling. Whacking through leaves, nicking branches, twisting, and sailing.

He hit the ground.

The back of his head bounced off the forest floor, splitting his vision. His spine cracked, and he lost feeling in his fingers. A bolus of vomit threatened to come up, but he forced it back down. His eyesight remained blurry, but what he saw above him was no mystery. The Twilight floated out from the tree leaves and began a slow descent toward him. It cocked its hood back and forth, hissing and, if it could, sneering.

Bendigo tried to move his arms, but they were numb. He attempted to move his legs. Nothing. Paralyzed. He was stuck on the forest floor as a Twilight came to kill him.

"Please," Bendigo gasped, and without meaning to, a name escaped his lips. "Dagon."

The Twilight floated inches away from him. The wind from its cloak softly blew his hair against his forehead. This was it.

Bendigo closed his eyes. He didn't want to see how he was going to die.

An abrupt disturbance of forestry made him whip his head sideways. Dagon exploded out of the trees with a knife in hand. All in a blink, he slit his own palm open, dove for Bendigo, and slammed the bloody wound against Bendigo's arm.

The Twilight reeled back, its cloak jerking upward like a jellyfish.

Dagon lay, panting on his stomach. His hand seeped blood against Bendigo's skin. Bendigo's eyes widened, trying to understand what was happening. He couldn't feel the warm red drops that drizzled down his bicep, but he watched in awe as the Twilight continued to move away. It hovered above the two for a moment longer before rising into the sky with the speed of a geyser, fading from existence.

Bendigo's mind raced. His chest expanded in frantic bursts. He was paralyzed. He was alive. One moment, he thought he was going to die, and the next, Dagon split his own hand open. Somehow, Dagon's blood had warded off the spirit.

Dagon pushed himself up and leaned over him. "Can you hear me? Bendigo, where are you hurt?"

"Dagon," was all he could say.

"Bendigo, can you move your arms?"

He stared at the blood that stained his bicep. "Your blood. How did—"

"Your arms." Dagon touched his hands. "Can you feel this? Do you feel my touch?"

Tears leaked out of his eyes and ran down to his ear. "No."

From behind Dagon, Willy and Shem came thrashing into view.

"Ben!" She dove forward.

Shem got a grip on her arm. "Willy, wait."

Bendigo looked up at Shem, who had a gash across his

cheek and a stiff expression.

"Willy." Dagon turned on his knees. "A Hyssop branch. I need a Hyssop branch."

"I saw one." She turned and bolted in another direction.

Shem squatted next to Dagon. "What happened?"

Dagon put a comforting hand on Bendigo's shoulder. "He's paralyzed."

"And you think you can fix that?" Shem didn't seem to want to look into Bendigo's eyes. "Dagon, I don't think a Hyssop branch is going to fix a broken spine."

Bendigo's eyes fluttered shut. Bile rose in his throat again. Pain in the areas he could still feel was beginning to make itself known now that his adrenaline had retreated.

Willy burst back to the men. "Here." She thrust the Hyssop branch into Dagon's hands. "What are you gonna do? Can you help him?"

"Back up a little," Dagon ordered the two in a gentle tone.

Bendigo watched Dagon's hands grip the plant and break it in two. A drop of moisture escaped from the break and fell onto his chest, though he couldn't feel that either. Dagon took one half of the branch and pressed it into his sternum with his wounded hand. His blood smeared over the branch and soaked through Bendigo's shirt. It mixed with the Hyssop branch's moisture and gave off a warmth. He brought his eyes up to Dagon's when he felt the sensation.

"Can you feel it?" Dagon asked only inches from his

face.

He nodded. "Is it going to work?"

"I'm not going to let this be your fate."

Prickling and tingling began in his fingertips, and soon, he could curl them into his palm. Against his control, his spine cracked and shifted, realigning itself into a position that eased his pain.

"How are you doing this?" Bendigo almost believed he was dreaming.

Dagon leaned into his sternum and exhaled across the branch. A wave of adrenaline pulsed beneath Bendigo's skin and soaked into his organs. Dagon reeled back and watched as he lifted his arms from the dirt, moving them through the air.

"How?" he whispered, pushing himself up to a sitting position. "How did you do that?"

Dagon let out a relieved sigh and helped him to his feet. "You were brave."

Willy left Shem's side and fell into Bendigo's arms, almost knocking him back down. "You're a fool, Bendigo Fletcher. Don't ever do something like that again."

Bendigo breathed in the honey suckle smell of her hair and closed his eyes. "I just couldn't let him get you."

"Well, stop that. We're here to fight too."

Shem stood off to the side, his arms crossed and his head down. "Why didn't you tell us you were a sorcerer?"

Dagon stepped in front of him. "I'm not a sorcerer."

Shem pointed to the ground where Bendigo had lain.

"Then what was that?"

Bendigo and Willy grew still. Shem seemed angry. Not amused. Not accepting of what had just happened. Angry.

Dagon bowed his head. "What you want is an explanation."

"What I wanted was the truth to begin with. Sorcery is dangerous and forbidden. Magic like that has consequences for *everyone* involved." Shem's arms twitched, as if trying to hold back rage.

"It wasn't sorcery." He stepped back. "But I do owe you an explanation. Let's set up camp for the evening. The sun won't be any help to us much longer since we're too deep into the forest. Nightfall will hit us sooner. Only get branches and leaves that are already lying on the forest floor; no need to disturb the trees themselves. Then I'll explain."

Ten

Bendigo sat on the forest floor, hugging his knees and staring into the bonfire. The flames flicked up toward the sky, curling at the tips before disappearing. He could feel shadows moving across his face as his cheeks melted in and out from a mild burn to a few moments of relief when the fire would lean away.

Willy sat next to him, semi leaning on his arm and zoning out. She had barely left his side since the Twilight incident.

To their right, Shem sat rigid like he was trying not to relax. Occasionally, he looked up through the flames at Dagon and gave a brief glare.

Dagon had one leg out straight and one bent up with his arm hanging over it. "I know you're all skeptical."

Bendigo stared across the fire at him. He felt no reason to question Dagon. If it weren't for him, he would still be lying on the forest floor, but Shem must know more about sorcery and its consequences than he does.

"I would never put you in danger on purpose." Dagon made eye contact with Shem. "I would never use sorcery to alter life."

Shem's shoulders relaxed a bit.

"It wasn't sorcery." Bendigo rubbed his shins. "It was your blood, wasn't it? You cut your hand open, so your blood could touch my skin. That kept the Twilight from claiming me. And the Hyssop branch only worked because your blood mixed with its moisture. Right?"

Dagon's shadow flicked over the ground. "You're right."

"Your blood." Shem dug a stick into the ground. "Your *blood?* Dagon, I trusted you enough to leave the Ports, and you didn't even tell us everything. Why would you keep something like that from us? Why did hiding it seem like the best decision?"

"All fair questions," he admitted. "I didn't want you to know what I was because I didn't want you to make decisions based on what I am and what must happen. I needed you to decide to join me in this journey by faith."

Willy leaned her cheek on her knee. "So, what *are* you exactly?"

A stick collapsed in the fire.

"I'm a product of The Book," Dagon breathed.

Bendigo furrowed his brows. "What does that mean?"

"The Book spoke me into existence. It wrote me into life." Dagon must've read their confused faces because he added, "I guess the easiest way to understand it is to think of The Book as my parents." He shrugged. "It created me to be different. To bring back the afterlife."

The flames illuminated Shem's weary eyes. "You aren't a man?"

"I am a man. Just spoken into being by The Book."

Bendigo threw a stick into the fire. "What makes you so different? What can you do to bring back the afterlife?"

"My blood. You saw what it can do. Yes, it has healing powers, but more importantly, it can't be destroyed by Twilights. *I* can't be killed by a Twilight. That is why I must be the one to defeat the Twilight army in Kalon. I'm the only one who they can't touch."

"This is unbelievable." Shem stood. "If you're untouchable, why are we here? Why are the three of us making this journey when the only people who could get killed *are* us?"

"Because that's not true." He rose to meet Shem. "I said a *Twilight* couldn't kill me. But people can. That's why I need all of you. I need fighters. I need people who have faith that Tarsha doesn't end with evil crushing every ounce of life. Have you noticed that there is *no one* willing to stand up? No one willing to fight?"

Shem's threatening stance sunk down, and he clenched his jaw. "All I've ever done is fight and protect."

"And that's why you're here," Dagon said, strained. "You have faith in a turn of events. Don't let doubt persuade you otherwise. Fight. Fight with me. Get me to Kalon. Help me eliminate the Twilights." He turned to the Whims. "Fight with me to pry the afterlife from their grip and return it to eternity where it belongs. Then we will no longer live in fear of death. Aren't you tired of living while knowing that your last breath can only lead to darkness?"

Bendigo had never heard such beautiful and profound

words. Such hope. Such passion.

Shem's eyes dropped. "I dread it every day. Death hangs over my head. Dagon, forgive me. I didn't understand." He lifted his head. "But you have my word. I will help you bring back the afterlife, and I will trust you."

Bendigo put an arm around Willy. "You have us too." He had never doubted Dagon, even though he should have. Something about the mysterious man made Bendigo submissive. Calm.

Dagon patted his chest. "And I am eternally thankful."

Dainty clicks and pops of the fire were the only sounds for the next few moments.

"Bendigo," Dagon said. "Do you mind keeping watch for the time being, while Shem and I see if we can find something to eat?"

"Will do." Bendigo patted his dagger to make sure it was still there.

Dagon picked up the cool end of a stick from the fire and held it like a torch. He and Shem drifted off into the darkness, fading from sight.

Bendigo leaned back on his palms. "You still holding up?"

Willy pulled her cloak over her lap. "I have moments of fear."

"So do I."

"Do you really?"

He drew back. "Of course, I do. Why would you assume I don't?"

"Back in Whimselon, when the Keeper said that you were the one who had to fulfill the prophecy, you didn't seem scared. Everyone else seemed scared, but you weren't." She gazed at his rigid eyes. "Why?"

"Willy, I was scared." He smiled at her freckles. "But at the same time, it was a relief. An aching relief."

"How?"

He inhaled a deep, calming breath. "I've been sort of...trapped."

"Trapped where? No one is bound to Whimselon, you know. Sure, no one leaves unless they *have* to, but that doesn't mean you *can't.*"

"No." Bendigo touched his forehead and smiled. "I've been trapped up here."

"In your brain?"

"My mind."

Willy tucked her knees up to her chest and rested her chin on them. "I don't think I get it."

He looked up at the black canopy of leaves. "I feel like my mind is a prison. I'm airy. Spacey. I don't really pay much attention to reality. Realities are so depressing, so hopeless. Because of that, I go to places I've made up in my mind, but the places I go to are lonely. Not always, of course, because I enjoy going to them, but when I come back here, no one here has gone to those places with me. I'm left reliving an adventure I have experienced alone. And I long to go back, but I can't just reside in a made-up space. So, instead, I feel sad. Detached. Like I want to lie on the ground in a closed-off room where no one can ask me what's wrong, because how can I tell someone I wish I was somewhere else without sounding ominous?" He swallowed. "I don't want people to share my burden; sharing my burden with someone else is a burden to *me*. So, I internalize it. Until it's so suffocating and mind consuming that I wish I were...dead."

She silently watched him. Her glassy eyes held back sorrow and shock. "So, you thought this task would let you live a real experience, one that would allow your mind to heal, because this time, you're traveling to a real place, not just a prison in your head."

"Yes." He gazed out into the woods that surrounded them. "I'm sick of feeling...sick."

She scooted closer to him and rested her head on his shoulder. "You aren't sick, Bendigo. You're just full of color."

He leaned his head on hers. "I like that. Full of color."

☾

Farther into the forest, deep enough that the bonfire was only a speck in the distance, Shem and Dagon scanned the trees for a fruit Dagon called Wittle. It was known to hold nutrients that could sustain a person for two days. Its existence though was, as expected, rare.

Dagon waved his fading torch across another mass of fruitless twigs.

"Is there anything else we can look for?" Shem spoke with a twinge of impatience. "I understand that the Wittle is ideal, but I don't think we should be wandering this far from the bonfire. We need to get back to Bendigo and Willy."

Dagon held the torch out to his side and faced him. "Yes, but I wanted to get far enough away to tell you something."

His mind swarmed with concern while the torch lit up only part of Dagon's face. "Tell me what?"

"I know about your wife."

A piece of his heart broke to the surface from the place where it had been buried. "How? I never told you."

"Revelation."

"That can't be your answer for everything."

"Though it seems to be the answer more often than not."

He clenched his teeth. "What about my wife?"

"Shem, you've waited eight years to hear from her, and although that's a long time, you still have hope that you'll see her when we get to Orenda."

"What if I have hope? That's not your business. How does that affect you? Or the Whims?"

"More than you know." Dagon kept his eyes fixed on the warrior's defensive expression. "What happens if we get to Orenda and you don't find her?"

"What are you getting at?"

He walked a few steps from Shem and blew on the

torch, creating a glow of embers before it faded again. "Something tells me she won't be there."

Anger filled Shem's heart, and he fought to keep it at bay. "How could you say that when all you talk of is having faith?"

He dropped the now useless torch to the ground and reached out for Shem in the darkness. "I'm trying to soften the blow."

"By discouraging me."

"By preparing you."

"I can handle heartbreak on my own."

Dagon brought his hands up and rested them on the sides of Shem's face, holding his head in a fatherly clasp. "But you are not on your own. You are to protect those Whims. If your hope is shattered with the truth of your wife's fate, you cannot let your sorrow affect your ability to protect them and even myself. We need you."

The back of Shem's eyes filled with moisture, and he blinked, trying to clear the emotion from view even though he could hardly make out Dagon's own eyes in the dark. "Yes." His voice quivered. "I told you. I'm here until the end."

"And I'll be here if the sorrow comes. Don't go through the pain alone when you have people around you who love you."

Shem drew back. "Love? I don't think I just speak for myself when I say I hardly think the four of us encompass love for one another."

Dagon let his hands drop. "Why is that?"

"We have known each other for mere days."

"Does love need a firm amount of time to grow?"

"What kind of question is that? Of course, it does."

"Love is not always the passionate kind. Why did you worry for Bendigo when he lay on the forest floor, unable to move on his own?"

Shem searched his memory, wondering what had caused him to become so distraught over Bendigo's paralyzed body. "I suppose it's just in my nature to care for another one's life."

"Love." Dagon's voice diffused in the air like a fog claiming its territory. "A pure love that you don't have to grow with time. It lives in actions. And you have a lot of it."

Eleven

Days faded in and out as the four made their way through the Orphic Forest. The seven-day journey was beginning to feel like a death march as the fourth day dawned. Bendigo tried to keep how badly his feet hurt hidden but his wincing gave it away. He *was* developing calluses on the more tender parts of his foot, and the pain, though subsiding, was still bothersome. What hurt worse was the pit in his stomach. All four days, the group's main source of nutrients had been wild plants that sustained them for two hours at most.

Knowing they couldn't function much longer under such conditions, the four had decided to split up for a short while to see if they could find something more sustainable to eat. During the search, Bendigo and Willy emerged into a field of orange trees. She wasted no time to pick one off a tree and enjoy the sweet taste of summer that they usually only got a few times a year when the Lhan produce cart would deliver oranges as a surprise. But a few bites in, Willy turned sour, insulting Bendigo, telling him how much she couldn't stand being around him.

"I don't care what you say. I still can't *stand* you." She threw an orange right at his head.

He ducked, covering his head with his hand in case he

wasn't fast enough. "Willy, what was *that* for?"

She grabbed another.

"Just hold on a minute." He kept his hands in front of his face. "What did I do?"

"You know what you did," she spat. "All you've ever done is make me feel worthless, and I've believed every word. You ruined me, and I *hate* you for it!"

He opened his mouth to retort right as Dagon and Shem broke into the clearing. "Dagon, look at this." He waved toward her. "I don't know what's gotten into her."

"Don't act so innocent!" She threw another one.

He crouched again. "See?"

Dagon scanned the field. "Did she eat one of the oranges?"

"Yes, and then she snapped."

"I see." Dagon heaved a sigh. "What did I say about eating before consulting?"

Bendigo threw his hands out, indicating how it was *her* who had failed to listen. Not him.

Shem squinted at her. "What's wrong with the oranges?"

Willy stood in the middle of the trees, clenching yet another round fruit in her fist.

"When an Orphic Forest orange is eaten, it brings out the emotion that is most deeply buried inside a person's heart." Dagon fixated on her with noticeable sympathy.

"Well can you fix it?" Bendigo twitched when she shifted a slight step.

Dagon shuffled toward her. "It usually has to run its

course. The only other way to turn the effects around is to show the person enough of the opposite emotion. What has she said to you?"

"She said I ruined her and that she hates me." His heart seized. "But we've been friends since we were kids, and we rarely ever fought, unless we were competing. What have I done to cause so much hatred?"

"It may not be toward you." Dagon took another step forward. "Sometimes, the emotions are the result of someone else's actions, but since you're the only one near, she'll see you as that someone else."

Bendigo gazed into her eyes from across the field. He saw a fire in her pupils that he had seen before in Whimselon. A fire that only became ignited when her parents tore her down. They always told her she wasn't beautiful and that she would be nothing. He had experienced it with her. "I know who it is." He looked at Dagon. "It's her parents."

At the mention of them, she lowered her chin, lifting her eyes up to a glare.

"You seem to be spot on." Dagon lowered his voice. "She has a lot of hate. We must show her love if we are going to alter the effects. Counterbalancing the curse is also exhausting on the one effected; she will need to rest after this. So much for trudging on till dark."

Dagon treaded closer to her, one inch at a time. He didn't hold his hands up in a protecting manner but instead walked like she held no threat. "Willy." His voice was soft. "Can we have a conversation?"

She dug her nails into the skin of the orange. "No." She threw the fruit, pelting him right in the cheek.

Bendigo cringed. "Dagon, I'm not sure that—"

"You don't know what I've been through," her voice broke.

Dagon didn't flinch upon the orange's impact, but his eyes did flinch at her painful tone. "No, maybe I don't know, but there is someone here who does." He turned to Bendigo.

Bendigo swallowed, fearing another strike of angry oranges, but saw what Dagon was trying to do. "Yeah, Willy. I know. Want to talk about it?" The awkward words escaped before he could muffle them. He was never good at emotional conversations, but he could try for the sake of breaking her of the orange's curse.

She considered his proposal in deafening silence. Then her hand dropped to her side, and an orange rolled down her fingers and onto the grass.

Bendigo took that as a yes. He straightened his posture and strode forward, never taking his eyes off her tense figure.

Dagon stepped back and turned Shem around by his shoulder. "Let's give them a few minutes."

Bendigo relaxed a bit, feeling more comfortable without an audience. "Hey. You know I understand."

"How could you understand?" she growled. "Your family loved you."

He stood directly in front of her, only an arm's reach

away. "They did, but don't you remember all the times I was with you through everything your parents did?"

Her glare dropped a little.

He dared to go on. "Remember that time you wanted to cover up your freckles because your mom told you they made you look dirty, so I stole some light potting soil from my father's herb cupboard, and we mixed it with water to make a skin-colored face mask? It ended up looking even more ridiculous than we thought. We laughed for hours."

A flick of ease passed over her eyes.

"Or that time your dad told you to stop spending so much time with me because you were only going to drag me down with you, so instead we spent every day together in June?"

"I remember that." She wrapped her arms around herself. She then blinked a few times, growing drowsy as her hatred began to descend.

Bendigo sat, crisscrossing his legs. He patted the ground next to him, and she plopped down, squeezing her knees into her chest and looking out at the orange trees.

"You've been there for me too, you know," he muttered through unexpected nervousness.

"I have?"

"Of course. I just do a poor job of telling you that. All the times I wondered what my life would be like if my mother was still alive, you would make up stories of memories I might have shared with her. It made her feel real again." He smiled without looking at her. "Then when my father died, you took care of Zach and my herbs, while we prepared for the burial. You did it without thinking twice."

Her whole body drooped forward, and her eyelashes fell toward her cheeks. Dagon was right about the exhaustion following the orange's curse.

Bendigo put his hands on her hunched frame and guided her to lay her head in his lap. He dropped his voice, so she could surrender to her slumber. "And you always pull me out of my sadness, even when I don't want you to." Without thinking, he ran his fingers over the hair falling across her face and tucked it behind her ear. "You're a really good friend. I never realized the depth of it until now."

The sun had tucked itself into the blanket of bulbous clouds that filled the sky above. All the blue had been pushed down toward the horizon, now replaced by shades of pink and peach as Tarsha prepared for another night. The orange trees gave the impression of dancing to a lullaby against the whimsical sunset's backdrop. Bendigo closed his eyes, smelling the twinge of fruit and feeling her warmth against his thigh.

This journey. This weird, unexpected, secretive journey. They had been away from Whimselon for over a week now, and he already felt that he had changed. He spent eighteen years wondering why he was so weak and enslaved by his depressive emotions. But in a few days' time, he had realized that he had something in him that was stronger: his ability to *love*.

Twelve

"So, it's like this." Shem held a long, knobby branch in his hand to resemble a sword.

Bendigo readjusted his grip on Shem's actual sword. "Okay. Got it."

"What do you do when I advance toward you like this?" Shem jabbed his stick high toward his throat.

He stutter-stepped backward and went for a jab.

"Nope." Sweat fell from Shem's brow. "Counter-parry."

"Right." He reset. "Do it again."

Shem swung the stick in another pretend attack. Bendigo drew a circular movement around Shem's branch with his sword and moved it away.

"Just like that!" Shem approved.

Willy watched from a rock that jutted out over the creek they stopped at. This section of the Orphic Forest opened more, allowing light to flood over the clear, cool water. A rainbow of color spread across every inch of the forest floor, wildflowers happy to be in the sun's presence.

"We need to get you a sword, Bendigo," she said. "Don't you think, Dagon?"

Dagon stood shin deep in the creek, rinsing his arms and cooling off the back of his neck with scoops of water.

"Sure. He's learning fast."

"Why don't you have a sword?" She tilted her head.

Bendigo turned an ear to listen.

Dagon gave her a thin-lipped smile. "I'll get one in Orenda."

"How do you know?" She crossed her arms.

He splashed water on his face. "Revelation."

Bendigo scoffed, smiling.

She scowled. "I don't like it when you answer with that."

"Seemingly, none of you do." He wiped water from his eyes. "What am I supposed to say?"

"I don't know. Isn't anything a mystery to you?"

"Of course. I just happen to have something called divine knowledge."

She dipped her bare feet in the water. "I've never heard of that. How do you get it?"

"Remember"—he strode through the creek's current in a slow-motion-like manner—"I was created through the words of The Book of Prophecy. Everything about me is not understood with logic. Although, if you ever need a little revelation, just ask me. I'm willing to share my knowledge for your benefit. I'll only keep it from you if I think it could cause you harm."

As if night decided to fall in the middle of the afternoon, a menacing shadow covered the sun, dimming the world to a gray hue. Bendigo paused, letting the sword hang at his side. Storm clouds the color of deep Whimselon mud rolled and twisted within each other, claiming every inch of the sky. A sense of danger whipped through his limbs, and he shoved the sword back into Shem's hands.

Willy stood. "What's happening?"

Dagon made a break for the creek's shore and jogged onto land. Reaching for her, he helped her off the rock. "Be still."

Bendigo stood facing Dagon and Willy with his back to the twisted trees. His body was stiff, heart rapping. The darkness consumed every bit of the air, and the creek churned like a rapid. A gust blew against his neck. Then another. The looks that overcame Dagon's and Willy's face forced him to turn around.

Tearing through the trees was what looked like a wall of water, like when a rainstorm makes its way across a plain. Only this wall of water wasn't rain. It was wind. *Visible* wind. It chugged through the forest, spreading out as far as Bendigo could see. With every inch it touched, it took the forest with it, uprooting trees, spinning up the grass, dispersing moss, and eating the flowers. It created a swirling mixture of deathly objects with inevitable doom.

And it was heading for the creek.

Shem pressed his forearm into Bendigo's chest and shoved him backward. "Dagon, what is it?"

A *thwarp, thwarp, thwarp* pounded in Bendigo's ears as the gale pushed its way closer and closer.

"It's an Execration Tempest," Dagon said with dread in his voice as he pulled Willy toward the creek. "A wall of wind so wide and strong that it destroys everything in its path, and nature only creates them under a curse. Move. Now."

The forest's canopy twirled, and dirt spun up against Bendigo's ankles as he dashed to the creek. The sound of their feet splashing across the water crashed in his ears. His pants clung to his calves, and particles from the forest floor suctioned to his wet feet as he scrambled out on the other side.

Thwarp, thwarp, thwarp.

He turned his chin over his shoulder to see a tree lifted from the ground as if it had been plucked like a carrot. His eardrums threatened to burst from the beat of the wind-storm. The wall chugged on, reaching where he and Shem had just been practicing on the other side of the creek.

"Quickly now!" Dagon yelled.

Full sprints carried the four through the forest. Tree trunks splintered, and branches sailed like birds through the open air. But the *sound.* The sound of the Execration Tempest screamed peril as it charged forward, nearing with every menacing second.

A tug yanked Bendigo's shoulder back. His backpack was becoming airborne, being vacuumed into the gust. He pulled forward, but it pulled back. He shrugged his shoulders free and threw the pack behind him, lurching forward toward Shem. But his lungs weren't retracting fast enough. The gulps of air weren't successful. He needed to slow down, but he had no choice.

A stampede of Orphic creatures charged through the woods, right alongside the four. Deer whizzed past, their fawns following close behind. Rabbits, foxes, and wolves. White, long-necked storks flew through the trees. Bendigo understood the severity of it now. Nature hadn't just turned on mankind.

Nature had turned on nature.

Up ahead, a gully cut deep into the ground. The creatures leaped right over it, continuing their desperate escape, but Dagon grabbed onto Willy and shoved her down into the ditch.

He waved Shem and Bendigo forward. "Here!"

Bendigo let out a yell, motivating his body to just *move*. He dove and slid into the gully, bumping into Shem as they collapsed against each other. The ground sat just a foot above their heads. A poor case of defense.

Dagon sailed into the ditch. "Heads down."

Bendigo knew they had no chance. He pulled his knees to his chest, tucked his head, and waited. Willy crouched next to him, breathing heavy. He grabbed her hand. A cry escaped from her throat.

"Willy." He could barely hear himself over the approaching wind. "I—"

A howling roar cut through the air, defeating the wind's sound. A woodland dragon, parading through the trees, hovered a few inches above ground. Its grayish purple wings flicked left and right, just missing tree trunks. It flew toward the gully where the four sat huddled.

Every other creature fled the wall of wind, this dragon seemed to be heading *into* it.

Bendigo squeezed his eyes shut, thinking of his worst nightmare: leaving this world the same way his father had. He had always feared it yet never thought such a day would actually come.

But upon opening his eyes, he realized that today was not that day.

The dragon's wings draped over the ditch, covering the four as the Execration Tempest arrived. The ground shook, and the dragon bellowed a menacing roar so deafening that Bendigo had to cover his ears. With the roar came fire, crashing into the wall of wind, pushing the tempest back, and holding it where it was.

"He's helping us," Dagon whispered. Then he snapped to it. "Get out! Go!"

Bendigo used Shem's shoulder for leverage and launched himself above ground. He reached back and pulled Willy up, dragging her behind him as he lurched forward. The heat from the dragon's fire sizzled in the air, crackling the leaves on the remaining trees.

"He can't hold it forever!" Dagon shouted. "He's losing control."

Bendigo turned sideways, not stopping his feet, as he watched the dragon struggle to hold back the wind. With one final breath of flames, it pulled away. With two flaps, it soared again, heading toward the four with nothing but an inch to spare above their heads.

"Get low!" Shem ordered.

Bendigo tensed and hunched forward. The beast's wings caressed the top of his head, nearly making an impact. It glided ahead of them, dropped to the forest floor, and threw its wing down to the ground, creating a ramp up to its back.

He slowed. "No way."

"*Yes* way." Willy shoved him forward. "Get on."

He sucked in a breath and was almost to the grounded wing when a root shot up, grabbed his ankle, and pulled him down. He kicked at it with his free foot, cursing it to set him free.

"Ben!" She stopped to yank on his arm.

The root tightened.

"Get on the dragon." Shem drew his sword. "I got him."

She sprinted for the dragon, climbing with all fours up its wing.

Shem hacked at the root with his sword, nicking Bendigo's skin in desperate slices to get him loose.

"Shem, behind you!" Bendigo warned.

Shem spun around and drove his sword right through a branch that had reached out to swipe at him. Another branch swung down, attempting to swipe the sword from his hand. He bent backward. The branch passed over his face, missing his nose by the thinness of a coin.

Bendigo's hands shook. He drew his dagger. With desperate force, he cut through the root around his ankle. He looked up and saw the windstorm nearing Dagon's back.

"I'm loose!" Bendigo shouted at Shem, pushing himself up from the quivering ground. "Go."

Dagon plowed into the boys, and the three of them made their getaway toward the dragon. Willy's eyes widened as they sprinted onward with the tempest almost touching the backs of their necks.

Bendigo leaned forward and dove for the wing. As soon as he made contact, the dragon lifted off, leaving him hanging onto the clammy, rough-skinned wing for dear life. Willy reached down and helped Shem sling his leg over to sit on the dragon's back.

The ground grew smaller. The windstorm warped from a wall into a circle, trying to immerse the dragon into its swirling mass. Bendigo's body wiggled in a wave from head to toe as the dragon pumped its wings, propelling itself upward.

Dagon clung next to Bendigo, shouting over the wind. "Link your elbow with mine!"

Bendigo shook his head. "I can't let go."

"*Now*, Bendigo!"

He released his grip and swung his arm under Dagon's, connecting elbows. Shem dragged Dagon and Bendigo up onto a sturdier surface, where the dragon's neck met its back. Willy clung tight to the neck. Shem sat behind her, holding her in place, while he placed Dagon behind him. Bendigo pulled himself into a sitting position and held onto the back of Dagon's tunic.

The tornado spiraled upward, twisting like a knobby finger reaching for the dragon's tail. The dragon pulsed upward and broke through the treetops. The setting sun's lavender and orange hues streamed across the sky, diffusing through the clouds. The dragon soared forward, carrying the four over the Orphic Forest and leaving the Execration Tempest behind to wallow in its failure.

Thirteen

Dawn's pale, white light stayed hidden behind steely clouds when the dragon quietly landed in what Dagon called the In-Between. The air had been chilly above the clouds and only turned to dampness upon landing.

The In-Between—where the Orphic Forest ended and collided with the forested outskirts of Orenda—had sad olive colored grass, damp with dew that never dried. The bark on the sparse trees were ashen, and the branches curved like lightning strikes, holding no leaves. The tips of the trees ended in sharp points. Dead. Hollow. Ghostly.

Bendigo's thighs ached as he stepped down the dragon's wing. He had been in a saddle position for countless hours. When his feet touched the grass, he wobbled a bit, flexing his muscles to keep standing upright. The soggy air suppressed his skin, sucking out any warmth his body may have spared from sitting so close to Dagon.

He looked around at the In-Between. It screamed death. There was no color. Only shades. This. *This* is what his mind looked like when he felt sad. He stood where he had to escape from daily, and it suffocated him. He slowly spun in a circle, hoping to find something different, but was met with the same horror: dead trees, drooping grass, and a sky that looked like it was about to cry.

Dagon stepped up beside him. "Are you okay?"

Bendigo cleared his throat. "Yes. This place just…feels desolate."

"It *is* desolate," he said. "The Twilights have already taken the life from here."

Behind them, the dragon let out a sigh as Shem helped Willy down. It looked toward Bendigo, blinking long and slow.

Bendigo gazed back at it. "Why did it help us?"

Dagon waved his hands around. "Nature is slowly growing cursed. The creatures see it, they feel it, and they understand it. This dragon sees that nature is an enemy both to humans and animals alike now. It picked a side."

"A side?" Willy shivered in the wet air.

"Yes. Life or death. It chose life."

Bendigo took a step toward the dragon. Its head hovered above the ground, and its neck curved in an *S* to compensate for the lower height. From head to tail, it was probably thirty feet long. Smaller than the one that had invaded Whimselon.

With an open palm, he reached toward its nose. It drew back and flared its nostrils, releasing a hot breath against his fingers. The two stood, staring at each other. Then it leaned forward and pressed its nose against his outstretched hand. He let go of his breath. The contact between skin and scales felt unusual in his palm, but he leaned forward, getting even closer to the dragon's muzzle.

"Thank you," he murmured, "for saving me and my friends. Keep choosing life."

The dragon pushed away from his touch and stretched out its wings. Its neck extended toward the sky, letting out a soft growl as if to announce its departure. With a swift stroke of its wings, it ascended, gliding above the In-Between. It nosedived downward before shooting back up again and disappeared into the rain-filled clouds.

Bendigo stood, staring up. The In-Between's silence gripped his chest. Then a hand slipped into his, and he turned to face Willy.

"You faced a fear," she said. "How do you feel?"

He drew in a quick breath. "Do you remember that night?"

"Of course, I do. I'll never forget what your father did. I'll never be ungrateful for it either."

"I feel like I betrayed him, in a way, by riding that dragon."

She shook her head. "No. I think he would have been proud."

Shem stepped forward. "Might I say something?"

Bendigo dropped her hand, thinking that Shem would make an unneeded joke about it later. "Yes."

Shem's hair had completely fallen out of its braid. It hung in matted tussles down his back and over his shoulders, fraying at his elbows. "I wasn't there the night your father died, but I know a woodland dragon took him from you."

He looked down.

"Your courage to trust something you should hate has made me contemplate some things."

Dagon crossed his arms, a warmth spreading across his lips.

Bendigo tilted his head. "Contemplate what?"

Shem clenched his jaw. "I've always hated Orenda. It took my wife from me. It bore hope for her, but it took her away."

Willy looked hurt. "I'm sorry, Shem."

He gave her a soft smile before his voice broke like the slip up of a stringed instrument. "I started to doubt that I was ready to know the truth, but I think it's just because…I'm…scared." He winced, as if it physically hurt to admit his struggle.

Dagon moved forward, joining his side. "Being scared is normal. Hiding it is no more painless than the fear itself. Remember what I told you: you are surrounded by people who love you. Let us share your burdens."

"He's right," Bendigo said. "The only reason I got on the dragon was because I knew you all were going to be there. I wasn't going to be alone. And you aren't going to be alone either. No matter what you find out."

A drizzle of rain fell, hitting Willy's nose. "Is that what we have for each other?" She squinted. "Love?"

"Brotherly love." Dagon nodded. "Something the world has lost because of selfish ambition and vanity. Let us never lose it because there is no fear in love."

Bendigo felt the flood of peace that he had experienced the first time he saw Dagon. It was like Dagon had a way of erasing all fear if he wanted to.

Shem nodded, rain dripping from his hair. "I'm ready to learn what happened."

"Then let's continue on toward the city." Dagon waved them along. "It's only a little ways ahead. Once we get to the city, we will have some rest. Some of our greatest allies live in Orenda."

"How do you know?" Bendigo trotted beside him. "Did you send word that we're coming?"

"No, but they know."

Bendigo and Shem shared a semi eye roll, agreeing in silence that they accepted Dagon's response yet detested its vagueness.

Willy wiped rainwater from her cheek. "Are we just passing through Orenda, or are we going there for a reason?"

"There's a reason." Dagon chuckled.

"What's the reason then?"

"Orenda is known for three things: their cobblestone architecture, their libraries, and their scholars. We are seeking their scholars."

Bendigo rubbed his arms, failing to warm himself. "How come?"

"Some of their scholars are dedicated to recording history and updating maps frequently. They have messengers and spies who have been tracking the Twilight's movements.

They can tell us what to expect once we reach Kalon."

"The Book you always talk about…" Shem turned to Bendigo. "You had said that it was originally in Orenda but hidden in Whimselon. Why?"

Dagon looked over his shoulder.

Bendigo caught his glance. "I only know what the legend says. The original Keeper tried opening The Book on his own, and a dense fog overcame the city, suffocating it for days. He knew then that The Book couldn't fall into the wrong hands, but too many people already knew where to find it, so he had to hide it. Right, Dagon?"

He nodded. "That is the story."

"Story," Willy echoed. "You say it like that's not what really happened."

"No, that is what happened," Dagon confirmed, "but some say that The Book's presence can still be felt in the city, and when the presence is detected, a dense fog rolls into the streets, searching for the Keeper."

Bendigo twitched a smile. "They do know that fog is a natural occurrence, right?"

"Oh yes." The lines on his forehead appeared. "They know that full well, but they say this fog is different. Cold. Alive. There for a purpose."

Shem wiped his eyes, clearing the rain that had collected on his eyebrows. "So we should continue to keep it a secret then? That we know where The Book is?"

"Yes," Bendigo said with haste, then frowned. "But…does it matter anymore?"

Dagon gave a slow nod. "We should keep it a secret. If The Book were to fall into the Twilight's hands, they could use it against us. Human eyes can only see the words written in The Book. Twilights can see beyond. They can see prophecies that aren't yet inked onto the pages."

"You were created by The Book." He sidestepped a puddle. "Does that mean you know the end?"

Dagaon looked up at the sobbing sky. "No."

He brought his eyebrows together. Something in Dagon's voice didn't sound convincing, but his conscience told him to not keep demanding answers. Dagon had told Willy back in the Orphic Forest that he would only hold back on knowledge if he thought the knowledge could be harmful, and he believed him.

The rain fell faster. Nothing like the storm that had chased them out of the Ports of Orphic, but Bendigo was on edge, wondering when nature would make its next move. Though he also doubted that the In-Between could create such force. Could a place so dead create *anything*?

A stream of smoke lifted from the lifeless treetops in the distance. Then another. And another.

"Look," Bendigo said, pointing at them.

Dagon brought his eyes up. "From the chimney stacks. We're almost there."

Dragging his feet from exhaustion, Bendigo's toe nicked the edge of something hard. He looked down. The grass hung like a wet blanket over a gray stone that peeked out between the blades. Except it wasn't just a stone. It was a gravestone. Bending down, he pushed the grass aside, revealing a name. *Braxton Lume.*

"Hey," he said. "I think we're in…" He lifted his head. All around him, jagged stones took over the wet, depressing landscape. Some stuck up, some cracked in half, and some laid flat underneath the overgrown grass. "A graveyard."

Pain laid like a smothering hand on Dagon's face.

They meandered through the stones, glancing at each one to read the names of people they had never met and giving the dead the respect of silence.

Willy stopped at one of the newer stones. "This one looks like it hasn't been here long. *Loretta.* No last name." She brushed some dirt from the bottom of the rock. "Oh but look. It says wife of…Shem…" Her bottom lip dropped.

Dagon closed his eyes.

Shem stood paralyzed a few feet away, looking at her like he didn't exactly hear her right.

"Oh, Shem." She clutched at her chest. "I'm so sorry."

Bendigo swallowed rising sorrow and stepped around the graves to get to Shem. "Remember." He stood next to him, as straight as he could. "We're here."

Reluctant, Shem approached his wife's grave with Bendigo at his side. He lowered to his knees and touched the name, *Loretta — Wife of Shem.* "I didn't want to admit that this was her fate, but I knew. Her sickness was too advanced."

Bendigo rested his hand on Shem's shoulder but said

nothing. He didn't know *what* to say. He knew the feeling of losing someone he loved. No amount of words would make the pain go away.

Dagon knelt next to Shem. "She must have been known and loved here for the people of Orenda to give her a proper burial. And she obviously spoke of you if they knew she was your wife."

Shem's fingertips clutched the gravestone. "I love her so much."

Willy's face broke, and she looked away, trying to hide it.

"She knew that," Dagon said.

"Did she?" A tear rested on his bottom eyelash. "I sent her off alone. What a terrible, awful thing to do to someone you love."

"She asked you to do that." Bendigo's voice wavered. "Maybe she knew what her fate was going to be."

"I don't care." He buried his face in his hands. "I regret it."

Dagon wrapped an arm around his shaking shoulders.

Shem's uncontrolled sobs made a few solitary tears drip out of Bendigo's own eyes. He bent down and reached his arm around Shem's other shoulder, overlapping with Dagon's. The two held him there, making sure he knew he wasn't alone.

Willy plucked a few wet strings of grass and tied them together to create a makeshift bouquet. She dried it with her sleeve and placed it on top of the gravestone, bowing her head.

Dagon glanced up at her gesture. The grass was a sad excuse for a bouquet, but it offered some acknowledgment of the pain that encompassed their hearts, Shem's especially. Placing a hand atop the bouquet, he drew in a cavernous breath and then exhaled, quiet like a humid breeze. He drew his hand away, revealing little white flowers that now danced on the grass tips.

Though it was magic they had never seen before, no one questioned how.

And though they were so close to Orenda, no one wanted to leave.

Fourteen

A stone archway marked the entrance to Orenda. An emblem of a lantern sitting on top of a book had been sketched into the rock in the middle of the arch. The letters in the name *Orenda* sunk deep into the stone, welcoming the travelers with a sort of foreboding power.

Bendigo shivered as he stepped under it, and for once, it wasn't from fear. The temperature had dropped to something between damp and icy, as the rain still fell. Dagon and Willy walked silently next to Shem, who hadn't said a word since they left the grave site. He hung behind them. Though he knew the city was famous for its architecture, Bendigo was still overwhelmed with its magnificence—of how every cobblestone building was solid yet held character in the way its windowpanes were shaped or how the doors were carved. Even the roofs had jagged edges and crooked slants.

A cold sensation slipped between his fingers, and he yanked his hand upward, startled. Turning around, he noticed a trail of fog had followed him into the city, hovering just high enough to run across his fingertips. It wasn't like the fog he was used to. Natural fog was more or less noninvasive. But not this time. This fog was lifelike.

"Bendigo," Dagon called from ahead. "Keep up."

Bendigo jogged forward. "Sorry, I just—"

"Saw the fog."

He nodded.

"It senses you."

He brought his voice down. "Why?"

"You have a direct relation to The Book. Just stay with us."

The streets weren't full. The rain had made sure of that. But light glowed in every window, affirming the life that thrived in Orenda. Some windows they passed had words painted on them like *tavern*, *cobbler*, and *apothecary*, but more than anything else was the word *books*. Every other storefront claimed to be a bookstore, and through the window glass, each one was bobbing with heads.

Bendigo stopped to peer into one of the windows. "They really do take books seriously."

Shem leaned over his shoulder. "How strange."

"Yeah, I guess." He was just glad Shem had spoken.

Willy joined them. "Why strange? Books are important."

"I've never read one for entertainment," Shem admitted.

"What?" Bendigo dropped his mouth slightly. "Why not?"

He shrugged. "Give me something worthwhile, and I'll give it a go one day."

Dagon cleared his throat, grabbing their attention. The three spun around, looking like kids who had been caught peering through a display case at a candy shop.

His arms were crossed, but a smile had spread across his

face. He lifted his chin toward the window. "They can see you."

Bendigo shifted his eyes back toward the bookstore and saw all but maybe two heads looking back at him. "Oh." He drew back. "That's embarrassing."

Dagon leaned his head back and laughed.

From across the street, a woman looked over her shoulder toward the laugh. Her hand rested on the handle of a red door that had a wooden sign hanging down in front of it. *Library*. She proceeded to lock the door and then looked back at Dagon again.

Bendigo caught her glance and nodded toward her. "We've attracted attention."

Dagon turned. "Oh?"

The woman had beautiful dark skin and black hair that was twisted into multiple braids that fell to her mid-back. She wore a brown and white robe that hung loosely around her arms. Her arms pressed a stack of books against her chest, and the keys to the library jingled as she slid them into her pocket. "Can I help you with anything?"

"Actually," Dagon said as he walked her way, "we are looking for someone who might be able to help us. A scholar, to be exact."

She shifted the books to one side. "I'm a scholar."

"You are?" Willy's jaw dropped. "But you're so *pretty*."

The woman glanced toward her and laughed. "Well, I do appreciate the comment, but so what? I've had my nose in a book since I could read. You don't have to look a certain way to be a scholar."

Willy visibly shook the disbelief from her mind. "Wow. Must be amazing."

"It's not like that where you're from?" The scholar gave her and Bendigo a sideways look. "Oh, you're Whims." Her voice perked. "Two Whims and...an Orphic Port merchant?"

Shem's eyes lifted. "From the Ports, yes. But not a merchant. More like a...watchman."

The scholar's head spun back toward Dagon. "And you...you're the one everyone has been talking about."

Bendigo whipped his head toward Dagon.

Dagon frowned. "Talking about?"

"Yes!" The scholar spoke faster now. "You're the one nature told us about. We've been waiting for you." She quieted down. "Well, *I've* been waiting for you. Everyone else sort of fears you, you know?"

"I *don't* know," he said, flat.

Bendigo squinted. "What's your name?"

"Oh, my apologies." She grinned. "I'm Sophia Esmeralda, number three scholar in Orenda and middle contact for the"—she held her hand over her mouth—"Kalon spies."

"The Kalon spies!" Willy smacked Shem's arm.

He glowered, rubbing the spot. "Yes, I heard."

"I knew it!" Sophia waved a slender finger in front of the four. "So, the rumors *are* true."

"Hold on a minute," Bendigo said, invaded. "No one knows about us, except for the people of Whimselon. How do *you* know?"

The fog swirled around Sophia's ankles, and she twitched. Looking down, she sucked in a breath. "The Book. Do you have The Book?"

Bendigo's spine tensed.

Dagon was nothing but calm. "What book?"

She bore into Bendigo's skull. "Don't tell me you're from Whimselon and don't know about The Book."

Bendigo tried to mimic Dagon's relaxed demeanor. "I know about The Book, but it's just a legend."

"Sophia," Dagon cut in, "we *do* need your help, and I would love to hear about these rumors. It doesn't feel like a coincidence that we have crossed paths."

"I'm more than happy to help travelers," she said. "Especially *this* lot. You have no idea what kind of hope you bring."

Bendigo, once again, felt the weight of their journey yet didn't fully understand it. The same underlying question penetrated his mind: why *them*?

Sophia lifted her lashes toward Shem. "You look familiar."

Shem's eyes still lingered with puffiness. "I don't know why I would."

She seemed to think about it for a moment too long but then shrugged. "Anyway, scholars here are paid good wages. I have three open bedrooms and a wonderful house hand. I can have her prepare a meal, and we can get you dry clothes."

Dry clothes. Bendigo didn't think he would ever be dry again between all the rain and the sweat.

"Your offer is kind." Dagon nodded. "We greatly accept."

Sophia led them through the cobblestone streets, the fog trailing them the whole way.

Fifteen

Sophia's house sat tall and narrow within a row of buildings that look just like hers. A spiral staircase inside the door led them up to a hallway that had the grandest decorations Bendigo had ever seen. The wooden floor was covered with a runner embroidered with gold thread, creating a vine-like pattern. Not one part of the walls were bare, filled with art. Paintings of wildflower fields and sunsets in gold frames. Paintings that looked real, their colors flooding his senses.

"You like the paintings?" Sophia asked, tilting her head at him.

He only nodded.

"You do strike me as the art type."

"I do? How?"

She stopped in front of a cherry-wood door. "I see the way you examine everything around you. The look of a true artist."

He felt embarrassed. "I've never created anything in my life."

"Of course, you have," Willy said. "You create images in your mind *all* the time. It's something you've always done."

Sophia pushed the door open. "See? You're an artist, and you didn't even know it." She stepped back for the others to peer into the room. "Now, this room has a bunk. Two of you can sleep here. The room next door and the room at the end of the hall holds one bed each, but the one at the end can get pretty chilly at night."

"I'll take the one at the end of the hall," Dagon offered. "I don't mind the chill."

"Guess we're bunking." Bendigo grinned at Shem, wishing he would at least smile.

And he did. "Oh joy."

☾

Bendigo slowly washed his body in the tub that Sophia had in the guest bathroom. He had never seen such a thing, and he wondered where the water went after he dumped the bucket over his head, and the little hole at the bottom of the tub sucked it away.

The dry clothes were like heaven against his skin, and he looked into the tiny, square mirror on the wall to adjust the buttons at the top of his cotton shirt. His mouth fell open. Facial scruff. It hadn't occurred to him once that he hadn't taken a blade to it like he routinely did in Whimselon. He wasn't aware that his facial hair could grow this much. Strange. He looked older, but he didn't mind that. Regardless, he took a blade to it, returning his face to its comfortable state.

Everyone met together around a dinner table covered with silver dishes full of chicken, potatoes, bread, green beans… Everything looked too good to be true.

"You mean we can have *all* this?" Willy said over and over.

"Yes," Sophia kept reassuring. "I treat my guests like family."

With full stomachs and tired eyes, they retired to a parlor that had so many decorations and trinkets lining the surrounding bookshelves that it was like they were inside a treasure chest. Pinstriped lounge chairs encircled a tea table in the middle, and once everyone was situated, Sophia examined everyone.

"I know what everyone wants to discuss." She pulled her braids to one side. "But I'm getting the feeling that an evening of rest would suit you well, and a conversation in the morning upon a fresh mind would be better."

"The *morning?*" Bendigo said. "But we didn't come all this way to relax. We need to know what's going on in Kalon, and once we do, we need to get going. I know I don't see the full picture, but from the looks of nature, the Twilights are cursing the land *fast.*"

Sophia looked to Dagon.

Dagon leaned back in his parlor chair. His hands crossed over his stomach. "Bendigo, it's okay. Travelers can't keep traveling if they don't rest."

"Sophia." Willy leaned forward. "I do want to know one thing. The rumors. We can talk about what they mean tomorrow, but I just want to know *how* you first heard them. Who told you we were coming?"

"The wind."

She nodded, then arched her mouth down. "I don't understand."

"It's hard to comprehend," Sophia admitted, "but sometimes, nature chooses to tell us what we need to hear. The people of Orenda heard whispers when the wind blew through the streets in sudden gusts. Anyone who could hear full sentences all heard the same thing: four travelers were journeying across the land, heading for Orenda. Two Whims, a man from the Ports of Orphic, and another man…" She trailed off, glancing toward Dagon. "Another man who, if he makes it to Kalon, can tear the afterlife from the Twilight's hands and return it to us, wiping away our constant fear of death."

A slither of warmth shimmied down Bendigo's back. The way she said it. The way she *believed* it. She spoke with such hope.

No one said a word. The parlor might as well have been empty.

"And that's that," Sophia whispered after a moment. "Just rumors, but I believe them to be true."

All heads turned to Dagon. He lifted his chin, unfazed. "I believe them to be true as well."

Sophia inhaled, sharp and giddy. "Well! I say this calls for a celebratory drink." She stood and meandered over to a standing, cherry-wood cabinet in the corner of the room. "The best wine in Orenda." She threw open the cabinet doors and drew out two bottles, pouring four crystal glasses to the brim.

Bendigo took one from her hand as she passed by, glancing over at Willy who stared into the black-red liquid in her own glass. He knew she had never had any before because neither had he. Whims only drank wine on *very* special occasions, and even then, it was reserved for the older townspeople. They were taught that one must be wise to consume it because of its mind-altering effects.

Shem turned down the drink in Sophia's extended hand. "I think I'm going to turn in for the night. It's...been a long one."

She drew her hand back. "I knew you looked more tired than the rest." It was a prying statement.

Shem stared cold and then glanced down.

"Hey." Willy looked to him. "Just stay for this one drink? Please?" She grinned. "It'll be good for you. That's what they say about this stuff anyway, right?"

"Hold on." Shem slowly took the glass from Sophia. "You're telling me you've *never* had wine?"

She shook her head. "Neither has Bendigo. Our people don't drink like your sailors do."

"In that case, I will take up your plea and stay." He brought the red to his lips. "I'm curious to see how this goes."

"What's that supposed to mean?" Bendigo took a tiny sniff of the drink. His stomach twisted with anxiety about trying something he had been taught to steer clear of. Shouldn't he at least think about how it might affect him?

Dagon took a glass and raised it toward him. "Just go easy."

Go easy. What did that mean? He brought the glass to his lips, not caring anymore. He was no ordinary Whim. He never was. Maybe the wine wouldn't affect him like he was taught it would.

It rolled over his tongue and shriveled his taste buds. It was bitter yet sweet and somehow dry. After just one sip, the insides of his ears burned, and his face muscles relaxed. How had he never had this before?

He took another sip. A big one. The burning sensation soothed him as the liquid flowed down to his stomach. Its fire webbed out around his core, and he realized that the burn replaced his anxiety, sadness, and tension. He, for once, didn't have to fight off negative feelings. The drink did it for him, and all he could do was keep guzzling it, wondering over and over why this had been kept from him for so long.

"Geez, Bendigo." Willy eyed his glass. "Slow down, will you? Don't you feel that buzz in your head?"

He struggled to keep his head upright. It kept wanting to fall backward. "Of course, I do. I like it."

Shem laughed into his drink. "Oh yeah. I'm glad I stayed for this."

Sophia chuckled in the corner. "Oh no. I didn't think he would feel it like this after one glass. I apologize, Dagon. I think one of your men might be down for the rest of the night."

Where Dagon usually laughs along, he seemed taught this time. "It seems that way, doesn't it?"

By this point, the conversations flitted past Bendigo's ears. He tried to grab onto words, but his brain couldn't track them fast enough. Like his conscience had taken flight and left his body behind to drag after it. That was the best part though: he wasn't oppressed by his own depressing thoughts. He felt happy. *Happy.*

When was the last time he truly felt like this?

"I have *never* felt like this," he said, answering his own thoughts.

"What do you feel like?" Shem asked, egging him on while hiding a smirk.

"*Happy.*" He laughed. Laughing felt so good. Almost uncontrollable.

Shem reached over and punched his shoulder. "I *like* you, kid."

"I'm not a kid," he corrected, bold, a little angry. "I haven't felt like a kid since my father died. My brother finished raising me, and even then, we watched out for each other. I'm not a kid."

"Excuse me." Shem raised his hands, his wine sloshing. "I retract the title."

Willy set her drink down. "You don't sound like yourself, Ben."

"It's because he isn't." Dagon stood. "Shem, quit provoking him. Sophia, could you please get Bendigo some water and maybe some bread?"

"Why are you upset?" Bendigo's head dropped forward, and he snapped it back up, trying to keep it steady.

"I'm so sorry." Sophia wrung her hands. "I just wanted to celebrate, not get him like *that*. It was just one drink."

"It's not your fault," Dagon reassured. He lowered his voice. "I believe there are some things Bendigo has never dared himself to face. Emotions that only a substance, like wine, can surface."

"Oh," she said, slipping from the parlor. "I'll be back."

"Shem." He gave a sideways smile. "Fun ends here."

"I suppose you're right." Shem set his glass down and rose. "I wasn't provoking him, just… Well yeah, I was provoking him. Took my mind off today. For a little while at least."

Dagon guided him to the parlor door. "Let me walk you to your room."

"I think I'll be fine."

"No. A quiet, lonely walk down a long hallway is enough for grief to penetrate back into the heart. Let me go with you."

Shem sighed but nodded.

"Willy." Dagon turned. "I'll be back. Don't let Bendigo have any more."

"Okay." She rested her elbow on the chair's arm and her chin in her palm as Dagon and Shem left the room.

Bendigo seized the moment with everyone gone and with her gazing at the doorway. He leaned over and snatched the bottle of wine off the tea table.

She caught the movement. "No!" She swiped at him.

He drew the bottle back faster than her swing and held it close to his chest, grinning. "It's *fine.*"

"No, it's not." She stood. "Put it back down."

Looking at her, he brought the lip of the bottle to his mouth and turned it up.

"Stop!" She lunged at him.

He jumped up from his chair and shimmied to the side, escaping. The sudden movement made his head spin, and he staggered. "Willy, what has gotten into you?"

"What's gotten into *you?* You're scaring me. Stop drinking it."

"It's making me feel better." He threw his hands out to the side, dumping some wine onto the floor. "Don't you feel it too?"

"No, I don't." She slowed her words. "I think you're using this as some type of…I don't know. Cover up. Medicine. *Something.*"

He plopped into another chair. "Why do you even care?"

"Because." She crossed her arms.

"Because why?"

"Because I care about you."

The wine bottle sat wedged between his thighs. "Then just let me feel happy *for once.*"

"It's not real happiness." Her voice sounded strained. "It's a stupid drink! You aren't yourself. I want the real Bendigo. Not this strange, bold, loopy one. Give me the bottle. We can talk about what's really going on with you."

"There is nothing to talk about." He took another swig. "You've known me your whole life. You know I feel sad all the time. Why would you want to talk about it now?"

"Because I didn't understand how deep it was. How constantly you struggle. Let's talk about it."

He lifted the bottle to his mouth. "No thank you."

"Bendigo!" She threw herself on top of him. Her legs awkwardly straddled him, as she yanked on the bottle, trying to pry it from his grip. "Give it!"

"Willy! Get off!"

"No!"

They made close eye contact, and his heart clenched. He had never noticed how speckled her eyes were. His grip loosened.

She yanked the bottle away and shoved his shoulder back into the chair. "I swear, Fletcher! You *infuriate* me. Why don't you just talk to me? I've always been here for you. When are you finally going to realize that we aren't kids anymore?"

"Huh?"

Dagon appeared in the parlor doorway. "Willy?"

She hurried to remove herself from atop Bendigo. "I was just…" She held up the bottle.

He walked in and put both hands on her shoulders. "Your effort is loyal. I'll take it from here. Go get some rest."

She glanced back at Bendigo, a hint of anger in her eyes.

She set the bottle down on the bookshelf as she left.

The happiness that had swarmed Bendigo's brain ran away, leaving behind a new feeling: guilt.

Dagon stared at him. "Let's take a walk."

The room spun for a moment when he stood. He gripped the back of the chair, regaining what balance he could. Nausea lingered in his stomach as he slunk toward Dagon, the last person he wanted to get reprimanded by.

From down the hall, Sophia hurried to Dagon with a glass of water and half a baguette. "Here. Again, I'm so sorry."

"You have been nothing but generous to us." He took the water and put it in Bendigo's hands. "And you have nothing to apologize for. They're tired. We're all tired. This is new territory for us. Get some rest, and tomorrow, we will sort out the next steps."

She hovered like she wanted something else but then nodded, heading down the hall.

"Eat this." He held the baguette out to Bendigo.

Bendigo took the bread but hung it at his side, looking at his feet. Dagon started walking, so he did too. The hallway was long but not enough for a leisurely stroll. When they reached the end of the red runner, they turned around and walked back the way they had come, only to hit the end and turn around again. They did this twice before Dagon spoke.

"I'm not upset with you."

Bendigo was scared to look at him. "You're not?"

"No."

"You're acting like it."

They reached the end and turned again.

"I'm not upset with your actions," Dagon said. "You had no idea what would happen."

Bendigo huffed.

His mouth sagged. "But I *am* saddened."

"Saddened about what?"

"How much you're hurting."

Bendigo clenched his jaw. He hated having conversations like this. They always ended with the other party not understanding and giving up on trying to reason with him. He never left these conversations feeling better, only more defeated than he was in the first place.

Dagon turned his head sideways, forcing eye contact. "You often feel sad. That's how you describe it, but it's much more than that, isn't it?"

He shrugged. "Sure."

"You don't just feel downcast; you feel utterly miserable. A depressing fog clings to your mind and numbs every pathway to joy. You *want* to feel alive, but no matter how hard you try, you can't. You spend days wishing someone can see the places you create in your mind. Wishing someone can understand the escapes you're capable of forming with your imagination. But no one can see how you think, how you view the world. You believe not one single person thinks like you or feels like you, longing for something more in life. You feel alone, so you seclude yourself. You never feel understood, and because of that, you never feel fully loved. Am I on the right track?"

Bendigo had stopped walking. Having his most vulnerable feelings described to him like they were physically noticeable shook his soul. *How* had Dagon known *exactly* the weight he carried day in and day out? But he couldn't ask how because the words wouldn't form.

Dagon pivoted, blocking him from walking any farther. "I see how hard you fight it."

He let his shoulders drop. "I don't know what to do anymore."

"Talk about it. Don't hide your sadness."

"No one wants to be around someone who is sad all the time. If I let people see it, I'll be even more alone than I already am."

"No." Dagon put a gentle grip on his arms. "That's a lie. The ones who love you want to know everything about you, and once you let them see, they will understand you more."

"But I've tried. No one will ever understand what goes on in my mind. I'm alone."

"Listen to me." Dagon strengthened his grip. "You are not alone. You have to believe that. Talk to me."

"What do you mean?"

"Talk to me. Tell me what is inside. I want to see it."

Bendigo blinked, the wine's haze still affecting his concentration. "My mind is full of good things. I just can't express them."

"Try."

Dagon stepped back, giving him room to breathe. To think.

"Well"—his inner worlds turned, bursting at the seams—"I see details. I see how Whimselon isn't just swampland and treehouses. It's speckled algae that swirls when something moves beneath it. It's fallen trees that have been consumed by moss, so soft that birds enjoy resting their thin legs on it after hunting all day. It's homes built in the trees by the very hands of the people who dwell in them. It's paint colors on the doors that mothers and grandmothers chose. It's the lanterns' glow that flicker on the boardwalks at night. The breeze that sometimes blows strong enough to tilt the flames sideways, reminding us that we ourselves are a mist in the wind. Here today and gone tomorrow. I see details for what they are. Intricate. Unseen. Perfect. Worth holding onto."

He let out a breath. His veins pulsed, and adrenaline throbbed through his arms. To his surprise, he *did* feel lighter. Less restrained.

Life flooded Dagon's pupils. "I see it. I see the beauty you described. The details."

"You do?"

Dagon nodded. "How do you feel?"

He shook his arms, wondering when the heavy feeling would return. "I feel airy. Like something inside of me was just let loose."

"And *that* is why you should never hide what you feel." Dagon strode forward again.

He followed, playing with the hem of his trousers. "What if you're the only person who will ever listen though?"

Dagon stopped at the bedroom Bendigo and Shem were to share. "I'm not. You will find the right people. Some are right in front of you. Like Willy."

That unfamiliar heart wrench made itself known again. "Willy?"

"Why does that surprise you?"

"I don't know. She's always the one who does all the talking."

"Try talking to her about it sometime. That's all she wants."

"Did she tell you that?"

"No," Dagon admitted. "But it's easy to see."

A nod was all Bendigo could offer. The wine made his eyelids droop, and his concentration wandered.

Dagon tilted his chin toward the bedroom door. "Go sleep. Sleep helps with the effects of wine, you know."

"It does? That's good to hear. I'm sorry for ruining everyone's night."

"You didn't ruin everyone's night." A flat smile curled behind Dagon's beard. "You gave Shem a fun time."

Bendigo cringed. "Good, I guess."

"Goodnight, Bendigo."

Turning the doorknob, Bendigo paused. "Hey, Dagon."

"Hm?"

"Thank you."

Dagon smiled. "You know, Sophia was right. What she said about you."

"What did she say?"

"You're an artist."

"You think so?"

"Think about it." He swayed off down the hall. "I think creating things could do some good for you. I'll see you in the morning."

"See you in the morning," Bendigo whispered as he shoved the door open.

The sound of steady, shallow breathing floated down from the top bunk. Shem had graciously taken the higher bed, probably assuming Bendigo couldn't maneuver his way up after his date with the wine bottle. Embarrassing to admit, but Shem was right.

As soon as Bendigo's head hit the pillow, the room spun, and he honestly thought his body was too. He squeezed his eyes shut, fighting the nausea in his throat. Lesson learned. He was not wise enough to stomach the red drink. Willy was right to force it away from him. In his head, he replayed the scene of when she dove on top of him, trying to rip the bottle away.

Her eyes.

Bendigo stared up at the bunk planks above his head. Why had he never noticed how beautiful her eyes were? They had never been that close face-to-face before. That was all.

He pressed his eyelids together and breathed deeply until he fell into a dream. A dream of Whimselon and all its detail.

Sixteen

While Orenda had been a damp, spooky scholar town filled with bookworms and libraries the night before, Bendigo found it to be totally different in the morning. Light streamed in through the glass-blown bedroom window and warbled on the floor in an aquatic-like pattern.

The festivities from last night lingered behind his eyes in a mild headache, but the nausea was gone. He felt groggy yet rejuvenated. Mentally rejuvenated, more so. Though his first night in Orenda had been humiliating, he felt known by someone in a deeper way than he had ever imagined possible.

"Shem, you up?"

There was no reply.

He rolled out from under the covers, stood, and stretched. He walked out to the middle of the room and looked up. Shem wasn't on the top bunk anymore. Walking to the window, he saw people bustling in the streets below. Several carts and carriages—filled with either fruits and vegetables, miscellaneous soaps and jewelry, or books— covered the cobblestone path. The way people wove in and out of each other, scurrying along like they had to be someplace *now*, amazed him.

The smell of coffee wafted in through the crack under the bedroom door. Bendigo remembered the smell from the Ports, and he realized why people drank it for pleasure. Yes, it was hard to get down, but it was grit in a cup. A good type of grit. The kind that motivated the body and soul to either get started or keep going.

He followed the smell down the hall as faint voices and clinks came from the kitchen. He turned the corner and stepped into the space where they had eaten dinner the night before. Dagon and Shem sat across from each other at the rectangular cedar table, drinking steaming coffee and laughing at something Willy had just said.

She stood next to Sophia, facing the counter and helping her place freshly baked biscuits onto a plate. They chatted, moving around each other to compose the breakfast tray. If their skin color wasn't totally different, Bendigo might have assumed they were mother and daughter. It was a scene he knew Willy wished she had shared with her real mother.

Shem spotted him hovering in the doorway. "Oh, look who it is. Fletcher in the flesh, but what version of him this time?"

Everyone chuckled.

His face turned red, but he forced a sheepish grin. "I'm feeling normal. Thanks." He caught a look from Willy, but she darted her eyes away.

"Glad you're feeling better." Sophia placed a tray on the table. "We have lots to do today."

"Really, Sophia." Bendigo dropped onto the bench next

to Dagon. "You feed us too much. I'm gonna dream of your kitchen table forever."

The surface was covered with the same serving dishes used last night, only they held golden biscuits; swirls of thin, sliced meats; bundles of grapes; jars of jams, honey, and butter; and a carafe filled with coffee.

"Hospitality is in my nature." Sophia joined them at the table. "And you all are *special* guests."

Willy climbed onto the bench next to Shem, across from Bendigo. She lifted her eyes to him but didn't pull them away this time. She offered an almost apologetic smile and then got into her breakfast.

He took a sip of coffee and looked to the window hidden behind drapes. "It's really sunny this morning. It's a good change of mood."

"I agree," Sophia said, "but we must keep the curtains drawn."

He frowned. "Why?"

"I went out early this morning to get fresh milk and overheard a few conversations. The town suspects that the travelers they have heard about have arrived, which is obviously true. But it isn't a joyous suspicion." She sighed. "It's better that no one knows you're here."

"But I thought you said Orenda has been waiting for us. In a *good* way."

"They have, only they were expecting a triumphant entry. A procession of sorts, confirming that you will end Tarsha's curse to death. And you didn't just bring yourselves; you brought the *fog*. Now, they aren't so sure about the travelers."

"I understand the meaning behind the fog, but how is it dangerous?" Shem broke apart a biscuit.

She considered her answer. "Through the years, we've started to believe that it's a pawn for the Twilights, on the hunt for The Book."

"So, why would the fog mean *we* are bad?" Bendigo asked.

She hummed. "Now, I don't believe this, but some people think that you yourselves could be Twilights." She looked to Dagon as if to ask: *are you though?*

"There is no way," Willy argued. "We don't even look like them."

"But they can transform to look like people, so it's a fair thought," Bendigo offered. "Remember the messenger we encountered before we reached the Ports of Orphic? He shifted right in front of our faces."

"Oh yeah." She rested her chin in her hand. "Darn. Sneaky little things."

Sophia straightened her back. "You mean to tell me that you've already had a run-in with a Twilight?"

"A few actually," Shem confirmed. "In different ways. Sometimes, it was their curse on nature that targeted us."

"Wait." She closed her eyes. "How? How do they know who you are or what you're doing? Wouldn't that mean they may know you're coming after them?"

"Not necessarily." Bendigo thought back to the night

The Book had opened. He had seen the Twilights coming in on the horizon. Could they have been in attendance that night and heard the prophecy?

She squinted at him. "What do you mean *not necessarily?*"

He squirmed under her hawk eyes. "Well, The Book only said—"

"Ben!" Willy thrust her hands out to the sides.

Shem leaned forward and rested his forehead on the table. "Fletcher."

"The Book is *real.*" Sophia almost knocked over her coffee. "Why would you keep that from me? Do you have it? Does it tell you what's going to happen? How could you not tell me?"

Willy rolled her eyes in Bendigo's direction. "Well, we *weren't* supposed to tell you."

"Hold on," Dagon said, calming the table in a fatherly fashion. "Everyone, just relax. Bendigo is right to tell Sophia. If we are going to work with her to get to Kalon, she deserves to know. Bendigo, tell her what you were going to say."

Bendigo felt even more ridiculous than he did last night with Willy and Shem looking at him like he had just destroyed their only chance at survival. "I was just going to say that the night The Book opened, I saw Twilights riding in with the sunset. We know they can shift their forms, and we know they have been manipulating and kidnapping people from multiple towns. They may have been in Whimselon that night. If that was the case, they may have heard what it said. The only thing is that The Book prophesied the start of the journey. Nothing else. It gave no insight about what was to come. Even *I* didn't know."

"What did The Book say exactly?" Sophia wrung her fingers. "I must know. I've lived my entire life surrounded by books, reading, writing, and learning. All I could ever dream about is whether or not The Book actually existed. Tell me what it said."

Though he hadn't tried to memorize what The Book had said that night, he felt the words had been written on his heart. "*Let his feet be swift. Let his heart be light. For the road ahead is eternal night. The shadows are unleashed, and the Twilights begin their reign. But now is the time to alter the end. Find the one they call Dagon. To the Ports of Orphic, he must go. The one who does the going is called Bendigo.*"

The window above the kitchen's water pump flew open. The lace curtains flapped and pulled against the curtain rod as a burst of wind ripped its way inside. Empty cups and loose utensils scooted across the counter, knocking into each other.

Sophia bumped her knees against the table, pushing herself up and hustling to the window. As she shoved the hinged windowpane shut, a dark cloud covered the sun, casting a shadow on her face. She yanked the curtains closed again.

Willy leaned toward Shem. "What just happened?"

Shem looked around as if he was trying to piece it together. "I'm not sure."

"You spoke the words out loud," Dagon said, weary. "Nature sensed it. The curse sensed it."

"The Twilights are going to find you." Sophia removed dishes from the table, frantic. "We need to get to the library, look at the war maps, and figure out the Twilights' plan. Our two messengers gave us useful information, but you're the only ones who can actually do something with it. We can't waste any more time."

Bendigo shoved a biscuit into his pocket, having not been able to eat much, and then helped clear the table. "Where is the library?"

"Where you found me last night." She yanked her leather satchel off a wall hook. "All the way across the city." She looked at the four, considering. "The only problem is that we can't all be seen together. Everyone is already suspicious, a little frightened, and skeptical. If we parade through town in a pack, it will give you away, putting you in even more danger."

"We can go one at a time?" Willy suggested.

Sophia patted her bag. "No. We shouldn't be alone either, in case we encounter a Twilight. And you don't know how to get to the library." She rubbed her temples.

"What about the rooftops?" Bendigo asked.

She tilted her head. "What about them?"

"We're Whims." He waved a hand between him and Willy. "We can climb really well. Fast too. So, we can take the high road, while you three take the low. We'll make sure we can see you and follow you to the library. That way, we are separate but together."

"Fantastic idea." Sophia flashed a grin. "The window in the bathroom leads to a ledge that can get you to the roof. We'll meet you outside."

Splitting into their group, Bendigo and Willy made their way to the bathroom. They walked shoulder to shoulder, but nothing was said. He had a feeling that she was still mad about last night, but from the way she wouldn't look at him for more than two seconds, he fought over if it was something more.

In the bathroom, he lifted a leg over the mysterious tub's ledge to reach the window. He drew back the burgundy curtains and swung the window outward. Though the sun dominated the sky, a cool breeze blew across his face, bringing the smells of fresh bread and coffee to his nose. For a moment, he closed his eyes, wondering what it would be like to actually enjoy Orenda's luxuries instead of hiding away. Maybe one day.

Willy sighed behind him. "What are you doing?"

He opened his eyes, remembering their real motive. "Pretending." He leaned out the frame and looked down at the five-inch ledge that wrapped around the building. Here, the house peaked in a long, pointy, cobblestone triangle. The bottom of the triangle met with the roof's level part, creating a perfect corner for stepping up. "Textbook." He drew his head back in. "This will be easy. You ready?"

Nodding, she joined him in the bathtub. A strange place to be together. They bumped shoulders, made eye contact, and shared a laugh.

"Bizarre way to leave the house." Her face morphed to slightly red.

Bendigo noticed. He could read her. He had *always* been able to read her. She only blushed under two circumstances, which he had told Shem before: when she was afraid someone would belittle her, or when she found someone attractive. He decided, since it was easier, that she must have been scared that he was going to belittle her.

But her words from last night seeped back into his mind, and he couldn't shake the feeling that she may have dropped some sort of hint. Then again, he was probably overthinking it. If she ever *did* feel a certain way, she would have mentioned it long ago. They've spent their entire lives together and never once talked about that kind of thing. It was sort of an unspoken knowledge that they were platonic soulmates. And he would use the word *soulmate* loosely. They were platonic. That was it.

"All right." He pushed aside his derailing thoughts. "The ledge is small, but we've climbed on smaller. I'll go first. Test it out."

He grabbed the top of the windowsill and swung his legs out, landing soundlessly on the ledge. Looking down, he saw an empty, shadowed alleyway. Facing Sophia's house, he pressed his hands up against the stone and inched his way to the side to give Willy room to come out. She appeared, flowing even smoother than he had, and was right next to him in seconds.

Bendigo gripped the step-up corner and tensed to maintain balance as his feet met the roof. Moving quickly, he scurried to the top, able to see the front of Sophia's house. Below, Sophia, Dagon, and Shem hovered in a circle, looking up. Confirming that Willy was behind him, Bendigo held up a thumb. The three in the street moved forward, heading toward the bustling crowds of people.

And the Whims were off.

Bendigo glided across the roof, not even having to look at his feet. He kept his eyes on the heads of their street team, knowing he would lose them if he looked away for one second. He came to the end of Sophia's roof, jumped, landed on the next, and kept moving.

Left, right, left, right, swing around the chimney stack, left, right, and leap.

Willy stayed behind him, mimicking his movements. They traveled like forest animals prancing through the treetops. The crowd in the streets below swarmed around each other like lost sheep, but three heads kept moving forward in a straight line.

Sweat ran down the side of his face, but he embraced it. The sun was getting higher, splashing the dark cobblestone city with a wave of life. Every storefront with glass windows reflected the white sunlight, flashing lovely beams into the streets. From up here, Orenda looked like a whimsical getaway with its bookstores, bakeries, and carts full of rainbow produce.

Willy passed him, using one hand to grip the peak of a

taller building and swinging down to a shorter roof underneath it. "Hey, daydreamer. They're waiting for us."

To remain stealth, Sophia opened an upstairs window for the two to enter. When they landed inside, she stood, grinning and looking at them like they were special. "You guys really *can* climb. I've never seen a Whim in action before. Forgive me for gawking, but you impress me."

Willy shrugged, hiding her satisfaction, but Bendigo's eyes were fixed on the *library*. It was two stories tall with a gold railing encircling the top floor. From floor to ceiling, books packed hickory wood shelves, leaving not one single space to add another. The ceiling started as an oval and coned upward into a peak like a twister.

Walking to the railing, he looked down at Shem and Dagon, who were strolling around and examining all the artifacts that sat in glass boxes atop wooden podiums. "Have you seen anything like this?"

Dagon glanced up. "I knew you would fancy this."

He *did* fancy it. Every inch. Nothing in Whimselon was this grand. Even the Keeper's tower was a skinny, shingled home, lit by lanterns that were in *everyone's* home.

A spiral staircase tucked in the corner guided them to the first floor. The best part though? A secret door inside one of the bookshelves. The books turned forward by themselves, hovering and connecting like puzzle pieces until a completed rectangle of pages and bindings meshed, forming an entryway.

He couldn't keep his bottom lip from dropping as Sophia pushed the door open and led them inside the hidden room. The door closed behind them, and the sound of books moving back into place thumped against the wall.

The room they had entered was circular and dim. No windows allowed them sunlight. The only source of light was the oil lanterns sticking out from the wall in the shape of a cane. A massive oak table—so tall that it came up to right below Bendigo's chest—occupied the middle of the room. Covering the oak was layers of detailed, paper maps tarnished with age. The top one was a map of Kalon, the specifics of its geography drawn perfectly with black ink.

Sophia waved the gang around the table. "Gather."

They moved in, their heads hovering in a circle and casting shadows on the map.

She waved her hand over the top illustration. "This is our map of the Isle of Kalon. We sent fifteen spies there to come back with information. Like I mentioned yesterday, only two returned. I'm the middle contact; the spies report to me, I update the maps and present the new information to the chief scholar, and the chief scholar organizes a plan of action if need be.

"The reason we sent spies in the first place was because Orenda got wind of a curse. It started on the outside of the city and has been slowly moving closer. You must've seen it on your journey in: the In-Between is dead. All life is gone. Death has been creeping toward us every day, forcing our hunters to travel even farther to catch game and plant crops. The full carts of produce filling the streets this minute? That's the last we have. We're clinging to nothing. We are about to have *nothing*. We will be the only living things in Orenda, and even *that* isn't promised."

Bendigo shuttered. Had he considered that the curse would kill more than just nature? Sure. Had he believed it? Not really.

What would even happen? Would he fall asleep and never wake up? That wouldn't be such a terrible way to go. Only what if it didn't happen that way? What if he wasn't the first to go, and he woke up only to find that Willy had? Or Shem. Or Dagon. And there was one other significant detail that he always forced himself to forget: there was no afterlife.

The Twilights' curse weighed heavy on his shoulders, consuming his lungs and gripping his throat. Death. Death gripped at his throat.

Dagon skirted his eyes to Bendigo's pale face. "But that's why we're here."

He drew back, alert that Dagon seemed to have just read his mind.

"That's why we have been waiting for you," Sophia added. "When we heard that travelers were heading to us on their way to Kalon, we sensed hope for the first time since the first plant died under the curse. You *have* to help us. You must get rid of death."

"Now, wait." Shem crossed his arms. "You can't just demolish death. People *will* die."

"Yes, but death will happen with the promise of an afterlife." Dagon didn't remove his eyes from the map. "That we can do."

Her eyelashes fluttered. "So, you're really going to do it?"

Without moving his chin, he looked up. "That's the plan. We just need your help to get there. Tell us what to expect."

"Right." She shifted the map toward her. "Look here." She pointed to the cliff in the middle of Kalon that held the rumored great stone castle. The starting point for all rivers across every land. "The Twilights have been building their army at the base of the cliff. Their numbers are not exact, but our spies reported about five hundred of them."

"Five hundred?" Willy held her chest. "That many? Bendigo broke his back because of *one*."

Sophia's face skewed. "You broke your back?"

Dagon was quick to cut in. "A minor injury. Don't exaggerate, Willy." He gave her a hard stare across the table, stern enough to tell her to quit talking yet easy enough to let her know that he was just trying to protect his secret.

"Well…" Sophia dragged her squint away from Dagon's and Willy's eye contact. "That's not all. Five hundred Twilights and six thousand people. Most with horses."

The room grew silent.

Bendigo was almost certain he could hear Willy's heart beating next to him. "I'm…I'm sorry." He closed his eyes. "Did you say six *thousand*?"

With a weariness in her eyes, Sophia nodded. "An army

of six thousand five hundred total. Approximately."

A long whoosh of air escaped Dagon's lips. For the first time, he looked worried. Truly worried. "What is their position?"

"Not advancing but guarding." She drew her finger around the bottom of the cliff. "All along here. For some reason, the castle seems to be of more value to them than anything else. We thought that by now, with the numbers they have, they would start their invasions. Overthrowing our cities. But they're not. Something is in that castle."

Willy tucked a loose hair behind her ear. "I thought it was empty."

She rolled her shoulders back. "I'm as lost as you are on that. It couldn't have always been unoccupied though. In one day and age, it was built for a purpose. Something about it is important to the Twilights and their army, and I believe the key to breaking the curse is in those stone walls."

Shem hovered over the map, arms crossed, eyeing all the little red dots that represented where the Twilight army supposedly stood. "Is the army posted around the base of the cliff the only thing keeping outsiders from getting to the castle?"

"Not quite." She pointed out a gold dotted line that encircled the cliff as well. "An iron gate surrounds the entire foothill. Twelve feet high. You could get beyond the army and still be stopped by the gate."

"Were your spies able to get a good look at where the

gate's entrance is?" Bendigo asked.

"Yes, but they said it was only opened once with a golden key during their mission. One of the horsemen holds it around his neck."

Shem rocked back on his heels. "Find the horseman. Get the key."

"Right." Willy rolled her eyes. "Good thing there are only *six thousand* to choose from."

He tilted his head back and closed his eyes, clearly agitated.

"Well…" Sophia held a palm up to the ceiling, weighing the thought. "The idea isn't too far off. Not *everyone* has horses. That at least dwindles it down to a more reasonable fraction."

"Let's say we do get the key," Bendigo played along. "How are we expected to make our way to the gate? Then actually pass through it?"

Dagon pressed his lips together, grimacing.

"I don't feel like I understand your question." She stood straight, shrugging her hair behind her shoulder. "You fight."

Bendigo dropped his chin. "Fight?"

"Yes."

Heat rose to fill his chest. "Can you tell me one thing?"

She bowed her head once.

"Who are the six thousand people?"

Willy watched with quizzical eyes. Shem shifted.

"They are the recruited," Sophia said, steady.

174

"Tell me from where." Bendigo leaned toward her, wanting her to understand where this was going.

She didn't budge. "From all over. By now, the Twilights have passed through almost every town or city on our continent, and when they leave, they take recruits with them, stealing them."

It didn't even phase her. He couldn't fathom it. "People from your own city are a part of the Twilight army."

She cleared her throat. "Yes."

"People from Whimselon are, by now, a part of it too."

"Yes, Bendigo. From every city." Her voice rose. "If we don't destroy the army they have now, the *rest* of us will be a part of their army—or worse, victims of it."

His voice rose moreover. "And the people who were stolen, taken from their homes? Are they not victims too?"

"Of course, they're victims. But not victims who know good from evil anymore. In their hearts lie evil, destruction, and murder. We must ruin them."

Clenching his fists, he mentally talked himself down enough to speak again. "You're asking us to kill our own."

Her voice dropped below a whisper. "I wish it didn't have to be like that, but there is no other way."

Though he ran through his mind's pathways, searching for another direction, he knew she was right. But that didn't stop him from provoking her. "Will Orenda be sending soldiers to fight with us?"

"Bendigo." Dagon put a hand on his shoulder. A signal to stand down.

"What soldiers?" She almost laughed. "We're *bookworms*, not warriors. No one here is trained to fight. Only trained to teach. To learn. That's why we have hope in you."

"But"—Willy played with her fingers—"there are four of us."

Shem tensed. "And six thousand of them."

"I know." Sophia leaned on the table. "But nature *spoke* of you. You aren't like everyone else. There is something special about the four of you, something that has power. Hope. Faith."

"You're believing in a fantasy," Shem said. "Rise to the challenge. Send some of your own with us."

A glassiness flooded over her eyes. "Even if I wanted to, our people wouldn't be compliant. They are smart, yes, but brave? Selfless? Fighters? No. I can't promise you soldiers. I'm sorry."

From the corner of the room, Dagon watched with wonder in his expression, probably sorting their words to use them as leverage. To make them question every doubtful thought. "What of power?"

Bendigo bit his tongue. Did he really just ask that? In this situation, power was everything.

"The only power the Twilight army has is evil." Dagon walked toward them, slow.

"And an army," Shem argued.

He drew his shoulders up, sighing. "An army that is only possible because of evil."

"So, what are you saying?" Willy asked.

"There are four of us. Though that matters little. It isn't four against six thousand. It's love against hate. Good versus evil. *That* is the true war. Power belongs to the ones who love above all else."

Seventeen

While the crew argued and agonized over a plan, the streets of Orenda cleared. A storm grew on the horizon. Thick, black clouds moved in across the sky, and a biting chill came with them.

Safe from suspicion in the now empty streets, Bendigo dragged his feet back to Sophia's house. He hung back behind the others while Willy slunk next to him. No one said a word.

Confusion and understanding clashed in his brain, clouding his judgment. He hadn't treated Sophia with the respect she deserved, and in turn, everyone had questioned her. There was guilt in his conscience yet fury toward her lack of empathy. To kill their own kind? Fight them like the manipulated weren't once *good?*

Though Bendigo struggled with this concept, Dagon hadn't pushed back on it. He hadn't come up with a different plan, backed Bendigo up, or even scolded Sophia for suggesting such a thing. That made Bendigo wonder if he himself wasn't thinking clearly. Did he perhaps not understand the evil they were dealing with?

Thunder rumbled in the distance as Sophia unlocked her front door. She paused with her hand on the knob, her head hanging low. "I'm really sorry."

No one spoke.

She turned to face them. "I wish it were different."

Dagon stepped in front of the others. "It isn't your fault that the Twilights have consumed our own. It's a reality that we must face, painful or not."

"It is painful." She looked at the row of skinny houses down the street. "Some of my neighbors…" She blinked, brought her focus back, and zeroed in on Bendigo. "You have a good heart."

The rage he held faded, leaving a gaping hole filled with regret. He couldn't respond with a thank you because he didn't believe it. He wouldn't have treated her the way he did if he had a good heart. Instead, he looked down, ashamed.

Splats of rain flattened against their skin, urging Sophia through the door. Everyone followed. The entry hall was dim, waiting for the lanterns to be lit for the evening. Shem maneuvered through the door, bumping into her arm. She dropped the book that was cradled in her elbow, and loose papers spilled out onto the floor.

"Oh." He bent down. "I'm so sorry."

She crouched, joining him. "It's okay. It happens more often than not."

He swiped up a stack of papers and realigned them between his fingers. He glanced down at the paper resting on top and stopped short. Like he had seen a ghost of his past.

"What is it?" she asked.

He held up a piece of brown paper, smaller than the rest of the papers in the pile. "Where did you get this?"

Seeming unsure, she took the slip from him. She held it out in front of her, gazing over the written words, and then looked up at him again. Her lips slightly parted as if she couldn't believe what she was seeing.

Feeling lost, Bendigo peered over her shoulder, deciphering the words in her hand. But upon reading it, he realized they weren't just words but a note. *I will always love you,* it read.

Shem stood, helping Sophia to her feet. "Where did you get this?" There was more awe in his voice this time.

Her voice was soft, airy. "I knew you looked familiar."

"This is my wife's handwriting." He pointed at the note. "Isn't it," he said more like a statement than a question.

Shoving the note into his hands, she smiled. "It is. And now it has found its rightful owner."

He gripped the paper, reading it over and over. *I will always love you. I will always love you. I will always love you.* "How?"

"She lived with me while she was in the city." Sophia looked almost past him, as if remembering the time she had spent with his wife. "Until she got *really* sick, of course. Then she moved to the sick house. I visited her every day though. I promise. I didn't let her pass alone." Emotion made her voice jump. "That was where she gave me the letter. She carried this drawing of you with her, always pulling it out to show me, to talk about you, and to tell me how lucky she was. A few days before she left this life, she gave me this letter, telling me that if I ever met her husband, Shem-Sakai, that I was to give him this note as her final goodbye. Of course, in the drawing, you had short hair, and you didn't introduce yourself with your full name, so I didn't put two and two together. But now…here we are."

He rested his chin on his chest, squeezing his eyes shut and clenching the note.

"And I didn't ever leave her," she whispered. "I stayed with her until the last moment."

Without looking up, he pulled her into a secure hug. "Thank you. Thank you, thank you, thank you." He smiled.

The tenseness in her voice relaxed. "Of course."

They drew apart, Shem still holding her shoulders. "What more can you tell me?"

"About her?"

"Yes. I want to know everything."

"How about over some tea?" she offered. "I would love to tell you everything."

While Dagon and Shem followed Sophia into the parlor, Willy split to wash her hair in the magical tub that she only could utilize for one more night since they would be leaving in the morning. Heading out of Orenda and into, well, the unknown.

Feeling run down, Bendigo ambled to his temporary bedroom to lie down until dinner. This may be the last time he had the luxury of resting in a bed. Might as well take full advantage of it.

Falling straight onto his back, he let his shoulders sink

into the cushy mattress. The pillow was cold beneath his head, soothing him. His body ached, and stress plunged into his soul. Nothing he chose to think about eased the unsettling worry that flooded his mind.

The rain hit the bedroom window in a constant rhythm, occasionally getting louder when the wind blew sideways. He propped his hands behind his head and shut his eyes. Could he kill? Did he travel all this way only to find out that he didn't have the stomach to shove his dagger into someone's heart?

Evil was such a broad term. Evil was, well, bad, something to avoid. But what if evil had always been a bigger deal, and he was just sheltered from its reality? Could the Twilights' evil really destroy *all* of Tarsha?

His eyelids parted. For a split second, he felt the flick of a fighting spirit. A moment where he saw himself swiping his dagger across people's chests, eliminating evil from the world one person at a time. Yes, he could destroy evil, but what about the person beneath? What would happen to them? They would lie slain, murdered by his own hands without the sanctuary of the afterlife.

He couldn't do that to someone.

Pressing his palms against his eyes, he groaned. If he let these thoughts fester, he would lose his mind. He already *was*. Why did he always torture himself with such detailed, crisis-filled contemplations? Sooner or later, he would drown himself in agony.

Unless he listened to Dagon's words. *Try talking to her*

about it sometime. That's all she wants. Another groan. Talk to *Willy?* Just *starting* the conversation would feel like biting iron nails between his teeth. Even if he wanted to talk to her, he *couldn't.* Nothing suffocated him more than vulnerability.

Suddenly he was on his feet with his arms crossed, staring at the bedroom door. He *had* to talk to her. He then was in the hall, padding across the floor toward her room.

He turned around. Bad idea. There was no way.

No. He dug his fingernails into his palms and spun around again. He was going to do it even if it killed him. He couldn't hide behind the walls inside his mind anymore. *That* would kill him before vulnerability ever did.

Sucking in a breath, he gently rapped his knuckles on her door, wincing.

It took a moment for her to respond. "Yes?"

"Hey." He shut his eyes, cringing so hard that he was worried he might pass out. "It's me."

"Ben?"

"Yes."

A brief pause. "Come in."

Thunder shook the entire house as Bendigo turned the knob and stepped through the door. He wasn't sure what to expect, but what he found made him look twice. Willy was lying on her bed with her feet propped up on the headboard, her head at the foot of the bed. Her damp hair was tightly wrapped in a top knot bun, and her hands were folded across her stomach.

He laughed, tilting his head. "What are you *doing*?"

She looked over. "Refreshing my blood."

"What does that even mean?"

"If you raise your legs above your head, the blood will circulate back to your brain and heart faster, which improves, well, everything. I do it every night. It's calming."

He walked to the side of her bed, examining her strange position. "And do you find that it works?"

"You tell me."

"How am I supposed to know?"

She patted the spot next to her. "Try it."

Anxiety gripped his chest. All he wanted to do was talk with her, not lie in her *bed* with her.

"Come on." She reached out and grabbed his wrist. "Try it. You look like you need it."

And so, he did. He propped his feet up beside hers, trying to control a nervous tremor in his fingers. He crossed his arms, trapping his hands between his biceps and chest.

"It takes a second," she explained. "Just breathe deeply and relax."

Impossible at the moment, but he tried.

"Why did you swing by?" She looked up at the ceiling. "Coming to get me for dinner?"

If only. "No."

She waited.

"I wanted to…talk. If that's okay."

She turned her face to him. "You *do*?"

He faced her too. "Yeah, I do."

"Is…everything okay?"

"I don't really know."

"What's bothering you?"

"This whole thing." Bendigo turned his eyes up to the ceiling, not brave enough to look at her anymore. "I'm having a hard time with how I feel about everything."

When he didn't go on, she prodded. "How do you feel?"

"Like I don't understand the extent of the evil in front of us. Like I should be feeling more malicious, more willing to fight." He glanced her way. "Why does it have to be people of our own kind?"

"Have you ever thought that maybe you'll be setting them free?"

He studied her. "Setting them free how?"

"Freeing them from the evil that has overcome who they really are."

No. He had never considered that. Not even once. Death to him was the end of everything. "But what about their families?"

"Getting rid of evil isn't a painless task."

Again, he had never thought about accepting that. "I suppose I'm afraid to do the wrong thing."

"Fighting for love and all things good is never the wrong decision."

"How do you feel so sure about these things?"

"Because I trust Dagon." Her cheeks were soft, relaxed. "Something about him fills me with confidence to follow his lead."

"I feel that too. What is it about him?"

"Right? What *is* it?"

"I don't *know*."

"Here we are." She laughed. "Traveling across the world, following a man we barely know, and trusting him with our lives."

He matched her chuckle. "But it feels so right."

"Yes, and to be fair, The Book *did* pinpoint him."

"True. We weren't *totally* blind."

"Only a little." She brought her pointer finger close to her thumb, squinting at the tiny space she created.

He smiled. "What you said about setting the people free, that makes me feel better, Willy. Thank you."

"You aren't the only one carrying the burden of mental conflict." She nudged him. "I had to think about it too. Then I realized...death isn't the end."

"What do you mean? It's always been the end. For the last four hundred years at least."

"Yes, but soon, it won't be like that anymore. We're stealing the afterlife back. When this is all over, there will be *hope*. No fear of dying. And those who lose their lives in this guaranteed battle of some kind will be free from this worldly evil and will rest in the afterlife that Dagon can somehow bring back."

Her words sunk deep into the marrow of Bendigo's bones, saturating his soul with a comfort that one can only *wish* to experience. She spoke of a future that was too good to be true. Only it *was* true, and he knew it.

"I believe in hope," he breathed. "I believe in Dagon and what he says about restoring the afterlife. Only…will the ones killed before the afterlife is restored be granted entry?"

Willy gave him an empathetic smile. "We may not know the answer to that. Like I said, getting rid of evil isn't painless."

It hit him like an avalanche: only by faith could he carry on. There was never a promise of certainty, never a full understanding to ground his decisions. Only faith. And right now, it was her faith pushing him on.

"Why haven't we talked like this before?" Bendigo stared at their feet that were still propped up on the headboard. "Well, not like *this*, lying in the wrong direction on a bed."

She gave his humor a beat of laughter but brought her feet down and rolled to her side, propping her head up with her hand. "The question is: why haven't *you* talked like this before? I always tell you things."

He repositioned himself to match her posture. "Yeah, but it's easy for you to talk about stuff." He grinned. "You never *stop* talking."

She rolled her eyes and then grew authentic once more. "It's not easy to talk to everyone. Just easy to talk to you."

Her eyes again. They danced in front of him like swirls of marble, catching a glint from the lightning that flashed outside the window. He couldn't fight a faint smile. "You're not so hard to talk to yourself."

"Took you long enough to trust me. We've only been friends for eighteen years, Fletcher." She reached out and playfully shoved his shoulder.

"Oh, don't give me grief about it. You know how I am."

"Yeah. Stubborn."

He chuckled. "Am not."

"So are."

"What of it?"

"You can be stubborn with anyone else, just not me."

"And what happens if I am?"

Willy paused as if searching for a respectable, torturous punishment. Her eyes widened. "The grapefruit."

He fell onto his back and tossed his chin up, consumed with laughter. "You can't *still* think about that. I won it, fair and square."

When they were no more than eight or nine years old, they had created an obstacle course in the woods to race through. The prize for winning? A grapefruit. Why? They were kids, and that was all they could sneak from her kitchen to use as a trophy. It was a silly prize, but what meant more than the trophy itself was the act of winning.

It *was* true that Willy's pant leg had gotten caught on a stick, slowing her down, giving him the lead and the win. But she complained all the way home, telling him that it wasn't fair. They actually had a real argument about it, but he was too young to give in and hand over the grapefruit to calm the waters. Instead, he rubbed it in her face for months, getting a devious satisfaction every time she would grow angry. Until one day, she had had enough and delivered a punch to his chest. A real punch. After that, he never brought it up again. Though as they grew older, it became their favorite, ridiculous memory.

Satisfied, Willy flopped to her belly, staring down at him. "I get the grapefruit if you're stubborn. That's that."

Her closeness made his heart speed. "That thing is rotting somewhere in a wooden toy box. You don't want it."

"Yes, I do. Otherwise, I might have to distribute another punch." She brought her fist up, and he flinched. "I'm not *actually* gonna do it."

His eyes sprang wider. "How was I supposed to know that? You're devious."

"What of it?"

"Nothing of it."

Lying on his back and looking up at Willy, he realized something: he didn't ever want to live without her.

His gaze must have changed because she furrowed her brows. "What?"

"What?"

"Why are you looking at me like that?"

"Uh…I was just thinking"

"About what?"

"About how I'm glad you came with me."

She seemed taken off guard. "Oh. Well, I couldn't let you have all the fun."

The way she avoided sharing a heartfelt sentiment eased

his increasing pulse. A tremor passed through his stomach when he noticed that he was reaching beyond the normal realm of their conversations. She must have noticed too because she sat up, facing away from him.

"I'll be right back." She stood.

"Where are you going?"

Stopping at the door, she leaned back and gave him her childlike grin. "To the bathroom, if you must know. So nosy, Fletcher."

A puff of air escaped his nose as she left.

He hadn't noticed how hard he was trying to breathe steadily. With her gone, he let his shoulders relax, relieved. Talking to her wasn't as intimidating as he thought it would be. In fact, it was exactly what he needed.

The wind smashed against the window, and thunder overtook the house's frame once again. Somewhere between the deafening boom and the glass window's rattle against the cobblestone, Bendigo heard a voice.

The thunder faded, leaving the room with only the sound of pelting raindrops. He inched to the edge of the bed and dropped his feet to the floor. He sat rigid, listening for a familiar whispered word. As he sat, a snake of cold air trailed up his spine, wrapping around his ears. Then came the voice again. *Bendigo.*

The house shook.

Where he would normally be skeptical—even fearful— he wasn't. The hushed tone drifting into his mind pacified him.

Bendigo. The voice moved away from his ears, floating toward the door. It fluctuated from an airy eagerness to an enticing giggle.

Again, Bendigo found himself enthralled with the voice, this voice that was a home to no one. He had to follow it, see who wanted to speak with him. Letting his feet carry him across the wooden floorboards, he followed the whisper out into the hall. The hallway lanterns cast a stretched-out version of himself on the wall of art. He and his shadow stepped into stride together, making no noise as they tiptoed to the room that Dagon had claimed. The drafty room.

Bendigo remembered Sophia saying that, but no matter how hard he thought, he could barely remember anything else. It was like his memories had been locked inside a treasure chest. He knew he had things worth recalling, but he couldn't reach them. Blinking, still inching forward, he couldn't even piece together why he was in Orenda. Was he even in Orenda?

In this moment, he was only sure about one thing. A voice wanted him.

Bendigo.

I'm right here, he thought.

The voice slipped under the door to Dagon's room and called to him from inside. Bendigo didn't hesitate to turn the knob, emerging into a room that was empty of Dagon but housed something else. The farthest wall, across the room, divided Sophia's house and the one next door. And it was *moving*. A spiral of blue and black steam seemed to penetrate the cobblestone wall, creating some sort of twirling portal that endlessly spun at a slow pace.

He moved forward, putting his hand out. He had to touch it. Had to see where it led. Nothing so mystical had ever crossed his path, but that wasn't the real reason he had to examine it. He felt like he had no *choice*. The more it spiraled, the more his head tilted, following the twirl. He was full of wonder and acceptance to what it was. Treading closer now, his hand was inches away. The wind from the mysterious spin grazed against his palm. One more step, and he would be there.

The bedroom door burst open behind him. "Bendigo!"

A set of arms collapsed around his chest, pulling him back. In that instant, the portal suctioned into a tiny black dot, disappearing.

The locked treasure chest of memories flew open and all of his awareness came running home. He was in Orenda, getting ready to leave for Kalon. Evil consumed everything. He was to fight. A flash of beautiful eyes sprang in amid his memories, and he remembered where he had come from but not how he had gotten here. The arms around him still clutched tightly. Strong arms.

"What was *that*?" Shem's voice shouted, though he could barely register the words.

"I-I'm not sure."

Shem pulled him to the door. "Move your feet, Fetcher."

He was still in a fog, not able to walk.

"Bendigo, move!" Shem dragged him.

"I'm trying!"

That was when he felt the heat. The explosive, threatening heat. The hallway was ablaze, nothing but orange roaring flames and menacing black smoke. He staggered back to reality. "Shem, what's happening?"

Shem wheezed, choking on the smoke. Without even pausing for a second, he pulled his shirt off, tore it in two, and shoved one half over Bendigo's nose and throat. "The whole house is consumed!" he yelled through the cloth now tied over his mouth. "Get outside! Dagon and Sophia will meet you there."

Bendigo ignored him. "I need to get Willy."

"Where is she?"

A piece of the cobblestone wall cracked, tumbling to the floor, on fire. Stone on *fire?* Magic. The Twilights had found them.

"The bathroom." Bendigo moved.

"Fletcher, get outside!" Shem ran behind him. "I got her."

"No, she's my family!"

The two braved the flames that engulfed the walls. The orange spikes creeped down to the floor, curling at the tips, reaching for the red embroidered runner. The men reached the bathroom door, and Bendigo gripped the knob, yanking as he burned his hand on the hot metal. It didn't budge.

He pounded on the door. "Willy!"

"Bendigo!" her voice cried back.

Flames seeped out from underneath the door and licked upward.

"Shem, it's burning in there." He tried the handle again, further scorching his hand.

"Willy!" Shem shouted through the door frame. "Get back."

Bendigo gasped, panic and smoke suffocating his lungs.

Shem crossed his arms over his bare chest and plowed his shoulder into the door. It rattled but remained shut. A gash busted on the side of his shoulder, and blood dripped down to his elbow. Again, he crossed his arms, shut his eyes, and drove his shoulder into the door with such force that a drawn-out groan escaped his lips. The door cracked in half, caving in. He caved with it. Willy burst through the opening, flames overflowing after her. She staggered over the broken door at her feet, reaching for Bendigo who held her upright.

Shem pulled himself to a stand as the doorframe collapsed, sending new flames spiking up to the ceiling. He took the cloth over his face and pressed it against her nose. "Go."

A roar wafted through the hall as an avalanche of cobblestone detached from the wall and spilled onto the floor behind them. Bendigo blinked, blinded by the sting of smoke that penetrated his eyes. He kept one hand on Willy's arm, his other limb dragged along by Shem. The walls groaned behind them as they descended the staircase.

The front door was wide open, flames outlining the frame. Shem's grip tightened around Bendigo's forearm as he yanked them through the burning rectangle.

Bendigo swallowed an unhealthy amount of night air, choking. The bleariness in his eyes jaded his surroundings, but he could see Dagon and Sophia hovering around him. Then his senses picked up on an unsettling scene.

Desperate screams and cries rang out through the air. The great cobblestone city was no longer standing as a magnificent creation of charcoal stone and twisted chimneys but caving under the suppression of fire instead. No building was spared. Relentless evil flames consumed the entire city, its stone architecture standing no chance.

Sophia gathered the crew. "The river at the east end houses all our boats. We need to head there; it will get us out."

They turned and morphed in with the flood of people, who all streamed in the same direction. Some carried last minute saved belongings, others shouted names as they looked for family members, and some ran with silent purpose toward the river.

A different scream echoed off the charred city walls, causing Bendigo to look. A boy, no older than two, stood in the middle of the street, tears streaming down his face. His mouth let out a continuous shriek, looking around for someone. But everyone kept passing by.

Bendigo's heart ripped out of his chest. He diverted from the group, pushing through the constant stream of people while running in the crisscross direction. Reaching the boy, he bent down and scooped him up. "I got you." Turning around, he saw that he had lost his group. The swarm of heads blended together, a stampede of unfamiliar people.

The boy kept screaming in his arms.

"It's okay. I'm getting us out."

Bendigo darted his eyes in aimless directions. None of his friends were even visible. The crowd moved too fast. Too frantic. But they were all going to the same place: the river. Even if he was alone, he knew where his people were going. He could find them there.

Stepping into stride with the crowd again, he propped the boy on his hip and held the child's head close to his chest to prevent a jostling shoulder or elbow from bumping it.

"Bendigo!" a voice floated over the chaos.

Bendigo shot his head up and searched the sea of bodies. "Here!" He hollered, even though he couldn't spot the voice's source.

"Bendigo!"

Spinning to the call, he spotted Shem and Sophia wading toward him. He changed direction yet again and plowed his way to them. "Where's Dagon? And Willy?"

Shem eyed the little boy. "Went another direction. Thought they saw you go down one of the alleyways."

"We can't leave without them," he demanded.

Sophia held her arms out. "Give me the child."

He transferred the boy over. "Go to the river."

Tears rested on the bottom of her eyelids. "And leave you all?"

"We were leaving in the morning anyway. Go. Get you and the boy out."

"He's right," Shem said.

Sophia clutched the child's small frame and leaned in. "There is a fork in the river. Go left. It will lead closer to Kalon."

"Thank you." Bendigo felt an urge to make things right with her. "I—"

"I know," she said. "I'm sorry too. I will miss you and your good heart, Bendigo Fletcher." She leaned in and kissed Shem's cheek. "Glad to have finally met my friend's spouse. I will miss you too."

He squeezed her shoulder. "Consider me a friend as well. Now go."

The back of her cloak floated behind her as she submerged into the masses again, disappearing in seconds.

"Where did you lose them?" Bendigo spun in a circle. The smoke suffocated every corner and every alley, billowing up to the clouds, claiming the life of Orenda. Taking it all.

Shem didn't reply. He was already charging his way across the street that was emptying as the panicked mass neared the river. Without hesitating, Bendigo followed, wiping ash and soot from his eyes. Black buildings, charred to the bone, stood ahead, but the fire still soared upward from the cracks. It didn't matter that there was nothing left to consume; the fire wanted to take more.

Between two charred buildings was an alley that had morphed into a tunnel of flames. Running through the center, toward the entrance, was Dagon and Willy.

"Shem, here!" Bendigo redirected.

"Get back!" Shem threw his arm out, stopping him from charging into the tunnel.

Bendigo bounced back, shoving away from Shem's preventive force until he heard the monstrous, crackling groan. The whole side of the singed building caved in, toppling downward. Stones fell like a waterfall, blocking any way out into the street. As soon as the rock hit the ground, an explosion of flames burst to life, creating a wall between the four.

Shem and Bendigo on one side.

Dagon and Willy on the other.

Bendigo's wide eyes connected with Dagon's, pleading with him to do something. Willing. Begging. Hoping he could stop the fire and join him and Shem. Then he focused on Willy. He grew desperate. "Dagon, *do* something."

The ground shook, threatening to shake the rest of Orenda's foundations to rubble.

"We will find you," Dagon spoke through the flames.

"What?" Shem pushed forward. "Dagon!"

"Shem." Dagon's voice was firm, authoritative. "Go. Get to the river. You two stay together. We'll find you."

Nasty orange swirls of heat seemed to laugh, proving it

was strong enough to tear bonds apart. To separate an army. To destroy a community's safety. To change plans. To kill hope.

Bendigo zeroed in through the flames. "Promise me you've got her."

Dagon's eyes pierced past the thickening flames. "I always have."

A deafening fall of cobblestone filled the alley again, cutting Dagon and Willy off from view. Bendigo's heart caught in his throat, and he stepped back, trying to process this. Afraid to move on.

"Keep it together, Bendigo." Shem grabbed his shoulders, pushing him east again. "A warrior keeps moving. I'm with you. I'm here with you."

Inhaling the toxic air and forcing the anxiety back down, Bendigo set his course forward yet again. He *would* keep going. The Twilights could set the whole city ablaze, but they couldn't stop him. They would have to kill him first.

At the edge of the city, the river's current cut and crashed, raging like the sea. And all the boats were gone. The people of Orenda had already made their escape and were long gone now, judging by the river's speed.

Shem dug his heels into the crumbling street where it met the dirt along the edge of the water. He leaned forward, cutting his eyes up and down the bank.

A rumble shook beneath Bendigo's feet, and he shifted, half expecting the street to swallow him up. When Shem turned around to look at him, his eyes drifted upward, widening and fixating on something behind him.

Noticing the alarm, Bendigo twisted around. A wave of fire and smoke raced through the city, advancing with purpose and washing over every last building, every last stone. A final act to claim death on Orenda.

Bendigo lurched forward, yanking Shem along. "Remember to fork left."

"Got it."

Then he dove into the furious river.

For a moment, there was silence. His body sunk deep beneath the whitecaps, the icy water penetrating through his clothes and curling around his skin. It stabbed the burn on his hand, stunning his core. The current threatened to sink him deeper, but he thrashed his arms, pulling himself to the surface.

He broke through, sucked in air, and was dragged back down again. Whirling water warbled in his ears. Escaping to the surface again, he saw Shem being thrown around a few feet away. He kicked hard, struggling to stay above the current, and scanned the river's pathway. In one hundred feet, it would fork, and he was set on the course for the right, while Shem's body tumbled left.

"Ben!" Shem choked through the water as he reached for Bendigo.

Extending his hand, he flailed, trying to contact Shem. Their fingertips were inches away, and the fork was upon them. A desperate thought screamed in Bendigo's mind: *I can't do this journey alone!*

Their hands made contact.

Shem pulled him toward his body, rolling sideways, just missing a collision with a jagged river rock. They tumbled through the water's anger to the left fork, toward Kalon.

Eighteen

The all-consuming fire cloud whipped through Orenda, dissolving whatever structures still stood, to ash. The hiss of the ashes whispering to the ground grew louder, nearing the side street that Willy and Dagon were trapped in.

She clung to his side, praying he could somehow stop the fate that was upon them. She didn't want to die like this. Not when they had gotten this far. But the cloud kept coming, and nothing in its path survived.

"I didn't see it ending like this," she choked. She brought her last image of Bendigo to her mind. Through the wall of fire, he had looked at her like he was seeing someone else.

Dagon guided her back down the way they had come. "It doesn't end like this."

Nothing but unquenchable flames burned all around. She wondered how she was still alive, not grabbed by the flame's fingers yet.

Dagon cut left and right, leading them through different streets that looked the same. Amber waves of excruciating heat, black cobblestone, and fire. Nothing but fire. It was *all* fire. There is nothing that screams death like running through a city consumed with red destruction. Yet as they ran, the fire thinned, eventually giving way to the outskirts of Orenda. Farmland. A cornfield, half burning and half still spared.

His figure bobbed through the spared crop, heading to a structure that wasn't, in fact, cobblestone but cedar planks. A barn. It was far enough away from the flaming corn stalks to be safe for at least half an hour, if the flames weren't so relentless. How he knew it was here, she didn't have time to contemplate.

The barn was home to one single animal: a muscular brown workhorse who lifted his neck over the stall wall, studying the strangers. A wooden plaque above the stall read *Mapalo.*

The stillness inside the barn sent an eerie wave across Willy's skin. She knew that the structure would be black dust by morning. She set her gaze on Mapalo. "Can we let him free?"

Dagon already stood inside the stall, patting Mapalo's neck and soothing him. "Let him free? He's coming with us."

She stepped back, giving him room as he guided Mapalo out of the stall and into the small open barn space. She backed up against a wall that was decorated with hanging farm tools, horse bridles, and a sad excuse for a sword. Doing a double take, she stared at the blade. Dagon's words from before ran through her head. *I'll get one in Orenda.*

Grinning, she yanked the sword off the wall, almost dropping it when its full weight fell into her grasp. "Hey,

Dagon." She brought it up, holding it in both palms like an offering. "Here is the sword you've been waiting on."

His expression brightened, and he bowed, reaching out to take the blade. "Ah, at last. Thank you, Willy. You remembered." Tucking the sword into his belt, he leaned over Mapalo's back and swung his leg around, mounting the horse. He reached down to take her hand.

"Of course, I remembered." She clung to his arm and awkwardly made her way up on Mapalo's back, behind Dagon. She grabbed his shirt to not tumble backward. "I believe everything you say will come true."

His muscles tightened beneath her knuckles. "Do you? Why is that?"

"You haven't failed me yet."

Leaning down, he mumbled something into Mapalo's ears and then twitched his thighs, sending Mapalo galloping from the barn. The night air rushed against her face, and she turned to watch the burning cornfield slide past her view.

The steady rhythm of Mapalo's hooves entering the uncharted wilderness was a sound she could relax into. She stared behind them as Mapalo carried them up a grassy hill. The smoke from the city was a quiet mist of misery against the horizon. She clung tighter to Dagon, a tear escaping down her cheek. Evil had done more than she assumed it could. It had attempted to take *every* life, no matter who. She prayed for Bendigo and Shem. Maybe somebody would hear her. Maybe somebody would make sure they survived.

"Willy." Dagon tilted his chin over his shoulder.
"Hm?"
"We'll find them."

Nineteen

Squeezing his lids shut, Bendigo moved his fingers, feeling the rough surface he was on. A cool, jagged platform. Probably a rock. A dry rock. Which brought him to his next realization: he wasn't soaking wet as he should be. In fact, his skin basked under a blanket of what felt like the sun's springtime rays.

Daring to look, he let his eyelashes lift. As they rose, a turquoise sky—one that was only this vibrant in his dreams—soared above him. And yes, the sun accompanied it. No storm clouds. No wind. No fire. Just turquoise and gold. He almost didn't dare to sit up, fearing that the sky might be a mirage, but the thought of Shem sprang to his mind. He propped up on his elbows, shoving himself to a sitting position.

His heart expanded, nearly bursting.

What surrounded him brought awe to his soul, saturating his mind's darkest corners that he kept private for imagining, creating. He was, as he had assumed, sitting on a rock but not just any rock. It was so pure that sparkles of crystal within the gray blended seamlessly together, reflecting the sun's beams. A calm, transparent river flowed along the edge, rushing into a basin that held a shimmering lake.

Surrounding the basin was something he had only heard of but never seen: volcanoes. From his textbooks, he thought volcanoes were brown, made of rock, and unpleasant to the eye. But not these. Different leveled ridges ran along their sides. There was no brown. No rocks. Instead, vibrant, plush moss covered its entire surface.

Nothing that Bendigo created in his mind had ever felt as real and fulfilling as this. For a moment, he found himself. His longing to escape to another world left his mind, and he was content.

"I was wondering when you'd wake," a familiar voice said.

Bendigo twisted around, leaning on his knees and staggering to stand. "Shem, *where* in the world are we?"

Shem leaned over a fire that he had created atop the rock shore, a vast jungle behind him. His top half, still bare, glistened with sweat in the sun. He had re-braided his hair, which had turned red from days in the sunlight. It hung down his back, two loose strands hanging over his eyebrows. "The river dumped us out here." He spun a stick over the fire, cooking some sort of animal. "I have no clue where we are."

"What happened to us?" His legs shook, weak, as he made his way to join Shem around the small fire. He sat. "I barely remember anything."

"That's because you were unconscious for quite some time." Shem reached down to a pile of aloe succulents and tossed one to him. "For the burn on your hand."

He turned his palm up and studied the circular, yellow and red blister. "Thanks." He broke open the aloe. "How long have we been here? You seem to have had enough time to do…a lot."

"It's been a few hours. When we got here, you had a lot of water in your lungs. I pumped out quite a bit. Not a fun experience, Fletcher. I thought you were done for."

"Geez." He massaged the aloe's gel into his palm, clenching his jaw from the sting. "Well, thanks."

"And then you were so panicked and hysterical when you came to that I had to find a Kalmia plant to knock you out for a while."

"Shem! You know those are poisonous, right?"

"They definitely aren't." Shem pulled the animal, which looked like a hare, out of the fire. "Only when consumed by the mouth."

A look of disgust encroached Bendigo's face. "If not by mouth, how did you give it to me?"

"Don't think the worst. I just held it under your nose."

"Oh." He rubbed his eyes, chuckling. "Well, thank you again."

Shem laid the meat on the rock and drew his sword, slicing it in half. "But it worked way better than I had imagined. You've been sleeping since sunrise."

Looking up, he judged the time of day. The sun was about two beats past the middle of the sky. Midafternoon. "How kind of you to silence me for hours," he said with a grin.

"I accept your thanks." Shem smiled, handing him half of the hare. "I will do it again anytime you wish."

"And get a couple hours to yourself? Never. I want to annoy you for the rest of our journey."

Shem's lips fully parted, revealing a whole beam. "I suppose I'll have to accept that, even though your presence causes little annoyance."

"How kind of you to say." He lifted his steaming meat up in a toast.

They dug into their meal, ceasing their banter. When they finished, they made their way to the gentle river to rinse the meal away from under their fingernails.

Shem bent down to submerge his hands. "Any ideas for a plan of action?"

Following his lead, Bendigo huffed. "I don't even know where to start."

"Don't you think that Dagon might have some way of finding us?"

"I have a lot of faith in him, but how are we sure that he and Willy actually…made it out?"

Shem stayed silent.

"We just have to think about that possibility." Bendigo watched his fingers move under the water's surface. Saying those words hurt, and if he didn't focus on something, he would lose control over the lump in his throat, and it might turn into tears.

Shem nodded. "If they didn't, what would you have us do?"

"I would say we try to find Kalon."

"You want to keep going if it's just us two?"

Bendigo frowned. "You don't?"

"Is it realistic?"

"Was the four of us realistic?"

"We had Dagon," Shem said.

"But The Book sent me."

"To find Dagon."

Bendigo stood straight. "Then that's what we're going to do."

Shem looked up at the sky. "I thought we were deciding what to do if he was gone."

"I've just decided. He's still alive."

"You can't just decide something like that."

"Yes, I can." Bendigo shook the water from his hands. "I don't think evil is strong enough to take him away."

Shem sighed. "He's not invincible."

"Says who?"

"Says he. He told us himself. The only thing that can't destroy him is a Twilight, so everything else isn't off the table."

Bendigo took a scoop of water and splashed it on his face. "If we don't try to find him, we will never know. Would you rather give up on him all together?"

"No."

"Then that's what we're going to do. We're going to search for him and Willy."

Shem paused. "And if we don't find them?"

"We reevaluate"

Shem only nodded again, wandering off down the river's shore and toward the lake. His eyes drifted upward, perhaps searching the volcanos for a clear route to take.

Bendigo meandered beside him. His insides were wrenched with a new wave of anxiety. "Have you lost your motives?"

"Have I what?"

"Lost your reason for coming along with us in the first place."

Shem looked down. "Finding my wife was what got me out the door. The evil we have seen is the only motivation I need from here on out. No part of me wants to bail now."

Relief washed over his stomach. "Good."

Shem rested his forearm on Bendigo's shoulder. "And of course, we're brothers now. I wouldn't leave my brother to fend alone."

"Brothers, huh?"

"If that's all right with you."

Bendigo nodded. "More than all right. What makes you feel that way?"

Shem gazed out across the water. "Family is someone you would do anything for, right?"

"In a perfect model, yes."

He groaned and then laughed. "Why are your answers never cut and dry?"

"Because I don't want to misspeak. I know of families that hurt their own. Like Willy's parents."

He crossed his arms. "You referred to her as your family when you insisted on getting her out of Sophia's burning house. Because you would do anything for her, right?"

Bendigo nodded and swallowed his clogged tears.

"I don't have a family anymore," Shem explained. "I was raised by my grandmother, and she passed away when I was fourteen, leaving me to fall under the fishermen's care. But you saw them. You can probably only imagine the way they raised me. I was more of a father to them than the other way around. I married the love of my life at eighteen. She left for Orenda when I was twenty. After that, I had no one to call family. Until Dagon showed up. Then for once, I felt like I had a father."

His story was unexpected, but Bendigo admired it. "I agree. It feels good to have the feeling of a father again."

Shem shifted his shoulders to face him. "You said something the first night in Orenda."

Bendigo cringed, thinking of the wine that exposed him. "I said a lot of things."

"Yeah, but one stuck with me. You talked of your brother. You said you felt more like a father to him at times. At that moment, I realized that you and I aren't too different."

He smiled a tad. "Not by much."

"So, why not be brothers ourselves?"

"I see no reason not to."

Shem lifted his arms. "It's settled then."

"I declare us brothers!" Bendigo shouted across the lake,

as if to seal a covenant.

A slight wind shimmied up the volcano ahead of them, waving moss like it was underwater.

Shem raised a brow, catching nature's sudden movement. "I think that worked."

"I'm more powerful than you thought."

"Spare me." He rolled his eyes. "It was luck."

"No such thing."

He turned and headed back to the dying fire. "If luck is real, then I would say you just misspoke."

Agitated that he posed a sound argument, Bendigo didn't object.

"All fun aside"—Shem stared into the jungle that lay before them—"we have to move if we're going to find Dagon and Willy."

"Through there?" Bendigo rested his hands on his hips. The jungle looked so thick that the dark greenery sometimes looked black. "I don't know if you're skilled with navigation, but that looks like an avenue to getting lost in."

"We're already lost."

"Can't argue with that."

They stood shoulder to shoulder, examining the looming territory ahead of them. Neither seemed to want to make the first move inward.

After a moment, Bendigo thwacked Shem on the back. "Well, how bad could it be?"

"Don't say things like that, Fletcher."

Scrunching his nose, he drew his hand away from

Shem's back, now covered in sweat. "Task number one: find you a tunic."

"Don't look so disgusted. I lost it saving *you*."

"Which I'm thankful for, but you are a fountain of sweat."

Shem opened his mouth to make a stab back but left it hanging when the vegetation in front of them moved.

At first, Bendigo thought a beast was thrashing through the jungle, about to emerge. But the plants didn't sway in chaotic angles; they parted right down the middle as if a wedge was driven inward, splitting the foliage to either side to create a pathway. Nature had created a trail to guide them.

"What did I tell you?" Bendigo moved in, shadows of palm shrubs waving over his body. "Dagon lives."

"I would reason, but I think you're right."

"Finally, nature turns to our side."

Shem drew his sword and walked behind Bendigo. "Isn't there a possibility that this path isn't nature leading us to Dagon?"

"There is always a possibility, but don't you feel what is pulsing through nature's veins?"

Shem glanced at a six-foot fern that leaned into the trail as if to touch him. "I feel different, if that's what you mean."

"Yes, different from what we've been experiencing. We've been witnessing nature under a curse, but here, nature hasn't been consumed yet. There is *life* here."

Twenty

The thought of traveling through unmapped terrain had made Willy anxious at first but not anymore. This land had endless life, a vastness she couldn't compare to anything else. She couldn't help but think about how much Bendigo would love to see what she saw.

Through the night and well into the day, she and Dagon had ridden Mapalo across the changing terrain that seemed to always be uphill. Now, they stopped to break on a wide mountain peak that was more or less a grassy plain spreading out for half a mile. Looking down, she saw waves and waves of hills, all covered in tall grass that was either a faded green or a hay-like brown. Herds of wild horses were scattered below in the sea of greens and golds.

Dagon poured water from his canteen into his hands and offered it to Mapalo, who accepted it sloppily before wandering away to graze.

"Do you see that thing peeking through the clouds out there?" She pointed, looking back at him.

He came forward, squinting. "Yes. Do you know what that is?"

"I would say that it looks like a mountain, but I've never seen the tip of a mountain cave in like that."

"That's because it's a volcano."

She thought back to her history book that had offered a drawn image of what a volcano looked like and what it did. "Doesn't that mean that we're in danger?"

"Not all volcanoes are active. And we're far enough away."

"Oh." She gazed out again, wishing even more that Bendigo could see this. She could already see the way his eyes would fixate on the volcano, fully enthralled in its beauty. She fought to see it like he did, but without his help, practicality and logistics swarmed her mind before awe could ever do a number on her.

Dagon positioned himself to stand beside her, observing the hilly plains. "I'm proud of you, you know."

She leaned sideways and twisted to see him. "Me?"

"Well, there's no one else here." He peered around as if he was actually seeking another person. "Unless you thought I was talking to Mapalo."

"No, obviously. I'm just— Thank you. Right? Is this when I say thank you?"

Dagon lowered his chin and laughed. "Oh, Willy."

She forced a grin through the cringe. "I'm sorry. I have no idea how to take those kinds of words."

"Which *I'm* sorry for," he said, growing serious.

"Why are *you* sorry?"

"I'm sorry that you haven't grown up with much love and affirmation. I hope it's not too late to introduce you to those things."

She crossed her arms, feeling uptight. "I don't know."

"You're a very brave woman with a lot of confidence and a willingness to learn. Those aren't characteristics you should take lightly. Be *proud* of that."

"Okay." Okay? That sounded ungrateful.

He looked down again, silently laughing. "Okay. I'll stop now. But just know that I mean it when I say I'm proud. You are strong and very trusting of me and the others."

"You said you were going to stop," she teased.

"*Now* I'll stop."

She sighed, looking down at her feet. She smiled from his words but was curious as to why she had forced him to quit complimenting her. A memory of six-year-old Bendigo floated into her mind. He had come outside to play, and she wore her hair down because her parents had put lemon juice in it to help the sun saturate the dusty color and hopefully make it blonde.

When Bendigo had seen her, he had said, "Willy, your hair is very pretty today."

With which she had responded, "It will be prettier when the sun makes it blonde."

He had seemed confused by her remark. "But my mom's hair is dark, and I think she's very pretty."

The memory cut off there, and she was drawn back to reality. Why she had tucked that memory so far back, she wasn't sure, but she could probably guess. Now though, the memory meant so much more. All her life, she had pulled her hair back into buns, slipped through crowds, hid her face, and lived alone because she was ashamed that she looked different.

She drew her hand up to the back of her neck. Why had she never dug deep enough to see that looks might mean everything to her parents and most of Whimselon but not to *everyone*? And that maybe—just maybe—if she was brave enough to love people as deeply as she wanted to, she wouldn't have to hide anymore.

She pivoted backward, glancing at Dagon. He had wandered back toward Mapalo, stroking the horse's neck and saying something she couldn't hear.

Moving her hand up to the bun resting against the base of her skull, she pulled a pin out, letting a few strands loose. She instantly felt a twinge prettier. Pulling the two other pins from the bun, she let all her hairs fall over her shoulders and down her back. They were looped and twisted from being in the bun, so she ran her fingers through them as they fluttered in the breeze.

She felt pretty.

"What do you think?" she called across the mountain top.

Dagon didn't look up. "About what?"

"Me."

"I told you already, and you begged me to stop." He lifted his hand from Mapalo's mane and brushed his palms together, bringing his eyes to her. "Oh."

She crossed her arms, picking at the elbows of her shirt, suddenly nervous and wondering why she had the boldness to allow herself to simply *be*.

"It complements your natural beauty very well. You look complete."

Her heart pulsed. "I do?"

"You've always looked beautiful, but your acceptance of it is what brings out its fullness."

"Wait. You mean when you first saw me, you thought I looked nice?"

He strode beside her again. "Of course."

She put her hands on her hips and huffed. "You're just saying that."

"I never just say anything." He gave her a teasing eye.

"Annoyingly, I know."

"So, you can trust me when I say I always saw you as lovely."

She fought against a blush. "Thanks."

He looked off but cut his eyes back to her. "I know someone else who thinks that too."

The blush won. "You do not."

"Must I convince you *again* that I don't speak lies?"

"Well, who then?" she asked even though she already knew.

He answered only with a tilted head and a devious smile.

"Did he say something to you?" Willy tried to make her tone sound more curious than hopeful.

"No."

Her shoulders dropped. "How do you know then?"

"I just watch."

"Right." She blew an exasperated breath. "That's a perfect way to misread situations."

He laughed once and put his palms up in a shrug. "Is it so unbelievable?"

"Not *entirely* but nearly. We grew up together. Any type of…different relationship would be…strange." Though the thought of it had been crossing her mind more than once a day. Every time, she ignored it, forcing it down.

Dagon hummed, leaving the conversation open ended. Willy wanted to hear more, but she didn't dare prod in fear of letting him see how interested she was. Instead, her mind ran back to here and now. Bendigo and Shem were out there somewhere. Yes, she had faith in their abilities to carry on, but she also knew they weren't invincible. Being with Dagon, she felt she had a better chance, but either way, two and two could go down faster than a bundle of four.

"How are we going to find them?" she asked, soft. "It feels near impossible. With us being in unknown territory and all. I just hope they're all right."

A cloud moved over the sun, casting a shadow over the mountain top. The natural breeze picked up, blowing stronger now. Mapalo lifted his head from his peaceful grazing spot, and Willy watched as the wind blew Dagon's hair away from his face. He closed his eyes, breathing in the new breeze and perhaps feeling something.

His eyelids lifted. Creating an *O* with his lips, he produced a long, drawn-out note, which rang down the mountainous plains.

Willy bit her lip. "What are you doing?"

Two wild horses galloped to the top of the mountain, heading toward him like they knew him. He brought both of his hands up and placed one on each horse's muzzle. He then whispered something.

She wanted to ask again but didn't. Especially when he removed the top layer of his tunic, revealing only a white, flowy undershirt. Yanking the rope that acted as a humble belt away from his waist, he placed his tunic on the back of the black horse and used the rope to secure it around the horse's midsection. Again, he whispered something to the black horse, tapped the speckled horse's side one last time, and the two steeds were off, striding back down the mountain and toward the volcano in the distance.

"What did you just *do*?" She couldn't believe she was still surprised by Dagon's antics.

Dagon leisurely turned an eye to her. "I sent those two off to Shem and Bendigo. They're going to need it."

Twenty-One

Bendigo.

His whole body twitched, and he jolted awake. He was lying on his side. Dirt gritted against his cheek and the darkness all around him screamed with the sound of night insects. The fire that he and Shem had built in the middle of a clearing was just an ember glow now, lacking warmth. The night temperature hadn't dropped enough to make Bendigo chilled, yet he had goosebumps running up and down his spine and arms.

Pushing himself up to sit, he drew his eyes in a circle, trying to find Shem. Spotting him leaning against a palmetto tree a few feet away with his sword across his lap, Bendigo exhaled. Shem had offered to take the first watch and let Bendigo sleep, but something had awoken him. A whisper. A name. *His* name. Just like that last moment in Orenda.

He stood, rubbing his arms to dissipate the goosebumps, and roamed over to Shem.

Shem slanted his chin up, spying him.

"I'll take watch now." He slid down against the same tree, leaning his head back and kicking his legs out straight.

Shem frowned. "You haven't slept for more than two or three hours."

"That's okay."

The silence between them must have told Shem that this was about something else, because Shem didn't transfer his sword over to Bendigo.

Bendigo turned his head, catching Shem already looking at him. "What?"

"Tell me what's got you distressed."

A pause. "You saw it, didn't you?"

"Saw what?"

"When you found me in Sophia's house, you saw that thing in the wall."

Shem's eyes grew, and a realization crossed his pupils. "In the midst of everything, I had forgotten about that until now. Fletcher, what *was* that?"

"Some kind of portal. Like if I reached inside, it would have sucked me in, taking me...somewhere. The worst part is that I *wanted* to go in, and it wanted *me*. It called me by name."

"You heard a voice?"

"I heard my name."

The crickets chirped around Shem and Bendigo's silence.

"It was evil." Bendigo's voice was foggy.

Shem's voice cut through that fog like a double-edged sword. "How do you know?"

"Here." He pointed to his heart. "I felt it here."

"Do you think that's how the Twilights have been recruiting their army?"

"It would make sense. How else are people disappearing without a trace if not through a spiritual portal of some kind?"

Shem tapped his blade, thinking. "It called you by *name*?"

"Yeah."

"Why you, Bendigo?"

It almost felt like an insult. "Elaborate."

"First, The Book singles you out, and then the Twilights try to take you but not the rest of us. What's different about you?"

"Listen"—Bendigo looked up at the sky through the thin jungle top, bouncing his eyes from star to star—"if I knew, I would tell you, but I'm also in the dark here. I didn't feel qualified in the first place, and I especially don't feel qualified now." That was true, however little drops of confidence had seeped under his skin along the way. He just didn't want to admit that. The thought of being a respectable, strong, fighter seemed too far-fetched, and half the time, his survival was because of outside help.

"What about the castle?" Shem rotated his chin to Bendigo.

He met his stare. "The Twilights are guarding it for *some* reason, but I have absolutely no guess as to what it could be. We learned about Kalon growing up, but the castle was always just an abandoned stone castle. Nothing more, nothing less. The water at the top, now that's another story."

"Do you believe that story is true?"

He changed his voice to carry a mystical narrative tone. "What? That all the rivers in Tarsha web from the mighty, life-giving river at the tip top of the mountain?"

Shem laughed, shaking his head. "It does sound ridiculous, doesn't it?"

"It does." He used his heel to create a shallow hole in the dirt. "But I think I believe it."

"I want to believe it."

"Then believe it."

"You can't just"—Shem waved his hands— "summon a belief into existence."

"Sometimes, believing in something takes blind faith." When he said it, the night The Book wrote his name flashed before his eyes. "Why do you think I left Whimselon in the first place?"

"Because The Book told you to."

"And I had to believe The Book, otherwise I would still be in Whimselon, hating myself for doubting it and wondering who Dagon was for the rest of my life." He imagined a life without ever knowing Dagon, and the thought became somber, agonizing even. At all times, Dagon seemed full of love, affirmation, and compassion yet equally filled with sternness, directness, and discipline. "I can't imagine my life any other way anymore. I want to be here."

Now, they both stared up at the sky, pondering.

A grin danced onto Shem's lips. "Let me ask you something."

Bendigo caught the devious look. "Oh no."

"Willy."

"I knew it."

"Come on, Fletcher." Shem repositioned himself to be square with him. "Why won't you just tell her that you care about her?"

"We're best friends. I tell her all the time. Why do you think she came with me? Because I care about her. She knows I do."

"Then let me put it this way: why won't you just tell her that you're *falling* for her?"

"Please, Shem. You're a hopeless romantic. Surprising, by the way."

"There is nothing hopeless about being a romantic, but there is everything hopeless about *avoiding* it."

"I don't avoid it. It's just not present."

Shem made a fist and socked Bendigo in the bicep. "Don't play. Tell the truth."

"Geez, Shem!" Bendigo shoved him away, then burst into a laugh. "That actually *hurt*."

"Not as bad as it will when you let her slip through your hesitant fingertips."

"Why are you so adamant about this?"

A wave passed over Shem's face, changing to the tense version of himself. "Because she looks at you the way my wife used to look at me."

Bendigo's heart twisted like a vine.

"And you look at her too. I've seen it."

He swallowed. "Well of course, I look at her. She's *pretty.*"

"Tell me what you think is pretty about her."

"Don't make me do this," he groaned, pulling at the sides of his eyes.

"Do it."

"Fine." Dropping his hands into his lap, he drew a breath. "She has beautiful eyes, which I just recently discovered. I like when she smiles. She knows how to make me laugh. Don't make me do this."

"Keep going."

A sigh. "She um...is the only person who sees beyond my sadness." His stomach churned, surprising him. "She is encouraging, witty, annoying, devious, heartfelt..."

"Come on." Shem brought his voice down, staring hard. "Don't fight it, Bendigo. You're going to regret it if you lose her."

Burying his face in his hands, he let out a steady groan. "It's complicated."

"Stupid phrase." Shem twirled his sword with his wrist. "*Life* is complicated, and that goes without saying. What *you're* dealing with is the fear of falling."

Wrapping his arms around his knees, Bendigo rested his chin on his forearm. He didn't have to ponder to know Shem was right. It was never the plan to see Willy any differently than the pesky, adventurous best friend that she was, but somewhere along the way, they had grown up.

The shift didn't even feel gradual; it felt sudden. Like the moment they left Whimselon was the determining factor if their friendship was bound by convenience or by genuine desire. And now, separated from her, he *wanted* her. Maybe he just wanted the familiarity of her, but maybe he just wanted…her.

"If you're right, what do I say to her?"

Shem stopped flipping his sword. "Are you admitting to—"

"Yes." Bendigo looked down, forcing a smile away. "Maybe."

"Well, well!" Shem gave him another punch, friendly this time.

"Don't make a big deal out of it." He let the smile come.

"Me?" Shem spun the sword once more. "Never. As for what to say to her, just tell her what you just told me."

That made Bendigo howl. "Yeah *right!* I've never said that kind of thing to her."

"So?"

"So…"

"No excuses. She needs to hear that from you. Especially since those kinds of words have been sparse to her, from what I gather at least."

He held his hand out, gesturing for the weapon. "Okay, Sappy. Hand over the blade and get some sleep. You've had your stab at me tonight. Now rest, so we can get moving as soon as possible. Kalon may not wait another day."

At the mention of the task at hand, Shem's loose side was drawn back in and replaced with his thick skin. "If you hear your name"—he slid the sword from his lap to Bendi-go's—"don't follow it."

Twenty-Two

Six days. It had been six days since the split between the fellowship of four. Maybe seven. It was hard to keep track when the days blended together.

Every morning, Bendigo and Shem would rise with the sun, and the jungle would rise with them to create a guiding pathway and then to form a clearing at nightfall. This ritual repeated day in and day out. Some moments, Bendigo feared they were walking in circles or that maybe the terrain never ended, tricking its guests to keep them lost forever.

But around day five or six—if today was day seven—the jungle had begun to thin, and the path broke through to another trail. An old, permanent trail of sorts. This pathway spiraled up the side of a massive volcano. So tall that clouds hid its peak. The rocky trail was too narrow to travel side by side, so Shem took the lead, and they began their upward climb, careful not to slip on the moss that could send them sailing over the edge and back down to the jungle they had just spent five or six days in.

Hundreds of feet in the air, this footpath spiraled upward yet not forward. They spent hours looping around the mountainous mass only to get closer to the clouds yet remain just as far from Kalon as they were hours prior.

"This seems so wrong," Bendigo panted behind Shem. The air was thinner this high up, and the humidity raged too, which didn't make sense, but uncharted territory was uncharted territory. Who said it had to follow the rules?

"I *know*." Shem had started to show ounces of annoyance the second day on the volcano and had stopped all conversation three hours ago.

The jungle below faded from view, masked by the clouds. Bendigo's eyes searched the sky. His view caught nothing other than steamy clouds and Shem's glossy back leading them up the continuous twisting trail. "What do you think is at the top?"

Grumbling, Shem attempted a joke. "Chocolate cake and red wine."

He tried to laugh but couldn't get enough air, so instead, his face just looked like he was in pain. "I wish."

"I don't know if there *is* anything at the top. This whole thing is starting to feel like a wild goose chase. I mean, what do *you* think there will be? A sign that says 'This way to Kalon. Hold your trousers and slide down?'"

"Geez." He exerted a little sound with his laugh this time. "You're funny when you're irritated."

Shem stopped and turned, sweat pouring down his entire upper body because, yes, he was *still* shirtless. And extra tan now. Borderline burned. Bendigo braced for one of his lashing comments, but instead, he held a hand up.

Bendigo stopped moving and searched with his peripheral vision, listening for whatever Shem had caught wind of.

At first, he heard nothing, felt nothing. But creeping under his toes was a slow, steady vibration. His first thought was that the volcano was erupting. The loose rocks on the path twitched and jumped with ever-increasing rapidity.

"Ben, move!" Shem shouted.

Yanking his head around, he realized the rumbling was from horsemen.

"I said move, Fletcher!"

The sound of hooves increased. He jolted forward, digging his toes into the path to sprint uphill and hoping he wouldn't slip.

Shem turned sideways. "Get in front of me. Quick."

He inched past Shem without slowing down, tensing as he worked with no more than four inches between Shem and the volcano's ledge. Shem followed behind, sword in hand. As he rounded the mountain, he looked down to the lower part of the path. He expected two or three horsemen. But no. A whole company strode up the volcano, single file, charging forward with weapons drawn. No territory flag flew, but black paint streaks ran vertically down each horse's face. Bendigo understood. They were close to the Twilight's territory, and those horsemen were a part of the Twilight army.

Giving it all he had, Bendigo continued the race to the sky. The parade of horsemen thundered closer, and the air grew sparse. Clouds wafted between his arms and legs as he cut through the air, propelling himself up to nowhere. Shem was right. The top would be a dead end, and the horsemen would catch up.

They had run into a trap.

A sharp whiz slung past Bendigo's ear, and he watched as an arrow sailed into the clouds and took a nosedive downward. "Shem, arrows!"

The ting of clashing metal made him turn just in time to see Shem use his sword to swipe an arrow in half midair and repeat the motion above his opposite shoulder.

Arrows struck the side of the volcano, darting against the rock, clattering to the ground, or rebounding off into the surrounding clouds. But optimism surged within him. Yes, the path was ending, but something else was beginning: a tunnel. One that stood agape on the side of the volcano. Dark, deep, and safe.

Bendigo made for the tunnel's entrance, ducking into the darkness. He halted when his eyes struggled to change with the lack of light. Shem dove in behind him, knocking him into the side of the inner rock.

"What are you stopping for?" Shem shoved him on-ward.

He blinked, tripping over his feet and nearly falling when the ground wasn't as level as he thought. It slanted downward, halfway vertical. Throwing his hand out, he felt the rock wall, steadying himself as he picked up speed.

As they descended into the darkness, faint shouts and echoes of thundering feet told them that the horsemen had dismounted and followed them into the underpass. Fear no longer tore through Bendigo's chest; the want to survive had replaced it. He swallowed air, forcing himself to not slow down. As he ran, he noticed a thin webbing of red streaks between the wall's cracks like lava had cooled in a constant glowing state. It provided enough light for him to see more than one pathway. Some tunnels that jutted left and right were too narrow, but three channels up ahead seemed promising. Promising enough to leave the horsemen guessing which one they had taken.

"Which path?" Bendigo panted.

"*Any*. They're almost on us."

He chose left.

Flooding down the tight pass, Bendigo second-guessed his choice, wondering if it would squeeze down to a space too skinny to continue. It thinned out, for a while at least, before expanding to reveal a wide-open cave. The red webbing of cooled lava glowed between every crease of rock, making it seem like they were inside a red crystal ball.

"Hang on." Shem grabbed Bendigo's arm, stopping him from continuing through the cave towards another tunnel.

"What?" Bendigo gasped, sweat covering his forehead.

He held a finger to his lips and pointed to the tunnel they had just emerged from.

Footsteps. The horsemen had chosen wisely, or they had split up. Either way, Shem and Bendigo couldn't outrun them. Even if the volcano had another exit, the horsemen would still be behind them.

Bendigo revealed his dagger, hands shaking and chest heaving. Shem took a stance beside him, gripping his sword out in front of him. For a moment, their staggered, uneven breathing whispered through the cave. It was an agonizing waiting game.

Then came the flood.

Pouring from the tunnel, the once horsemen were now a ground army, flying toward the two with weapons waving and shouts.

Bendigo froze. The army wasn't just evil pawns. They were Whims, port merchants, Orendan scholars, Lhanian farmers, and others he couldn't identify. They were Tarsha's people. Some of *his* people. Now, the blood of the leading man, a native Orendan, sailed through the air, flinging off Shem's sword. And Shem kept going—swinging and slicing to *slay* the army.

A spear in the hands of a towering, male Whim drilled its way through the militia, on target for Shem's side. Losing all sense of self, Bendigo launched himself forward. He shoved the spear up and away and drove his dagger into the Whim's chest. He closed his eyes, yanking it out again and swinging it behind him. He knocked another body away from Shem.

Shem spun around Bendigo, dragging his blade across a line of attackers. Bendigo ducked as a sword sounded like a thick swoosh above his head, and he used the low leverage to drive his dagger into the weapon carrier's side. As the body tumbled down, its eyes passed over Bendigo's face. A woman. Clothed in Lhan farming attire.

He reached for her.

Arms pulled him back.

"Time to move." Shem pulled him toward the new tunnel. "*Now!*"

Everything in his heart screamed, but he followed Shem into the inclined tunnel. The top of the incline exposed white light from outside. The Twilight soldiers who had survived the momentary bloodbath continued to pursue Shem and Bendigo, shouting, snarling, and seething behind them.

Bendigo begged himself to get to the light, fearing he may collapse. He burst through the opening, squinting in the daylight. He wheezed, temporarily relieved. But the army behind them exploded out too, only a few feet to their rear.

Then he saw an opportunity. "Shem, there!"

Ahead, in the grassy plains that overtook the landscape, were two horses. One black, one speckled. The black one carried a piece of cloth tied around its core. They paced like anxious friends, clearly expecting the two.

"Dagon," Bendigo whispered, a warmth flooding his shattered heart.

When he and Shem wrapped their arms around their horse's necks and pulled themselves up, the horses took off, leaving the Twilight army behind. The four-legged creatures were now *their* advantage.

Twenty-Three

The speckled horse glided beneath Bendigo's weight, shifting him forward and back in a rhythm as its hooves galloped over the plains. All the way to the horizon line, tan and olive grass rolled over the ground, following the hills. Besides steady thumps from the two horses' hooves, he had nothing else to listen to. Nothing else to focus on. Just the quiet air.

A moment of peace was what it should have been, but he was far from that. His fingers were wrapped in his horse's mane, and every time he looked down, he tried to bury his fingers further beneath the hair, so he didn't have to look at them.

He didn't want to see the blood. The blood from the Whim. The Lhanian woman. The other unknown body he had pierced. Their blood had dried, seeping into his own skin and crusting like a permanent stain. It felt as if their deaths had been engraved within his fingerprints, forever hovering to remind him that *he* was responsible.

"Steady," Shem's voice said, calm, as he slowed his horse.

Bendigo's horse followed suit, and finally, he looked up. Another forest. Pine trees this time. He had been so focused on his hands that he didn't even realize the change in scenery or the passing of time.

Shem slid off his horse, his muscles protruding beneath the long-sleeved tunic that had been tied to the horse's black coat. He faced the woodland, examining the dimness between the pines. "The forest will provide cover. Let's move in."

Bendigo landed on his feet and patted his horse's neck. There was the blood on his hand again.

Following Shem into the forest, he led his steed, and the gradual change in temperature ran up his arms, inducing a shiver. The air felt moist but not from a warm humidity; it was a wet chill, mixed with a crisp pine scent. The flutter of a crow's wings disrupted the eerie air as it took off farther into the woods.

"Let's not go too far in." Shem stopped, guiding his horse to a small yet rich patch of grass amid the damp dirt. "Something tells me that Dagon and Willy haven't reached the forest yet."

Bendigo showed his horse to the grass too. "Why do you think so?"

Squatting, Shem scooped up a palm of dirt and rubbed it between his fingers, scraping off the blood on his own hands. "When Sophia showed us the war map, I noticed a forest of pine trees called the Kalon Pinewoods. It was the last territory to pass before reaching the cliffs where Kalon's castle sits. Dagon wouldn't have gone in without us. He would have waited."

"So, that's what we should do then?" He stooped down. "Wait?"

"What do you think?" He asked it for real.

Bendigo pressed his hands into the dirt, digging his nails in and imagining the dirt replacing the dried red under his fingernails. "I don't know what to think anymore."

"Hey." Shem's voice sailed smooth like a single breeze.

He glanced up.

"You did good back there."

Bendigo looked back down. The blood *had* to come off. No part of him could stand it any longer. Gathering a clump of dirt, he scrubbed as Shem had, using the grit and mild dampness to eliminate the dried-on death. Some blood chiseled off; some was harder to remove. It lined his finger-nails and stayed in the deep, hard to reach crevasses. He rubbed more intensely. It *had* to disappear.

A wallow of desperation washed over his soul, and he dug his nails into his skin, clawing at the dried blood, ripping away the stain. It stung, and it burned, but he kept going. Get off! The words shouted back and forth between the walls of his mind. He was angry. So *angry*. He had *killed*. No. *Murdered*.

He hated himself. Then he justified it. Then he screamed at himself. But when he focused on his palms again, he saw that *more* blood had appeared. Warm. Fresh. His own. He had clawed through his own skin, and though he realized that, he kept going. It felt good. It felt like a form of justice. It felt—

"Bendigo! Bendigo, stop!" Shem dove toward him and ripped his bloody hands apart.

The sudden movement made him tumble sideways, and he tipped from a squat onto his knees, not able to catch himself as Shem kept a firm grip on both wrists.

"I have *blood* on my hands." A cry snaked up his throat. "*Their* blood!"

Shem rested on his own knees, squeezing his wrists. He forced a stare into his hysterical eyes. "Brother."

He gasped, in out in out, trying to focus on Shem.

"Brother," Shem said again. "We are in a war."

"But I *killed*."

"No. You protected. You protected yourself, and you protected me."

He focused on his breathing and refused to let the tears move from behind his eyes. "Why does it hurt *so bad*?"

"Because you've never killed before."

"You have?"

A shadow crossed Shem's eyes. "Times come when you must decide what is most important to you, and you usually choose based on who it affects. You had to fight back there. Otherwise, you and I wouldn't be here."

Bendigo's arms went limp and slipped to the forest floor as Shem released his grasp. They sat on their knees, staring at each other. The air between the pine trees swirled overhead.

"Is the first time the worst of it?" Bendigo asked, desperate.

"By far."

"Am I going to be okay?" The question was genuine, childlike even, but he had been altered. He truly felt like the burden would never leave, reminding him of his actions for the rest of his life.

"Yes. You will be changed but not tortured. The initial shock will pass. Just give it time."

Bendigo's heart slowed. "Okay."

Shem sighed. "It's going to be all right."

Trusting Shem, Bendigo stood, offering his arm to help Shem up. "I don't know if I'll ever *not* have to tell you thank you."

"So polite, Fletcher. But really, it's not needed."

He exhaled, calm now, and noticed the horses still grazing on the same patch. "It's wild that Dagon could get them to us. Even wilder that he thought about giving you a tunic." The world felt lighter as he thought about Dagon possibly being near. "He must have known you had to stop walking around like a toned warrior, making me look like the twiggy sidekick."

"The presence of my tunic doesn't make you less of a twig."

"Give me a break. I'm a Whim. My chances at bulkiness have been slim since birth."

"You're getting some though." Shem pointed to his chest.

Bendigo snapped his chin down. "I am?"

"Yeah. Don't you feel stronger?"

"I do. I just didn't think about it too much."

Shem twitched his lip upward. "Willy might notice when she sees you too."

His stomach ran rampant. "Quit."

"What? Nervous to see her?" Shem collapsed against a tree and shut his eyes, folding his hands over his lap after he placed his sword within reach.

"No," he lied. "Just expectant." He joined Shem against the tree.

"And you called *me* the hopeless romantic," Shem mumbled through shallow breaths that usually proceed sleep.

Bendigo didn't answer, but with Shem's eyes closed, he let his smile show—only to force it away with his hand in fear that Shem might flick his eye open and catch him. But now steady, drawn-out breaths escaped Shem's slightly parted lips. He had fallen asleep that quickly.

Slowly reaching over him, Bendigo grabbed the sword. He would take first watch. But before he knew it, he closed his own eyes and didn't have enough time to remind himself that he and Shem were alone on the outskirts of the Twilight's claimed territory.

☾

Meanwhile, in the waves of the grassy plains, Dagon and Willy rode Mapalo across the terrain towards the Kalon Pinewoods, arriving just in time to see a Twilight drift out from the shadows of the forest and make its claim on the sleeping Bendigo Fletcher.

Twenty-Four

Dagon was off Mapalo before the horse even stopped. "Bendigo! Wake up!"

Thrashing through the pines, he raced to Bendigo. A Twilight had its hands gripped around Bendigo's eyes, hugging his head. But Dagon's call caused the spirit to jolt backward, pulling back its wispy fingers.

"Be gone!" He thundered over Bendigo, driving his sword toward the Twilight.

The Twilight let out a scream before reaching for Dagon, attempting to grab his throat. But its cloak grazed against his fingertips, and in that second, it hissed to dust. Its being dissolved into a frail, gray particle midair and fell heavy to the forest floor.

A scream erupted from Bendigo's throat. He opened his eyes only to realize that he couldn't see. His world was black. He blinked over and over, only to see darkness. "Shem!" He screamed. "Shem!" A rustling sounded around him, the shuffle of feet, and he flung his hand out to touch whoever was beside him.

"What happened?" Shem's voice hollered, but Bendigo felt like he was facing the other way, not toward him.

"A Twilight," a familiar voice said. "It just tried to claim him. Give him to me."

Bendigo's heart burst. "Dagon!"

A firm set of hands reached down and gripped his biceps, pulling him up.

"I can't see!" Bendigo pressed his hands against the body holding him up, feeling the firmness of Dagon's chest.

"Relax," Dagon hushed.

He gripped the front of Dagon's shirt, entirely vulnerable. "I'm *blind*, Dagon."

"Listen. Relax."

Trying to follow orders, he breathed through his nose, letting the air flood his lungs. Dagon's thumbs rubbed over his eyes. He let his lids shut, allowing Dagon to push his thumbs slightly inward. With the pressure came a soothing flow of orange light, filling his vision before webbing away to reveal darkness again.

Dagon's thumbs dropped. "Look at me."

Bendigo hesitated, but after some deep breathing, he parted his eyelids. As he did, light shone through, blurry for a moment but then focused on the one in front of him. "Dagon," he choked. He collapsed forward, hugging Dagon like he was his father returning after years of being dead.

Dagon returned the hug just as firm. "What are you doing sleeping with the Twilights?" His voice had a hint of a smile.

He drew back and kept blinking, making sure he could still see. "I didn't mean to. I just—"

"I'm teasing." Dagon chuckled, but then his voice dropped to a serious tone. "But you need to be diligent from here on out. They can blind you from seeing the difference between good and evil. They'll claim you like that." He lowered his voice to a hush that was only audible to Bendigo. "And they want you most."

Shem stood to the side, looking dazed. "Nothing like the phrase 'in the nick of time' right about now."

Dagon stepped toward Shem and offered a strong hug to him as well. Bendigo smiled, toiling over Dagon's last words for a second before pushing it aside. He felt whole again. They were all back together.

He spun around, his eyes falling on Willy, who hung back by a horse. At the sight of her, everything inside twisted up, more extreme than from Shem's comments.

She seemed nervous, fiddling with her shirt sleeves. "Hey, Fletcher."

He moved toward her, and she did too, a grin expanding across her mouth.

"I'm so happy you're here." The words tumbled effortlessly from his lips.

He pulled her into his arms, securing her in his grasp. She squeezed just as tight around his midsection, and he let his face fall into her hair. Her hair was down, flowing over her shoulders and brushing against his arms. He hadn't seen it like this since they were seven. Maybe younger.

Drawing apart, he had to force himself not to run his fingers through her locks. "Your hair... It looks..."

Fear flashed in her eyes.

"Pretty," he said through a beam.

The fear faded to a relieved bashfulness. "Thanks."

He wanted to say more but didn't know how, so he just stared instead. She had changed. A new sense of confidence eased from her, even though she still looked down and away like she was afraid to make eye contact with him.

Dagon cut the tension by calling everyone together. Bendigo was glad to be saved from forcing himself not to reach out and pull her into him again. The four assembled as the sun hung low, leaking gold through the tall pines.

"We are nearing Kalon." Dagon scanned each face in the circle. "As you may have realized, the Kalon Pinewoods are the only thing that stands between us and the castle, meaning the army is closer than ever."

Dread touched Bendigo but passed by when courage took over. "So, what's the plan?"

"Rule number one." Dagon held up a finger. "Two of us will always keep watch during the nights. We must have no repeats of what just happened moments ago. The Twilights *will* take you." He set his gaze on Bendigo.

He nodded, furrowing his brow at how he was subtly singled out.

Dagon pulled his eyes away. "As for a plan, we will have to assess our tactics when we find the army…" He trailed off. "I know going in blind is not the way of warriors, but you three show tremendous faith, trust, and drive. There *will* be an end to the days of evil."

Bendigo held his breath.

"Don't give up on hope," Dagon added. "Even when it seems like evil has won or when it feels like you aren't strong enough anymore. Look at how far we've made it."

Yes, he was right. Against all odds, they had survived. They had power in their presence, faith in their hearts. And at times, nature may have done them a favor. Even as they set up camp for the night in the pinewoods, the night chill held off, offering them a sense of comfort.

As the four sat around the bonfire, exchanging their stories of what had happened during their separation, it was made even clearer that nature fought to hold onto the good in the world. Even though evil had seeped into Tarsha's soil and dispersed itself, good still held on, waiting, perhaps, for the final battle.

☾

"Does your horse have a name?" Willy spoke softly as to not wake Shem and Dagon, who were sprawled out on the opposite side of the fire.

Bendigo watched his speckled horse, who hung his head low beside Mapalo and the black stallion. "How should I know?"

"You just name him." She pulled her knees to her chest. "Duh."

"Well, help me name him then."

"It has to be something majestic." She waved both

hands in front of her like she was creating an invisible rainbow. "It *is* Bendigo Fletcher's steed."

"Oh, that doesn't mean a thing. He kind of looks like a river stone though, doesn't he?"

"He does."

"Can't we just call him River?"

She tilted her chin up. "River. You know, that's fitting."

"I know." He brought his hand to his chest, grinning. "Thank you."

Rolling her eyes, she pointed to Shem's black horse. "What about him?"

"Shouldn't we let Shem name him?"

"No. That'd be no fun. And we couldn't let *you*, the best horse-namer in the world, miss out on such a fitting moment to do your work."

"Right." Bendigo sat forward, straight and all business. "Let's see what kind of magic I can summon this time."

She watched him as he squinted at the horse, visibly trying to pull something together.

Then he smiled. "Meesh."

"*Meesh?*" Her upper lip stretched in disgust.

"Come *on*, Willy." He tried to hold his voice below a normal volume. "Please tell me you remember Meesh."

"Wait." She brought her hands to her temples and shut her eyes before shooting them open wide. "Like our pet beaver, Meesh?"

"Yeah." He quieted a laugh, remembering the day they had found a beaver in one of the ponds almost outside of

Whimselon's territory. Being too young to know that a beaver isn't a practical pet, they had spent all day trying to catch it. When they weren't successful, she cried all the way home, saying how much she was going to miss Meesh. They spent the whole summer visiting the beaver. He usually came up with stories of what Meesh had done while they were away.

"Meesh it is then..." Her voice trailed like pipe smoke.

"You all right?"

"Hm?" She rotated her head to him. "Oh, yeah. Sometimes, I just...I think about how much time we've experienced together, and I..." She looked away, smiling faintly.

"You what?"

"I'm thankful."

"Oh. Me too." He nodded, not wanting to tread too far. "Definitely thankful."

She didn't say anything.

He didn't say anything.

Then they spoke at the same time.

"Willy—"

"Ben—"

They both laughed. She leaned her head on his shoulder, closing her eyes and grinning.

"You go first." He turned his head slightly to feel her hair on his cheek.

"Must I always be the bold one?" she asked with a hint of mockery in her voice.

"I can be bold." His words came out softer than he intended.

"Can you?" she whispered.

He exhaled. "I'm trying to be."

"I want to hear what's on your heart."

Her words struck him like a sudden summer storm. She wanted something he had always assumed no one would ever want: his innermost thoughts, feelings, longings, contemplations, and fears. But he had never rehearsed this. All too often, he had rehearsed conversations where he may need to defend himself *about* himself in his head, but he had never practiced what to say if someone ever asked him to share *what* it was about himself that he felt he had to defend.

"There's a lot in my heart," he said. "And some of which I'm not sure how to say."

"Tell me just one thing." Her voice was sweet, trailing down his arm that she was leaning on. "One thing from your heart. We can take it slow. What's the first thing that pops into your head?"

He could have simply said *you* or *us* or something along those lines, but instead, the image of his hands driving his dagger into the Whim and the Lhanian flashed in his mind. He pressed his teeth together, clenching his fists and bringing them to his eyes.

Willy removed herself from his shoulder. "What is it?"

"I'm never going to unsee it, Willy. Ever."

"Unsee what?" She placed a hand on his back.

"What I *did*." He let his hands drop to his lap. Turning to meet her eyes, he wondered if she could even picture him doing something so evil.

The hair around her face fluttered backward, away from her eyes, as a breeze swirled through camp. Glancing down, she peered at his hands. The stains were faded, but the dark red still outlined his fingernails, clinging to the roughness of his cuticles. Without asking, she reached down and took his hands in hers.

He yanked them back, folding them against his stomach. "Don't, Willy."

"Stop," she whispered, reaching forward to touch them again. As she enveloped her hands around his and pulled them into her lap, his heart raced. "If it wasn't them, it would have been you." She traced his palms.

His chest wanted to explode. "I can still see them. Feel them."

She reached behind her and grabbed her canteen. She unscrewed the lid and tipped the lip downward, drizzling water over his hands.

He winced. "Please… You don't have to do that."

She pulled his hands closer and draped the loose part of her shirt over his fingers. "I want to."

"Why?"

As she etched away at the creases around his nails, the blood lifted from his fingers. A faded brown stain appeared on the front of her shirt. "Your burden is my burden," she said, strong.

"No, it's not."

"Yes, it is," she cracked. "When have I ever let you go

through something alone?" Her glassy spheres of marble looked up.

Her presence overwhelmed him. "When did you grow up?"

Her hands slowed. "We grew up together."

"I must have missed it until now." His voice shook. He had said too much. Went too far. This was something he wasn't ready for. And was it him, or were her hands trembling in his?

"Well, good thing we still have time left." She looked down again, getting back to removing the burden from his skin.

Time. Bendigo had lost all sense of it. And though he wanted to believe that they still had it, he also had a sudden realization that it may actually be running out.

Twenty-Five

The morning brought chilly air and a blanket of dew, but the sun was crisp, glinting through the branches to wake Bendigo. He and Willy had switched with Dagon and Shem at witching hour and fell asleep a few feet away from one another, but now a warmth pressed into his spine. They lay back-to-back, their body heat colliding to ward off any impending chill. Afraid to have her notice their body position upon waking, he scooted away and sat.

Blinking, he watched Dagon pour the last bit of his canteen into his hands to offer to the horses, while Shem rotated another rabbit over a new fire. Rising to his feet to make his way to the warmth, Bendigo rubbed his arms, noticing the drastic change in temperature.

Shem peeked up at the sound of him approaching. Without saying a word, his eyes asked a question.

"No," Bemdigo answered, leaning toward the flames. "I didn't tell her what I told you."

Shem only shook his head.

"I'll get there." He huffed. "I'm not a blunt fella."

That drew a smile out of Shem's otherwise distraught expression. "That you aren't."

His brows met together. "What's ailing you?"

"Other than the usual?"

"Your usual is generally levelheaded. You look troubled."

Shem cut his eyes toward Dagon, who was still preoccupied with the horses. "He says we may reach Kalon in two days' time."

Weight fell onto Bendigo's chest, but he fought through the seize. "We did come for this."

"That doesn't make the task any lighter."

"No, but the sooner it comes, the sooner it will be over. The anticipation is usually worse than the battle itself, or so I hear."

Shem touched the sword by his side, gazing into the fire. "How are you feeling?"

"Tired."

"I mean since yesterday."

Bendigo looked away for a second, but Willy's words from last night became his own. "If it wasn't them, it would have been us."

"Yes," Shem breathed. "Exactly. I'm here because of you. You understand the weight of that, right?"

"I do. And I'm ready to protect you again."

Shem created a fist and held his forearm over his chest. "My brother."

Bendigo mimicked the motion. "Brothers."

The connection was cut short as Willy teetered over to the boys, not fully awake yet. She waved her hands, trying to get their attention.

Shem stood, drawing his sword. "What is it?"

Dagon spun at the sound of the commotion.

"Horsemen." She reached for Bendigo.

He grabbed her and shoved her behind him, wanting to protect her from what she was protecting *them* from.

"Where?" Shem flared out, ready to pounce.

She pointed through the trees, back toward the open plains. "There. A lot of them."

The sun lit up the grasslands, highlighting the dew that hung to every olive blade, but that wasn't what drew Bendigo's attention as it normally would. Against the sky's morning glory, a menacing swarm of horsemen thundered over the last hill, making headway for the Kalon Pinewoods. A cloud, but not one made of vapor, hung above the army's heads. It was a swarm of faint colors, made up of little flying objects. Like a group of birds. It stayed with the horsemen as if it was a part of their herd.

And so it was—Bendigo gripping his dagger, Shem standing with his sword, Willy tucking behind. They stood as a tripod, waiting for the approaching doom.

Dagon looked to the horizon, his feet carrying him to the three with urgency. "Wait."

Bendigo did not wait. He didn't lower the dagger. He didn't step away from Willy.

Dagon placed a hand on Shem's sword. "Bring your weapons down."

"And accept our fate?" Shem's muscle pulsated on the side of his neck.

"Yes." He still hadn't pulled out his own sword. "Because this fate will change our chances. Look. These horsemen are of *good*."

The tip of Bendigo's dagger dropped slow, his mouth parting when the approaching army grew close enough to recognize. Leading the pack was a familiar man with a flag draped on the side of his horse. The *Whimselon* flag.

Willy moved up to be level with Bendigo's shoulder. "Is that...*Zachary*?"

He could barely verbalize. "Ye...yes."

But that wasn't all. There were more flags. The horse beside Zachary's held an Orendan flag with Sophia riding its back. Then a Lhanian flag, a Ports of Orphic flag... The swarm of "birds" were actually Orphic Forest fairies. An army of *good*.

The horsemen thundered into the forest, flooding through the pines and filling every space. They stopped after Zachary raised his hand directly in front of the four.

Bendigo left Willy's side. "*Zachary*."

Zach slid off his horse and met him with a hug that almost knocked them both over.

"What are you *doing* here?" He broke the hug and held Zach in front of him. "*Really*. What are you doing here?"

"You can't battle six thousand five hundred forces of evil with only the four of you." Zach stood steadfast, not an ounce of hesitation. "Not when you have all of us who want to stand beside you."

"How...how do you know of the numbers?" Bendigo

258

looked at the army before him. Hundreds. There had to be hundreds. Maybe a thousand. More than a thousand?

Another rider left his horse and made for Bendigo. It was Len, the Keeper. Strapped to his chest was The Book itself. "The Book did not close after you left," Len explained. "With every passing day, your actions and locations, Bendigo Fletcher, were updated with the emerging ink. We've been gathering every night to learn what you have been doing to get rid of this evil encroaching upon our world."

Shem stepped forward. "You brought The Book *here*?"

Sophia stepped down, joining the grounded crew. "Don't worry. We are all aware to protect it."

Zach drew his eyes to Shem. "Shem?"

"Yes."

Then all eyes diverted to Dagon. He stood in the back, watching the scene play out.

"You're the one who can restore the afterlife," Zach stated with awe.

Dagon positioned himself beside Bendigo. "With the help of a few good warriors, yes."

Willy moved up and lightly hung at Bendigo's other side.

Seeing her, Zach visibly drew back. "Willy."

"That's me."

"You...you left without saying anything."

Bendigo tensed, getting ready to defend her.

"I did," she admitted. "I knew that if I offered to go, I would be cut down and held back. I'm done with being held back. Done with being manipulated. I am worth more than Whimselon ever taught me I was."

Her words created an audible shift, and a set of heads in the middle of the masses strained to set eyes on her, to get a glimpse of her. To see their daughter.

Bendigo noticed her parents and stood taller. "She's been a strong addition." He said it to Zach but used it as a blunt force to her parents. "She's a great warrior."

She blushed a little, concealing it by forcing cold eyes.

"When did you leave Whimselon?" Bendigo tried to put a timeline together that made sense. "How did this army *happen*?" He cut eyes at Sophia. She had said that no one from Orenda would be willing to fight, yet here they stood.

"Bendigo." Zach was in noticeable agony. "Everywhere you've been has been plunged into darkness. There is destruction in every city, every town, every port—"

"The Ports?" Shem perked up.

Zachary nodded, while another member of the army made his way to the front. He walked with a limp yet made his way quickly. The wrinkles under his eyes looked more from a lack of sleep and too much sun than old age, and his ragged attire pointed to him as a fisherman from the Ports. Shem's recognition of him confirmed it.

"Silas," Shem's voice fell to shock.

Silas looked upon him with admiration and wit. "I may be old, but if I can still fight the stormy seas and drag in full nets, I can fight for the termination of evil."

"What happened to the Ports?"

Silas hesitated. "The Ports still stand, but the seas are empty of fish. There hasn't been a single catch, even on our long days, and no rain has filled our buckets. Our people have been rationing, and soon, we will run out of everything we have preserved."

Bendigo swallowed, feeling a pang of responsibility for their toils. "And Whimselon?"

Zachary blew out a long breath. "Whimselon remains, though not as you left it. It now houses Whims *and* Lhanians."

Willy gasped. "What happened to Lhan?"

He glanced at her. "A few days after you left, floods of Lhanians arrived in Whimselon. Their farmlands had been set ablaze in the middle of the night. Every single one of their plots. When the fires had spread to their homes, they had nowhere else to go. It was during their refuge in Whimselon when me and Julius over there"—he tilted his head toward a man, who nodded in return, that sat on a horse with the Lhanian flag—"decided to form an army. When evil reaches your homeland, it's not easy to just pray that it passes." His voice grew soft. "I didn't expect to come across all that destruction. And I didn't anticipate the army to grow."

Dagon passed his eyes over the army in a swift gaze. "How many do you have in total?"

Zach held a hand to his heart. "We started with eight hundred Whims and seven hundred Lhanians, eventually growing to three thousand eight hundred total. Not equal to the Twilight's numbers but better than four. Our plan was to use The Book and retrace Bendigo's steps in time for battle." He pointed upward. "Did you spot the next recruits?"

Bendigo tilted his head back and scanned the pine branches. Decorating the bristled greenery were dots of colors that flicked their wings occasionally. "They're Orphic Forest fairies, aren't they?" He didn't give Zach a chance to respond. "What happened to the Orphic Forest? Was it the windstorm?"

"Completely wiped it out," Zachary confirmed. "At least parts of it anyway. The fairies slowly banded together over our heads as we rode through. It was a silent recruitment really. No words exchanged. They simply hovered above us and became one with our purpose."

Bendigo brought his chin back down. "You don't communicate?"

Willy crossed her arms. "They *can't* communicate. Fairies don't speak loud enough for people to hear. You'd know that if you paid attention in school."

"How do you relay information to them then?" Bendigo asked.

Zach held an easy smile. "Perception and body language. So far, we've worked with each other. Something I never imagined possible."

Shem waved a hand toward Sophia. "How did you come across Sophia and her people? The last we saw of Orenda was during its last hours."

Sophia shuddered but held a steady look. "We took the river east and ran ashore in the Land of None."

"None?" Bendigo said.

She nodded. "A territory of soil and nothing else. Goes on for miles. Easy to get lost in, but a safe place to avoid evil. There is nothing in the Land of None to destroy."

"So, that's where the army found you?" Bendigo guessed.

"No." Zach took over. "We went to Orenda but got there too late. Everything was charred. Gone. The Book plotted you in places we had never heard of, so we blindly moved onward. That was when we ran into Sophia and the Orendans. They were on their way back to the city to see if anything was spared or rebuildable."

"Which it isn't." Sophia looked down, a hush floating from her lungs. "It's completely gone."

Without thinking, Bendigo stepped back, feeling small. His movements had brought about destruction. Evil wanted him dead, and it cost others their homes. Their lives.

Dagon placed a hand between his shoulder blades, preventing him from shrinking any further back. "Death would have come eventually. To blame yourself is a wasteful task."

"Oh, yes." Her eyes fluttered wider. "Please don't blame yourself. The turn of events is what changed me—changed us. We want to fight. We want a world where darkness is not the only thing to welcome us in death."

"What about the children?" Shem didn't see any little legs draped over the sides of the horses. "You didn't bring *everyone*, did you?"

"Of course not," Zachary said. "Any Orendan who didn't wish to fight is on a trek to Whimselon, led by some of our own. They will find a haven there."

Bendigo clenched his fists. "For now. Evil won't spare Whimselon forever."

"Especially with The Book removed from the village," Dagon added, attracting all eyes. "They most likely spared Whimselon out of fear of destroying The Book. Destroying it would mean eliminating any possibility of knowing the end."

"*How?*" Zachary pushed. "The end isn't written yet."

Dagon held out his hand. "May I be the holder of The Book?"

He reacted like someone had slapped him. "I'm sorry?"

"I would like to be the Keeper."

"For what purpose?" He stood aghast. "Len has successfully held The Book for years without letting it fall into the hands of the wrong company. And like I mentioned, the end is not written."

"Not written for *your* eyes," Dagon said, stricter. "Spirits can see beyond what we are able to see. The Book in the hands of a Twilight could mean the ultimate reign of death over our world."

His jaw tightened.

Bendigo made his voice as steady and demanding as he could. "Trust him, Zach. Dagon is the only person who can offer true protection against a Twilight. Give him The

Book."

Len put a gentle hand on Zach's arm. "It's okay. I see protection in his eyes."

And so, in the Kalon Pinewoods, The Book was transferred without the usual Festival of Passing that Whims anticipated every eighty, ninety, or even a hundred years, whenever the current Keeper's time was up. Instead, The Book was simply placed into Dagon's outstretched, rough, worn-out hands.

Facing the new recruits, Bendigo saw ready, fighting spirits. Everyday warriors who wanted goodness to reign. He didn't believe that kind of spirit existed anymore. Until leaving Whimselon, he wasn't sure *he* carried that kind of hope in his heart. Now though, hope surged.

"Okay, Bendigo." Zach stood as a submissive follower. "What's the next move?"

Bendigo froze, feeling all eyes on him. The entire army. People he knew, people he didn't know. They all looked to him as if he was to take over.

Dagon set a hand on his shoulder. "You know what to do."

He knew where they were *going* and what they *planned* on doing but as for getting there?

"I'll be here with you. You won't be guiding alone."

He knew that. He knew that more than ever. And so, he faced the army. "We are estimated to be two days out from Kalon. We ride during the day and break at night. The fairies will fly overhead and be on the lookout for Twilights.

Zach, communicate that to them in whatever manner you have adopted. As for the rest of us, have weapons handy and don't underestimate the sudden changes in nature. We fight for each other. That's the only rule."

A couple agreements and exaltations rose from the masses, cheering him on.

He felt a surge of empowerment. "Let's ride."

Those on foot scattered to mount their horses once again. Willy turned to follow Dagon, but Bendigo caught her arm, pulling her toward him gently. She blinked through wisps of hair, not resisting his touch.

"Want to ride with me?" he asked.

Her very Willy-like grin shone through the attempted coolness in her response. "Sure."

He mounted River, and she joined him, clutching the back of his shirt at first but then slowly wrapping her arms around his waist. The position was needed so she wouldn't topple off, but he liked the feeling of it.

With her arms warming his core and an army behind him, Bendigo Fletcher thundered forward through the forest, Dagon gliding by his side, and Shem riding on his other.

Twenty-Six

Night fell and so did the army's visibility, even though they had lanterns to illuminate the darkness between the pines. Every member went to work to set up camp, utilizing what they had brought and tapping into their skill sets. One-third of the army sectioned off to surround the entire camp and take first watch, while the other two-thirds pitched makeshift tents out of cloaks. Those skilled in forestry created multiple bonfires throughout the camp, and the food carriers walked about to give out the rice rations. The fairies spread out, found resting spots in the pine branches, and illuminated their wings like fireflies to provide a glow for the warriors below.

Bendigo wandered between the fires, stopping at each campsite to make sure everyone was okay. With thousands of people, the campsite was vast. Fires dotted the woods like little night mushrooms. He eventually found Shem and Zachary sitting around their fire, chatting and laughing. *Laughing.* In a time where they should be…cringing? Panicking? Their laughter surged through the camp, and he couldn't help but smile as he approached.

"Ben." Zach waved for him to join, eyes still crinkling.

Bendigo sat, searching for Willy but didn't see her. "I

have the most absurd feeling that your laughter is about me."

Shem ran his hands through his long, free hair. "Oh, how your hunch proves to be true."

"Don't tell me," he groaned. "Wait, do. It was the wine, wasn't it?"

Zachary bent forward and grinned into the fire, letting out a rowdy laugh. "I still can't believe *you* tried it. You were always hesitant about doing anything you weren't supposed to. And then you drank it and got *fuzzy*." His laughter egged on Shem's, and the two howled again.

"Oh, *geez*." He found himself chuckling with them. "Come on. It's not *that* funny."

"It is." Zachary leaned back on his hands. "My little brother. *Fuzzy*. When did *you* get so bold?"

The way Zach asked made him feel small, as if Zach thought he was so meek before. It struck the wrong chord in Bendigo's chest, and all his feelings of being misunderstood and written-off came flooding back. Where he had been learning to express his emotions, he no longer knew how. He bit his tongue and swallowed his hurt. It was like he had reverted to who he was when he was in Whimselon. Hidden.

Shem seemed to notice. His laughter died down, and he gave an apologetic look.

Dagon strode up behind Bendigo and tapped his shoulder. "Can I borrow you?"

His appearance made Bendigo jump, but he was glad

Dagon had come to save him from this wave of uncontrolled, emotional reversion. "Absolutely."

Dagon guided him away from the firelight and drifted into a corner of shadows. "I need you to climb one of these trees and see if you can spot the Kalon castle in the distance."

Spot it. To *actually see it*. He almost didn't want to. "You think we're that close?"

"That's what I need to find out."

"On it."

Calculating which tree was highest and could provide the best view, he chose one not far from where he stood and shimmied up the side. No branches stuck out for his convenience, but the pine trees here were easier to climb. Since they were thin, he didn't have to wrap his legs around the trunk but instead grasped with both hands and planted his feet on the bark. When he reached the top, the branches held him, but the stiff greenery poked through his clothes and left mild scratch marks on his face and neck as he shoved his head through the top of the canopy, emerging into the open sky.

For a moment, he forgot why he had climbed up here. The stars above him seemed close to his touch, like he could steal one if he reached out. And they were everywhere. Some hung in clusters, creating masses that looked like clouds. He let himself sit in awe for almost too long, but a fluttering to his right yanked his attention away.

A fairy had shot up through the branches and sat beside

him, resting her delicate, grain-sized feet on the tip of a single pine needle. Her wings illuminated a golden glow, exposing the spiderweb-like veins that wove through them. Her face was about the size of his pinky nail, and the only reason he could make out her facial features was because they were so animated. Through the dark, the light from her wings exposed her beauty, and in her beauty, he saw a warning look in her two pools of blue.

"It's okay," he whispered. "Dagon asked me to do this." He didn't even know if she could understand him.

Then her head tilted to the side as if to ask why.

"I'm looking for Kalon. Want to look too?"

She fluttered her wings and rose to meet Bendigo's shoulder. He felt nothing when she landed. Her weight was air. But even so, he noted a sense of friendship, a sense of trust.

Back to the task at hand, he stared out over the treetops to where the black silhouettes of branches met the even blacker, star-dotted sky. His eyes adjusted to the night, and he saw lines of trees ending in the far distance. Almost too far for him to see, a single turret protruded the sky. His heart sank.

There it was. The first piece of evidence that Kalon's castle was, in fact, waiting for them.

The fairy seemed to sense his rising uneasiness. She lifted from his shoulder and hovered in front of his face. She hung midair, examining his eyes and perhaps trying to communicate with him, but he couldn't figure it out.

"It's just so close. That's all," he said. "Are you scared?"

The tiniest smile softened on her lips, and she gave a gentle nod, but her hand moved over her heart while the other moved over her eyes.

Bendigo turned his mouth down. "Your heart? And your eyes?"

She removed both, and then, one by one, she placed her hand over her eyes, paused, and covered her heart.

"Eyes. Then heart." He laughed at his own confusion. "You can't see? And you can't feel?"

The fairy might have rolled her eyes.

"I'm *sorry*." He was amused. "I'm trying. Okay. You can't see, so you're blind?"

Her wings shot upright, and she nodded.

"Okay, blind and…" He got it. He *felt* it more like. She wasn't *actually* blind; she was using it as a description. "Blind faith."

She spun around as if on an axis and clapped her hands together, though no noise was produced.

"Blind faith," he said again. "We go forward because of blind faith."

Then she pointed at him.

"Blind faith…in me?"

Her single nod brought him floods of anxiety upon realizing that the whole army saw him as some kind of hero. Some kind of leader. But he was *not* that. He was rarely assertive, if ever. But maybe that was what made him different. A different kind of leader. He *had* led the army here in a way. They followed his actions through The Book and used him as their guide, but why did they need him now? Now they had stronger people like Zach and Dagon and Shem.

Why *him*?

Whatever the case, Bendigo had to tell Dagon the news. They were close. Too close.

Dagon's response to the find confirmed it. "We are near, as I suspected."

He stood beside him, the fairy leaving to return to her post as a night light. "What does that mean for us?"

"It means"—Dagon's voice was soft as he leaned in—"battle is tomorrow."

Tomorrow. The words were a spear. Right between the space where Bendigo's ribs came together. "Are you sure?"

Dagon bowed his head. "As sure as the sun will rise."

"What should we tell the others?"

"Let them sleep in peace tonight. We will rise early to tell the news and prepare the battle plan."

Bendigo nodded as a wave of emotion almost knocked him over. *Tomorrow.* He had to find Willy. He had waited too long to tell her. Waited too long to tell her that he had grown up too. With war on the horizon, their time left together could be on its last leg. A morbid thought but a realistic one. "Dagon, where's Willy?"

Dagon smiled, almost relieved. "I haven't seen her, but you should find her."

"I know."

"You need to tell her."

Their eyes met, and he realized that Dagon *knew* him. Like really knew him.

"Go." Dagon moved his chin upward, as if to nudge him on. "Tell her you love her."

"What if she doesn't love me back?"

"Would that change if you love her or not?"

"No."

"Go."

So, he did. The pace at which he traveled through the camp drew heads, but the campsite was a blur to him. There was only one person he sought, and he couldn't find her quick enough. She wasn't around a single fire nor mingling with any group. Panic slid down his throat as he thought something bad had happened to her, but then he saw her standing in the shadows, looking out into the darkness of the woods, alone. The ring of watchmen on their horses outlined the perimeter a couple hundred feet away, probably not even aware that she was fairly near.

Before he could get a grip on his emotion, Bendigo opened his mouth. "Willy."

She spun, seeming alarmed at the tone of his voice. "What's wrong?" She made for him in a panic. "Are you okay?"

His breathing was labored. "No. I'm not."

She stopped before she reached him. "Did something happen in camp? I left for a minute to get some solitude. How did something happen that—"

"Nothing happened. Not to anyone but me."

Her eyes softened, voice drifting. "What do you mean?"

"I feel out of control, Willy. I've never been bold enough. I waited too long."

"Bendigo." She moved forward, placing her hands on his shoulders. "Waited too long for what? You're not making sense. Just calm down."

"I can't calm down, Willy. I—" Air caught in his throat, closing the pathway to his lungs. "I can't get it out, but I *need* to. *Help me.*"

She looked frightened. "Ben. What do you need me to do?"

He no longer had control over his words. "Don't leave me when I tell you. I'm afraid you'll leave. I'm afraid to lose you."

"Bendigo, never." Her voice was a whisper but strong. "*Tell me.*"

The words were like rushing water bursting through cracks in stone. "I *love* you, Willy."

Her hands went limp on his shoulders, and her mouth dropped. "You...you do?"

His heart thundered so fast he worried she might be able to see it jumping beneath his shirt. "It's...it's okay if you don't, but I...I had to tell you. I just can't imagine a version of my life that you aren't a part of. I can't *live* without you."

Her hands moved to the back of his neck, though their bodies were not an inch closer. "Bendigo?"

Without thinking, he put his hands on her waist and pulled her near. The front of her pressed into his chest and stomach, her arms draped around his neck. "Yeah?"

"I want to be yours."

Her words evaporated from her lips and found a place to condensate around his ears, flooding his heart. "You mean it?"

He held her against him, never having deliberately touched her like this before. As if touch wasn't new enough, their noses were all but three inches from each other. He felt her breath, her heartbeat, her passion.

"I mean it." She fluttered her eyelashes, never taking her gaze off him.

He moved his nose an inch closer, but she tensed, so he stopped.

"I'm sorry," she whispered. "I've just never done this before."

He stared at her lips. "Do you want to?"

She nodded, still looking at him.

"May I?"

She nodded again.

He moved his hands up the middle of her back and pulled her forward, closing the gap between their lips. Her body relaxed into his, and he had to tighten his arms just to keep her upright. Her body trembled, and shivers through his palms radiated up to his core, crippling him. He grabbed onto the back of her shirt, so his hands wouldn't travel. He couldn't do that to her. Shouldn't at least. Not that he *couldn't.* But even so, her lips were enough. Even as they parted, adrenaline still surged through him.

They looked at one another.

"*Bendigo,*" she breathed.

"Willow." He touched her cheek.

Her face looked stricken with surprise at the sound of her real name.

"You are worthy of your beautiful name. You've always been worthy of it, and you've always been beautiful. I'm sorry for not telling you sooner."

She reached up and pulled his tunic's collar, dragging him closer. "You don't have to apologize. You always made me feel wanted."

Their lips met again, longer this time.

And it seemed that the terrors of tomorrow had disappeared.

Twenty-Seven

The camp was quiet. All voices had died down, fires had been dimmed, and warriors slept in peace, unaware of tomorrow. Bendigo walked Willy back to the center of camp, both slightly blushing and smiling every time they made eye contact. They stopped at Shem and Zach, who were passed out near their fire, their cloaks draped over their shoulders.

He could have walked her back to where her parents were, but ever since the army's arrival, she had little contact with them. It was like they didn't know how to approach her. She had made no effort either though. On top of that, Bendigo, Willy, Shem, and Dagon had become safe with each other. Separating, even in sleep, would feel unstable.

But one was missing.

Bendigo peered about. Dagon was definitely not sleeping on the ground, and he wasn't in the first watch group, so where *was* he?

"Is something wrong?" she hushed, trying not to wake the boys. "Besides the fact we reach Kalon tomorrow?"

He, still reeling from the experience of letting someone love him like that, faced her, while also floating in the midst of his sudden alarm. "No, don't worry. I'm just going to find Dagon for a minute. I'll be right back."

Her face dropped. "You're not running, are you?"

"Running?"

"Running scared."

He loved her worried eyes. He pulled her into him again, holding her head against his chest. "No, Willy. I'm not afraid of this. Don't you worry. Besides, I'm bravest around you."

Her breath penetrated through his shirt, her chest retracting with an exhale. "Good. Because I will gladly hold you captive if I have to."

He laughed and kissed her hair. "That's the Willy I know."

They withdrew. He didn't want to part, but he had a nudge in his mind that he needed to find Dagon before he could try to sleep. He made sure she was comfortable and walked away from the fire's faint glow. A maze of shadows weaved through the camp, between the other dying flames. He wasn't sure where he could find Dagon, but his feet seemed to guide him. Almost at the camp's perimeter, under a pine tree, sat Dagon. His face in his hands.

Bendigo paused a few feet away. He had not expected this. *Strong* Dagon was hunched over, clearly in some sort of pain. And alone. He knew the feeling of solitary wallowing all too well. That was the only reason he moved toward Dagon, stopped right beside him, and bent down to his level. "Dagon?"

When Dagon brought his face out from his hands, Bendigo noted tears dripping down, smearing in wet spots along his jawline. "Are you...are you all right?"

"I feel afraid."

The words hit him like a knife to the chest. His lips parted, and he dropped to sit shoulder to shoulder with Dagon, the one he saw as untouchable. "Afraid? Of battle?"

"Of the evil ahead."

"But we have encountered evil this whole journey. What makes the evil tomorrow any different? If anything, you should be afraid of the numbers, not the evil."

Dagon brought a hand up and placed it on Bendigo's cheek. "You are one of the bravest people I know."

A surge of peace rushed through his veins. "Because of you. Of Shem. And of Willy. I'm not brave, but you've all given me a reason to be."

"Ah." Dagon brought his hand down. "No fear in love. See?"

"But doesn't that mean you shouldn't be fearful either?"

Dagon hung his head, staring at his feet. "Yes, yet I find myself mourning."

"Mourning what?"

"Bendigo." His voice flipped, flatlining. "I need you to promise me something."

"Of course."

"Tomorrow, there is only one thing that matters most in battle."

"Staying alive?"

"Well"—Dagon puffed a laugh—"*that* but also something else." His laughter disappeared. "You need to get me to the castle."

The castle. What was *in* there? "Me specifically?"

"Yes. You will have to take me up there. Just us."

"Why? What *is* it with this castle? Do you know?"

"You just have to trust me."

Bendigo gritted his teeth. "I *do* trust you, but if you know something, why won't you tell me?"

"I only keep things from you if I know it may hurt you."

"So, what you're saying is that whatever is in the castle may hurt me?"

"Not *it* but the *knowledge* of it."

Bendigo shook his head, dropping his chin. "How are we going to find the right horseman with the key? If what Sophia had said is true, doesn't it seem impossible to find one specific man amid the thousands? That will be like looking for a needle in a haystack."

"It is impossible, isn't it?" Dagon kicked at the dirt. "It might help if we had a visual of what the horseman looks like."

Looking up, Bendigo felt that he was about to release information.

"The one who carries the key is the one with the red-chest plate." He tapped his own sternum.

"You know what he looks like?"

"Only that."

"You keep too much to yourself until the last minute."

He leaned to the side, examining Bendigo, and then

threw an arm around him like a father would a son. "Yet you still trust me."

"Of course, I do." Bendigo's heart had ached for moments like this since his father's passing. "I've trusted you since I met you."

The tears that had once streaked Dagon's tan skin had disappeared, and an easy wave lay over his gaze. "Your presence has chased away my fears."

"It has? That's good I suppose, though I'm not sure what I did."

"You simply *came*. And now I remember why I should not be afraid."

"Why shouldn't you?"

"Because tomorrow is going to bring about a new era. And you'll be with me."

Bendigo agreed, but a question pinged back and forth in his temples: an era of light or an era of dark?

Twenty-Eight

In the morning, Bendigo's warriors weren't the only ones to figure out that battle awaited them that day. Nature knew too. Clouds had rolled in overnight, bringing thunder and splotches of rain that hurt when they landed. The entire campsite had turned into a pit of gray mud, sloshing beneath their feet as they bustled about, packing up the camp, securing their things to their horses, and giving smiles that were meant to encourage but showed the fear within.

Bendigo wiped water from his forehead as he slid on his cloak. He patted the inside of his clothes to make sure his dagger still rested against his side.

Shem plopped through the mud, his hair tightly braided against his scalp. "I came to give you this." In his hands was a sword—golden, pristine, and used maybe once—along with a belt and a scabbard.

Bendigo hesitated. "For me?"

"Yes. As handy as your dagger has been, you are going to need something bigger. Stronger."

The metal hilt was heavy in Bendigo's grasp, and as he twirled it, a glint of light specked off the blade, though the sun was not shining. "Where did you come by this?"

"The Whims." Willy appeared, holding one of her own.

"They brought them."

"And they trusted you with one?"

She swung the blade, eyes widening when its weight slung her arms about. "Whoa. I'm glad I did that now and not for the first time in battle."

The thought of her fending for herself, wielding a sword in the chaos of war, gave him a rush of consuming worry that made him want to yank the sword from her hand and tell her to stay behind. To sit back and wait. Wait for the terrors to be over because he would be back for her, and she would be safe. But he knew better. He knew her. She would use the sword on *him* if he ever suggested that. So instead, he showed her the right way to hold the sword, which Shem had first taught him.

"So, this is it, huh?" Shem stared around camp.

Feet on the ground dwindled, the hooves of horses being the main source of the sloshing mud sounds. Zach rode through the camp, calling orders and organizing the ranks, and the warriors obeyed, lining up in rows, all facing the same way. The horses stamped their feet, antsy in the slick mud and irritated by the rain.

The thump of Mapalo's hooves approached, and Dagon looked down from the horse's back. "Time to mount. You ready?"

Bendigo yanked the scabbard around his waist and slid the sword in. "I'm ready."

"Good," he said. "They're waiting for you."

Looking over at the layers and layers of horsemen lined

up, Bendigo noticed Zach hovering out front, facing his direction. They must expect him to lead them like he had through The Book's narration.

"You'll all stay with me, right?" he asked.

Shem reached up to pull Meesh toward him by his mane. "All the way through."

"Me too." Willy didn't smile.

Dagon and Bendigo met eyes.

"Until the gate." Dagon didn't pull his eyes away. "Then Bendigo and I go at it alone."

"*What?*" Shem hissed. "You and Bendigo are going up to the castle *alone?*"

The sting in Dagon's voice pierced the air. "It *must* be done that way. Under no circumstance are you or Willy to follow. There will be a battle for life or death on the surrounding plains, and you will be needed down there."

"But there's a whole army," she argued. "Why can't we stay together? Make sure you make it?"

"Trust me." He closed his eyes. "Once we make it to the iron gate, we will be okay. Just help us get to the gate."

Shem's jaw was firm. "I don't want to trust you."

His stare had a compassionate look. "Shem, you are one of the greatest fighters in the land. *Use* those skills to help this army. *Show* them what to do. They will need you. They are everyday people with good hearts, but a lot of them have no war experience. We can't leave them to fight on the battle grounds alone."

"But first, I will get you to the gate." Shem stood firm.

He gave a shallow nod. "Yes. And we will need you to, but after that, trust me. Willy?"

Her eyes enlarged as she looked up at him.

"Don't doubt yourself. You have this in you."

She nodded. "Thank you."

Bendigo and Dagon connected once again, Dagon's stare gripping Bendigo's soul. "Trust me."

Bendigo's heart had no doubt. "I do."

"Then let's go."

He clicked for River, who pranced over and stopped at his shoulder. Dagon and Shem rode up toward the waiting army as he pulled himself and Willy onto River's back. For a moment, they sat there. Her arms curling around his waist, his sword dangling at his side, and her breath swirling at the back of his neck.

Closing his eyes, he placed a hand on hers at his waist. "I want us to both come out of this."

"Me too."

"But if I don't—"

"Bendigo, stop."

"If I don't, I want you to know that you have been the best part of my life."

She leaned into his neck and rested her mouth against his skin. "And you mine."

He swallowed and gripped River's mane. "I love you."

"I love you too."

Letting air extinguish from his lips, he turned River toward the army waiting for him. Zach, Dagon, and Shem stood out front, each on their horses. As Bendigo and Willy made for the front of the pack, a voice rang out from somewhere in the sea of warriors.

"Yeah, Bendigo!"

Then more.

"Bendigo!"

"We follow Bendigo!"

Then cheers. Hollers. Shouts of readiness.

Chills intruded upon every inch of Bendigo's skin as he halted River in front of the masses. They were willing to follow him, and he had to get Dagon to the castle, and in this moment, he believed that with them, the task was possible.

The shouts died down, and all eyes were on him.

"I feel...very honored," he said in a conversational tone. "But we couldn't do any of this without all of you. Good has brought us together, and good will bring us through. The evil ahead wants to smite us, so let us not hold back on them. Fight to cleanse our lands of this curse and fight so that we may have the afterlife again. An end to hopeless days!"

Shem raised his sword. "An end to hopeless days!"

Every sword rose in the air. "An end to hopeless days!"

Bendigo gave Dagon a sideways nod. "Let's move."

Twenty-Nine

The storm clouds thickened, bringing walls of rain. Mud grabbed at the horse's hooves. Fear waved through the traveling army like a suppressing smog that choked out any sense of courage, quieting the warriors. The day's trek felt long, agonizing, and edgy. With every passing minute, fear stacked like brick and mortar. Bendigo led the thousands, fighting off his own dread and shivering from the endless sheets of water. Willy leaned into his back, shielding her face from the storm.

Then a melody penetrated his mind, a minor tone waltz he had learned as a kid. A song his long-lost ancestors had sung as they fought their way through Tarsha's lands to claim their freedom from magic. He parted his lips and mumbled the lyrics.

"*I hear a whisper of salvation. That is why I march ahead.*

Family beside me. Our king to guide thee. One day, I'll be free instead.

March on to the scene. Battle is calling me."

Willy lifted her head. Some warriors drew their eyes up, watching him through the cascade of rain.

Shem drew in a breath. "*I hear a whisper of salvation. That is why I march ahead.*"

Voices from the army wafted through the air. "*Family beside me. Our king to guide thee. One day, I'll be free instead.*"

Fuller now.

"*March on to the scene. Battle is calling me.*"

The warriors' waltz drifted up into the trees as they waded through the forest, a mass of fighters. Fighters who were once gardeners, scholars, farmers, and fishermen. Their presence was a sudden springtime rainstorm, trailing for miles. With every muddy hooved step, the warriors grew louder, gaining confidence, power, and fire. It would only be a few more miles until they came face-to-face with the evil that awaited them.

But now, they filled each other up with hope. Hope that the battle was theirs for the taking. Hope that their strength could withstand the war.

Thirty: The Battle

When the trees faded to few and far between, the forest gave way to a sage green, rugged plain that expanded toward the base of a cliff with a castle looming at the top in the foggy distance. The turrets hid in the white vapor as if to reign over the land *and* the air. On the side of the cliff, carved out steps traced upward to the castle, providing the only way up. A twelve-foot iron fence surrounded the bottom of the cliff, blocking the entrance to the steps with a bulky, rusted gate. It was shut, locked, and heavily guarded by a sea of recruited horsemen.

Bendigo's warriors emerged from the pine forest, layered in their ordered ranks with their swords in hand. Bendigo halted River, and Dagon and Shem stopped next to him. They had all expected it: the dark mass of horsemen waiting for them across the valley. All six thousand of them. *Their* people. Once *their* loved ones. And hovering in the air over the manipulated hearts were the Twilights themselves. All of them. So many that it seemed like a black sheet lay rippled over the rival horsemen's helmets.

They were staged for battle.

Bendigo closed his eyes. He inhaled. In the last second

of silence, he heard Dagon's voice inside his head. *Trust me.* His eyes slung open.

Willy leaned into his ear. "You can do this. *We* can do this."

Drawing his sword, he spun River around to face his army. "You know what to do! I want the fairies to take care of the Twilights. Keep them away from the warriors on the grounds."

The fairies swooped into a clump and folded into each other like a mushroom cloud to acknowledge and accept his orders.

"The rest of us, *slay* those who fight us on land." He clamped the uneasiness in his throat. "I know they are our people—our loved ones—but they are not free. Save them from evil's grip with your swords! We *will not* leave here until the curse is broken."

A voice echoed from the army. "An end to hopeless days!"

He raised his sword. "An end to hopeless days!" He yanked River to face ahead and let out a shout.

Behind him, the army sent waves of their battle cry over the rugged plains to the frontlines of the Twilight's army, who responded with their own shouts.

River charged forward.

The clouds' thunder above was no match for the thunder of hooves against the plain. Good charged toward evil, evil charged toward good, and time slowed with each beat of Bendigo's heart.

Thump, thump.
His body rose and fell with River's stride.
Thump, thump.
The two sides grew closer.
Thump, thump.
Shem took a single breath.
Thump, thump.
Willy drew her sword.
Thump, thump.
Dagon leaned forward.
Thump...
Thump...
Then came the clash.

A dissonance of good and evil smashed together as the battle erupted. It was almost too sudden for Bendigo to grasp. The first sword that swung toward him nearly ended it all. But Shem's sword clashed against the incoming blade, saving his life.

Shem screamed into his left ear. "Fletcher, right!"

He pivoted his wrist, driving his blade into an oncoming horseman. He drew it out, blocking another attack. Then another. There was no end. The flood of horsemen, shouts, cries, and *anger* erupted for miles.

The body of a manipulated Orendan and his horse slammed into River's side. Bendigo jolted sideways. Willy gripped the back of his cloak. Her body teetered to the side, and she fought to stay upright but lost. She crashed to the ground.

A sword slung past his face as he yanked River around. "Willow!"

But Dagon was already there. His horse leaped in front of her as he fought off the oncoming waves of horsemen.

Bendigo skittered toward her, but a horseman blocked his way. A Whim. One he knew. Closing his eyes, he slashed his sword in a horizontal motion across the Whim's midsection.

On the ground, Willy emerged from behind Dagon's horse. By the look in her eyes, Bendigo knew she was about to do something ridiculous. She was fixated on something. On some*one*. He followed her gaze to a horseman in the distance. He was thicker than the rest, a native to Lhan, and wore a red chestplate. Bendigo remembered that he had made the mistake of telling Willy that the red-chested warrior would be the one to hold the gate's key.

She drew her eyes up to him. He saw fury and fire in her. He knew what she was about to do.

On foot, lower than the rest of the warriors, she bolted forward, leaving Dagon's protection and charging into the sea of battle.

"Shem!" he shouted.

Shem emerged, blood dripping down the side of his arm.

"Follow me."

Bendigo and Shem galloped toward her, plowing their way through the blurs of war. The red-chested warrior saw them coming though. It was obvious they were targeting him, and he pulled his horse's reins, backing up from the front lines. His menacing eyes were on Bendigo and Shem, but Willy remained unnoticed to him.

She wasted no time, weaving between knobby horse legs and dodging blade swings that weren't meant for her. Bendigo's throat knotted as she drew closer to the keyholder. She wasn't slowing down, but her sword wasn't sturdy in her hand. He foresaw what was about to happen, but he still shouted when she used her Whim advantages.

She leaped and pulled herself up onto the horse, now riding with the red-chest horseman, who was not expecting her. He employed his sword, making a hasty swing at her. She blocked it with her own.

"Bendigo!" Dagon exploded into view beside him. "*Get her!*"

Bendigo leaned forward. "River, go!"

River obeyed. He clung to his mane, eyes fixated on the one he loved. The keyholder and Willy were in a tangle, trying to force the other into submission. She was obviously losing, her wrists now clutched in the red-chested horseman's hands.

Squeezing his knees inward, Bendigo shifted his body up, moving to stand while hunched over to keep his hand placement on River's mane. He was almost upon Willy and her opponent. He had about two seconds to make his landing. And that two seconds was now.

Bendigo let go of River and lunged toward the keyholder. He made sturdy, forceful contact. The keyholder let go of one of her wrists to grab at his horse, trying not to fall. But the fall was imminent. Still having a hold on her, the keyholder sailed to the ground, bringing her with him. Bendigo fell with gravity, landing over both of them.

They all scurried to their feet, trying to gain the advantage, but their bearings had been rattled. Now, they stood facing one another.

In a moment of stillness, the battle around them seemed to grow quiet.

Then the keyholder's lips curled into an arch. "Bendigo Fletcher." The words sounded like the hiss of steam.

Hearing his own name seep from the keyholder's mouth felt like serpents coursing through his veins. He had never met this Lhanian in his lifetime, yet he knew his full name. Evil knew his name.

Bendigo held his sword in front of him, not panicking but robust. Evil knew his name for a reason, and if there was ever a moment for evil to dread his name, it would be now. The key hung around the keyholder's neck, and there was no way Bendigo would leave without it.

With no warning, the keyholder made the first move, driving his sword toward Bendigo's chest while shouting. Bendigo sliced his blade upward and clashed with the oncoming metal. The keyholder tired again, slashing downward in a hack of fury.

Again, Bendigo blocked it, but the keyholder kept pushing forward. His arms shook from the weight. Both swords neared his face. If he let up, they would slip and slice his throat. He knew he wasn't strong enough. He drew in a breath, gave a grunt, pushed off, and spun to the side. Bad choice. His back was to the keyholder for half a second, and that was enough for the Lhanian to make another swing. The tip of the keyholder's blade grazed his back, and he felt his skin split open, filling his shirt with warmth and dampness. Turning, he jabbed at his opponent's core but was blocked and shoved backward.

He stumbled and crashed downward. His shoulder blades met with the ground, his head slamming hard. The blurry vision that took over didn't block out the view of his opponent diving on top of him. The keyholder had won. He pressed his body into Bendigo's, holding his sword under Bendigo's chin. He pushed it light enough to not break skin but hard enough to show it was on the verge.

"You thought you could stop this." The Lhanian's words drooled out. "There is no power greater than *us*."

Squirming, Bendigo tried to bring his sword up, but the keyholder pressed his hand into his bicep. He was completely vulnerable. There was no move that Shem had taught him to get out of this one.

The blade dug further into Bendigo's neck, and the keyholder leaned in closer. "You were supposed to be our greatest threat, but here you are." He grinned. "And I'm going to get the glory for killing you."

Bendigo stared into the keyholder's eyes. "Do it. There are thousands more like me."

The keyholder's expression changed. At first, Bendigo

thought it was shock, maybe a realization, but the light faded from his opponent's eyes. The sword's pressure under Bendigo's chin let up, and the keyholder slumped forward. Dead. A blade stuck out of his back.

Willy stood over him, her hand still on the sword's hilt.

"Willy," Bendigo moaned, rolling the dead body to the side and gasping in relief.

"Get the key." She shook, stepping back. "Hurry!"

Another wave of horsemen were approaching from the base of the cliff. Fast.

Bendigo's fingers shook like a violent storm as he slid them beneath the keyholder's shirt. His heart clenched when he saw the face lying still. A face that had spent his last days serving evil against his will. He didn't deserve to die like that.

"Bendigo, get it!" she cried, visibility processing the severity of what she had just done.

His fingers wrapped around the gold prongs, and he yanked it. The chain broke loose. "I got it," he whispered. His legs wobbled, and his breathing was heavy. Standing was harder than he remembered.

All around him, the war raged on, though he and Willy found refuge in being lower than the rest of the attackers. They could move undetected and get to the gate faster.

The gate. All they had to do was *make* it there.

With Shem and Dagon.

"Willy." Bendigo grabbed her wrist, forcing the key into her hand. "All you need to do is unlock the gate."

"Wh-what? *I* can't do that." Tears swamped her face.

He pulled her close. "Yes, you can. You're faster and swifter than me."

"How will I make it through the horsemen?"

Grabbing her arm, he drew her forward with him. He moved with haste, breaking into a run. "Shem will hold them off. Just *don't stop.*"

He didn't let go of her. They were mere seconds from the next wall of attackers, and he knew that once they broke through, he would have to release her. Now those seconds turned into milliseconds, and fear for her life ripped through his soul as he let her go.

She kept treading forward, her hair floating in the wind of her sprint. His army and the Twilight's horsemen created a maze of legs for her to cut around as they killed above her.

The thud of Dagon's horse warbled in Bendigo's ears, and he reached up, swinging onto the horse as Dagon rode by.

"Shem!" Dagon shouted. "Hold 'em off!"

Shem rode ahead of Willy to slay her attackers. Every next second was a perfectly timed moment, ensuring Bendigo's and Dagon's success. Shem struck the last defendant in front of the iron hinges. She dove and slammed the key into the gate's lock.

The Twilights' screams overhead erupted in panic as they dipped down to stop her, only to be consumed by the fairies who had created a wall between her and them.

The gate swung open.

Dagon and Bendigo burst through. She slammed it shut behind them, the lock clicking closed again. As horsemen encroached upon her, Shem cut his horse across the front of the gate, snagging her up into his arms and tearing away from the base of the cliff.

Only now, as Dagon led Mapalo up the steep slope of uneven, jagged steps, Bendigo didn't know what kind of victory waited for them in the castle.

Thirty-One

There was a quiet that didn't settle right with Bendigo's soul. As Mapalo's hooves clacked against the carved rock stairs, it seemed like no forces of evil were up here. The higher they climbed, the more drowned out the battle became. The fairies contained the Twilights, and the ground army prevented entrance through the gate. It was just Dagon, Bendigo, Mapalo, and a feeling of dread that suffocated his spirit.

He hadn't had the chance to tell Willy that the shame of ending someone's life would fade and that she wouldn't feel like a murderer forever. Watching her cry without being able to comfort her was a scene that played over and over in his mind. Now, he was up here, and she was down there, and Dagon offered no explanation as to what was in the castle. For all he knew, that could have been the last time he saw Willy.

The top of the cliff flattened into view. The castle that seemed so daunting from the ground looked majestic in the sky. The turrets climbed into the open air, mixing with the pale clouds above the gray, stormy ones. Likely lively once, the castle now sat abandoned, vines penetrating every crack in the stone. The wooden drawbridge was shut up, its rusted chains hanging like ghosts. But as monumental as the castle was, the backside of the structure was what made Bendigo leave Mapalo's back. Mouth hanging open, he glided across the cliff and looked over the edge.

The sea. It crashed against the cliffside, breaking into white speckles of salt and water, swelling in mountainous peaks, and flowing down again to be consumed by the dark deep. It went on beyond the horizon, blending with the royal blue sky. He was so mesmerized that he almost missed the fountain of water that cascaded down the side of the cliff, crashing into the sea below his feet. Its source was a shimmering, clear river that flowed out from beneath the castle's foundation. The wide ravine passed through the dead courtyard garden and sped between the rocky terrain that separated the castle from the waterfall.

Bendigo twirled to face Dagon. "The river. It's true. The legends are true. It really *does* start up here."

"It does." Dagon dismounted and stood on the edge of the riverbank. "This river clashes with the sea to be swallowed up and taken through waves throughout the world."

"How does it feed the rivers?"

"This sea touches the lands here and the lands on the other side. All the seas and rivers connect, don't you know?"

"I suppose I do."

They both faced the river, watching it move like a magnificent, graceful beast. Anxiety threatened to eat away at his stomach, and he looked up at Dagon, who closed his eyes and let his hair lightly flow behind his ears in the breeze.

"Dagon," he whispered.

When Dagon lifted his lids, wetness hovered in front of his pupils.

His anxiety increased. "Should we go in? Face whatever it is we must face?"

"Bendigo." Dagon reached out and grabbed onto his shoulders. "You are so brave."

"I—"

"Listen to me." Dagon's voice had a catch. "Step into the river."

Shaking, he slid his feet under the water's cool surface and over the smooth stones lying at the bottom. He followed Dagon to the middle of the waterway, where they stood waist-deep, facing each other.

No words were spoken, but Bendigo allowed Dagon to pull his father's dagger out from under his clothes. The whole time, his heart slammed against his rib cage, increasing even more so when Dagon pressed the dagger into his hand.

"What are you doing?" He looked up, holding the dagger with a death grip.

"Your faith and trust in me have been worthy of praise."

"I do trust you."

"I know. Which is why you were chosen."

"Chosen for what?"

Dagon lifted his arm, drawing back his sleeve to reveal

his bare forearm. "*I chose you. I knew your heart. I saw in you what I need now: Strength. Faith. Obedience. Perseverance.*"

His eyes twitched over Dagon's forearm. "What are you showing me?"

Inhaling the thin, crisp air, Dagon closed his eyes, held a small breath, and exhaled over his arm. As his breath touched his tan skin, words appeared on the surface, fading into existence. It was the poem that set Bendigo into motion back in Whimselon. The words of The Book.

"Dagon…how…"

"The Book lives in me. I am the physical being of it."

Bendigo slowly lifted his gaze, studying the man in front of him. His friend. His protector. His hope. "You…you're The Book."

Dagon nodded. "And I have come to Tarsha to steal back the afterlife."

The dagger in his hand suddenly felt like a weight trying to drag him down. "How are you going to do that? Why do you need me?"

Hanging his head, Dagon stepped closer to him, sloshing the river's water against their stomachs. They stood inches from one another. Dagon slid a hand around Bendigo's wrist that held the dagger. Lifting Bendigo's hand, he pulled the dagger toward himself and rested the tip of the blade over his heart. "Put the blade through me."

Childlike anguish erupted from Bendigo's voice. "Dagon, no!" He yanked the dagger back, moving it away from the heart of the man who was supposed to be the survivor in all this.

Dagon threw his hands forward and grabbed the sides of Bendigo's head. "Bendigo Fletcher."

A sob escaped from the depths of his emotional well. "Dagon, I *can't.*"

Their foreheads touched.

"My warrior," Dagon soothed. "It's going to be all right."

"No, it's not!" The corners of his eyes scrunched, and his lips crumbled with his sobs. "You can't leave us. We need you here."

"I know. But only one thing can clean evil footprints from good lands: blood. In this case, my blood. It's the only thing that will cleanse Tarsha of the Twilight's evil."

He shook his head against Dagon's. "*No.*"

"It must spill here in the river, so it can flow down the waterfall and into the sea to reach every land, every village, every family, every*one*. Without my death, there will be no victory over the Twilights, and I can't claim the afterlife back. My blood breaks the curse and will wash away any footprint the Twilights have left on Tarsha." Dagon smiled. "I was created for this. This has always been the way."

"But why does your entire being have to shed blood?" He scrambled for solutions that would keep Dagon with them. "Can't you cut your hand again? Or just do something *else*? Please!"

Dagon held his head firm in his hands. "It must be a

full-fledged sacrifice. Evil isn't weak, and I am stronger in the spiritual realm. The spirit can withstand more than the flesh."

"But I don't want you to die," he choked, leaning against Dagon's forehead.

"Look at me."

He could barely see through the tears flooding his eyes.

"If I don't go, there will be no life after death."

"Can't I go with you?"

Dagon gave him a soft smile. "You will follow me there, though not yet. Your time hasn't come."

Squeezing the dagger, he tried swallowing the continuous rising tears, but he had no reign over his emotions. "What if I have to wait a lifetime to see you again?"

"At least you will have hope that your lifetime on Tarsha isn't the only life you'll have." Dagon drew his head back enough to get a better look at Bendigo. "You must send me to the afterlife. You must let me go."

The sound of the river ceased in Bendigo's ears, and all he could sense was Dagon's presence. He had trusted Dagon with everything. From the moment they collided at the Ports of Orphic. This time was no different. Dagon was The Book, meaning Dagon was a prophet, giving Bendigo all the more reason to put his hope in him.

"I know you need me to," he cried, lifting the dagger back up to Dagon's heart. With one hand on the dagger and the other clinging to Dagon's shoulder, he paused. He looked right into the eyes of his friend.

Dagon stared back, a light smile protruding. "It's going to be okay."

Torment passed into his soul like a shadow covering the moon. "You've become my father. I love you, Dagon."

"And I love you, Bendigo Fletcher of Whimselon, the son who trusted me."

His chest heaved. His fingers wrapped even tighter around the dagger. "I'll see you soon."

"I'll prepare a place for you."

He pushed the blade forward.

Dagon clung to his arms; his eyes pierced with the shock of pain.

As the dagger went deeper, Bendigo's mouth fell open, and he let out an excruciating wail of agony that lingered so long that he wasn't sure when it turned into screams. He cried. Sobs of misery, of heartbreak, and of anger. He buried his face in the chest of Tarsha's sacrifice and held him up, feeling the weight of his death: the way his muscles tensed only to relax and grow cold, the way his death grip on his arms released, and the way he no longer stood on his own but slumped over Bendigo, cradled in his arms. Dagon's heart beat once against Bendigo's body. Twice.

Then nothing.

The river rushed around the meshed two friends. Bendigo held Dagon, shaking with tears. Dagon's blood seeped from the dagger and soaked into Bendigo's clothes. The sight of it pulled Bendigo back to what needed to be done. Dagon's blood had to flow into the river, not flow onto *him*.

"I'm so sorry." Bendigo dropped to his knees, the water rising to his chest. Sorry for what, he didn't really know. Sorry for making the right decision? For doing exactly what Dagon told him to do? There was no clear answer in his mind, but he didn't need one. It was in his character to place blame on himself even in situations where he shouldn't, but deep inside, he knew this decision held no blame. Hurt, yes, but blame? No.

He still held Dagon against himself, but slowly lowered the sacrifice into the water. The river trickled over Dagon's face and soaked his hair, causing his brown locks to float gracefully around his head. The long tunic around Dagon's body consumed the water and soon, the weight was heavy enough to take Dagon fully underneath the surface. He slipped from Bendigo's grasp and the river capsized over the dagger, creating a mini peak of water, then settled.

Through the water, Bendigo watched as the blood from beneath the dagger slowed its flow against the river's pressure. It twirled upward, slow and steady, like a dance. But it didn't float to the surface. Instead, it webbed out and trailed around Dagon's body, spinning around him like vines on a rail. Bendigo stepped back, hands soaked and quivering. He felt a jolt beneath his feet and threw his arms out to steady himself. The world around him vibrated. His eyes darted left and right, watching the trees shake, as storm clouds roared with unnatural thunder.

When he drew his eyes back to Dagon's body, wonder exploded from his chest to his fingertips. As the blood engulfed Dagon, his body dissolved but not to nothing. Rising from beneath the water were swirling lotus flowers, petals colored white and the pink of amaranth. They took over the river, covering the surface as they floated with the current.

Bendigo turned to face the edge of the cliff. The flowers curved around his legs and continued toward the waterfall. The masses of pink and white rushed faster now, racing with the river's ripples.

The water's force slowed him as he attempted to run. Scrambling up the riverbank, he staggered, catching himself with his hands. He pushed back up and kept moving forward. The flowers neared the waterfall, and he couldn't miss it. What would happen once they got there? Something massive? Extraordinary?

Rocks spewed over the edge as Bendigo skidded to a stop.

The flowers met the curve of the waterfall's tip and collided with one another, slipping over the edge to join the falling river. Another tremble hit the world as the flowers— or Dagon—cascaded down the side of the cliff, falling to the sea where they broke the curse.

Thirty-Two

A roar rumbled within the sea, sending concussions into the air. A wave broke so high up the cliff that white foam exploded in front of Bendigo's face. He stepped backward, turning slightly and catching a glimpse of Shem and Willy. They stood side by side, covered in smears of dirt, blood, and fatigue.

He noticed a sense of knowledge in their expressions. They *knew*. They knew of the sacrifice. Not because someone told them or because they had witnessed it but because of revelation. A divine knowledge, as Dagon would call it.

Bendigo faced them, his arms falling limp and his chin dropping to his chest.

Willy, as calm as a summer wind, brushed her hair behind her shoulders and moved toward him. Blood caked her arms and neck, and a gash sat behind her ear, but she was sturdy when she reached him. "You did it."

He collapsed into her arms, burying his face in her neck and hair. "I didn't want to."

"I know," she soothed him. "It's okay." But her voice cracked.

Shem's muscles twitched with fatigue, but he managed to wrap his arms around both of them, holding them tight.

Letting them know that he was still there. Making sure they knew he felt the pain just as much as they did.

In the battlefield below, the sun split the clouds, chasing away the thunder and flooding the terrain with white light. The Twilights' screams rang out through the sky as the light hit them. They wailed, dissolving into thick gray smoke while rising into the clouds. Those who were manipulated under their control dropped their weapons, falling to their knees and blinking in the light as the fog left their eyes.

Willy lifted her head. "Guys, *look*."

Bendigo stood straight now. A warm wind ripped through his clothes, sailing his cloak behind him. The clouds folded into themselves, vanishing and letting the sun pour out over the clifftop. The brown vines that had ebbed from the castle's cracks burst into a rich, lively green, growing higher and expanding to a lushness that brightened the abandoned structure. Whereas the courtyard had been overrun by brittle, dead twigs and parched florae, it now exploded into living colors as plants of all kinds rose from the barren grounds. The pinewoods expanding along the horizon shot taller, spreading their branches to new heights as birds emerged through the tops and sailed toward the open turquoise sky.

Nature was alive again. *Free.*

Bendigo watched the new breeze twirl Willy's hair and send ripples through Shem's loose shirt. The three stood in the moment, too dumbfounded to speak, while not knowing that what they were seeing was only the half of it.

☾

What they didn't know was that the ruins of Orenda stirred. Ash swirled like fog, rising from the ground, recreating, reforming, and rebuilding. The walls that had once stood took shape again. The stains of fire and smoke vanished as if it had never been.

The fallen, split trees lying desolate on the Orphic Forest's floor moaned, leaning upward and awakening toward the sky. All the magical creatures that remained burrowed inside their homes, afraid to venture into their destroyed land, peeked out into the sunlight. They placed their paws, feet, and claws over the soil, rich with dew and soft with a mysterious fresh till.

In the Ports of Orphic, the gray waters capsizing over the rotting boardwalks swirled to a calm, receding to a blue color that matched the sky. Fish leaped out of the water, glinting in the sun's rays, as fishermen threw open their windows and shouted to one another that life had returned.

Lhan no longer was a farmland of ashes. Their black, charred harvest dissipated into the air, fluttering away like the wings of moths, as new crops burst forth from the ground. Their apple trees twisted and knotted into a dance as the red, ripe fruit grew from their arms, replacing what had been lost and more. The barns thundered back into place. Homes reformed like a set of hands placed the pieces back together.

All over the world, restoration poured down like a rainstorm of joyful tears.

☾

In Kalon, an eruption of cheers and shouts from the battlefield below traveled up the cliff to meet Bendigo's ears. The winds of nature's freedom subsided. The river's trickle and birds' songs lingered in the air. Comfort grew like a flourishing vine in his heart, and the sacrifice was suddenly *beautiful* to him. Dagon's blood had brought about life. Hope. To shut your eyes and not wake up was no longer a nightmare to constantly push out of mind. Now, death meant the beginning of life in eternity.

"You were so *brave.*" He grabbed Willy's arms, wincing when the diagonal gash on his back stretched with his movement.

"She was strong down there." Shem gave her a nudge. "A warrior if I ever knew one."

He held his arm over his chest. "Shem. We couldn't have survived without you."

"Something tells me otherwise, but you know I would protect you no matter what."

His eyes bulged. "Zachary?"

"He's safe."

He looked at Willy. "Your parents?"

"My father's gone to the afterlife." She swallowed. "Mom's still here."

"Oh, Willy… I'm so sorry."

She forced a soft smile. "I spent my whole life hating them, only to lose one in a battle we fought in together. There is a sense of closure in that, in the fact we were fighting for the same thing. Proves that there is more to them than I thought. Maybe amends are in the future." She rubbed her arms, awkward at her own words.

"Whatever you decide, I'm here to support you. What about Sophia?"

Willy tilted her chin up toward Shem.

He just shook his head.

"Oh." Bendigo glanced out at the sea, seeing Sophia's face in his mind. He blinked. "I didn't think the wake of something good could be so painful."

"But in time, it will subside," Shem said, exhaustion riding on his breath. "Though it may linger, it won't grip you forever. We have new hope."

The weight of it being just the three of them settled in a little deeper. Their conversation grew mute as they naturally waited for Dagon to make a comment, to say something to lighten their spirits.

"Was he scared?" Willy asked, mournful.

"No." Bendigo drowned a sob before it could form. "He was not. He was willing. Hopeful. Excited to grant us freedom. He loved Tarsha and the people in it."

"The King of Souls." Shem's words meshed perfectly with the sounds of nature. "That's what our warriors have started calling him."

"The King of Souls," Bendigo echoed. "That's what he

is."

Willy looked sly. "They have a name for you too."

He frowned. "They do? What is it?"

She lifted her nose, standing straighter. "Leader of Lands."

The label made him draw back. "Leader? But the battle is won. It's done. Over. I don't have anything to *lead* anymore."

"What do you mean?" Shem pivoted and waved a hand toward the castle. "Kalon, the land of the victory and home to all tribes. The first of its kind. No division between peoples."

He ran a hand over the top of his head. "You mean some fighters want to stay here?"

"They want to build a life here. A city where people of all kinds can live together. Orendans, Lhanians, Whims, Portman, and Orphic creatures." Shem stared up at the stone walls covered in luxurious vines. "It will be a long process, but it's togetherness they want. No more divisions and fear of one another. Magic and realism can collide."

"But that's what our ancestors fought *against*," he said, skeptical. "What if this new generation grows to hate one another again?"

"Our ancestors fought out of fear of one another," Willy disagreed. "Us coming together to take victory over a common evil...that has changed everything. There is a new aura between everyone."

"Love," he exhaled. "It's a love that covers fear."

"That *is* what Dagon told us." Shem nodded. "There is no fear in love."

Bendigo felt affirmation in what he was supposed to do when Dagon's words left Shem's lips. "If they want me to lead, I can't do it alone. I'm too young."

"Who said you'd be alone?" Shem squinted. "I'm with you until the very end. Always." He turned to Willy and gave her a playful raise of the eyebrows. "And don't forget about your lady."

She opened her mouth to protest, but Bendigo cut her off.

"He *knows*, Willy. He knew the whole time."

"Oh." She looked down but then broke into a laugh. "Well, Shem's right. I'm not gonna let you do this alone. And you don't have a choice, Fletcher. Did you *really* think you could get rid of my pestering presence after all these years?"

He grinned. "Wouldn't even dream of such a thing."

Thirty-Three

Biting his lip, Bendigo peered over his shoulder as much as he could to pull the layers of medicated leaves off the gash on his back. He tried to examine the wound by using a mirror that hung in a gold frame.

Every room in the castle had been furnished when he and the army entered through the creaking drawbridge three days ago. Dust laid in films over the furniture, and a lot of wooden pieces were lost to rot, but each person took up the task of restoring the ancient shelter.

Of course, the castle wasn't large enough to hold all three thousand eight hundred of Bendigo's warriors plus those from the Twilight's army who had been released. But after the battle, they only had about two thousand to house. The castle could accommodate that number slightly better, but many warriors took to sleeping on the floor in the supposed ballroom or even outside in the courtyard.

The warriors had become like family to one another: giving up beds and rations for each other, using their skills to tend to the wounded, and putting the kitchen to use with the game the skilled hunters had brought back. It was like each group had something to offer, and together, it made a stable community.

Bendigo examined his back and figured that the stitches a Lhanian woman had woven into his skin were working well. It itched, but that was a sign of healing. She had told him that he was lucky the blade didn't penetrate any further, or he may have severed his spine.

He shuddered at the thought and walked over to the glass door with a green wooden frame that led out to a stone balcony. Lush vines covered the balcony that overlooked the grassland where the battle had taken place. When he stepped out into the air, the sun softened over his face and bare chest, and the sea smell trickled into his nose.

Yesterday, the rugged plain still held bloody red stains from the battle, but a monstrous storm had swept through last night, washing away any evidence of violence. Now the terrain was less menacing, and the pinewoods in the distance rocked with the summer breeze.

It was all so surreal to Bendigo. How he got here. How he had even *made* it. When he left Whimselon, he had thought that he would pass the message on to Dagon and head back home. He never had an ounce of confidence in his soul that would have prepared him for such a journey as the one he had endured.

A wallow of heartbreak clutched at his heart when he thought about Dagon. It had only been three days since the battle, and the pain hadn't subsided. It felt like losing his father all over again.

"I miss you," he whispered to the air.

As a flutter of wind caught his words, a single white

cloud passed over the sun.

Bendigo squinted, leaning forward, and focused hard on the pinewood tree line. A figure stood at the edge of the forest. Tan skin, familiar clothing, and hard to make out in the distance but known well enough for Bendigo to figure it out.

Dagon.

He almost fell over the balcony's edge. He wanted to shout Dagon's name, tell him to come to the castle and reside with them in their new home. Yet as he opened his mouth, no sound came out. As if something prevented him. To his aching heart, the sight of Dagon was a sweet, sweet relief, but he knew Dagon wasn't here to stay. It was displayed in the way Dagon didn't move from the tree line and how his hair wasn't moving in the breeze. Nor did his body cast a shadow. He was here to say goodbye—or his spirit was.

Dropping his shoulders, Bendigo rested his elbows on the balcony's edge and smiled across the terrain. Though they were far from each other, their eyes met. Rays of sunlight surrounded the balcony, and the clouds parted over Dagon's head. With a slow raise of his hand, Dagon gave him a final wave.

He lifted his hand into the air. "Goodbye, King of Souls."

Dagon's spirit dissipated into thin air and vanished like smoke rising from a chimney. Though this time, watching him go didn't hurt as much. Death had taken Dagon from *this* place, but death had not destroyed him. In fact, it was quite the opposite. Dagon had defeated death, and that was worth the pain.

Light footsteps crept up from behind him, and Willy's smooth arms slid around his waist. She stood on her tiptoes and leaned into him, careful to avoid his wound. Bringing her lips to just behind his ear, she gave him a gentle kiss. "What are you doing up here?"

He grabbed her hands and pulled them up to his chest. "Saying goodbye one last time."

She brought her eyebrows close together but dropped the manner and smiled against his skin. "I have a surprise for you."

"Oh?"

"Hold on."

She pulled her arms away and reached behind the door frame where she had hidden her gift: a stack of blank papers held together by bits of twine and a leather satchel of pastel colors and assorted brushes.

His mouth fell wide.

She grinned. "It's an artist's set."

"Where did you *get* this?" He touched the leather bag.

"Sophia. She had brought it with her from Orenda. She was going to give it to you after the battle."

"Wow…"

"She knew you were an artist. Now you can at least give it a try."

He took the kit and marveled at the opportunity in his

hands. "Thank you, Willy, for making sure I got this."

"Of course. I just want you to be happy."

He placed the kit at his feet and grabbed her hands. "I *am* happy. I may battle sadness, as I usually do, but I'm happy."

"Me too."

"We're different people than we were in Whimselon, aren't we?"

She snickered. "Oh yeah. In the best way possible though, don't you think?"

He ran a hand through her hair. "Without a single doubt. Tell me something."

"Yeah?"

"Did you love me in Whimselon?"

There was a hint of a blush. "I don't know if I would call it love at first, but I was definitely…attached to you. And I may have imagined what it would be like to kiss you one too many times."

Laughing, he moved his lips to hers but stopped right before they touched. "Are the real ones as good as the imaginary ones?"

"Better."

He was livened as her lips connected with his. The feel of her body in his hands was more than he could handle, but he continued.

She lifted her mouth and stared up at him. "I'm glad we're staying here."

"So am I."

"And as much as I want to keep kissing you, everyone is waiting for you downstairs."

"Is it that time already?" He drew back slightly.

"Yeah. Your brother will want to say goodbye."

"Then I guess we must go."

Willy left his arms and trailed away. "I'll meet you down there. I promised the travelers that I would help pack their horses."

"Okay. Let them know I'll be right there." He shrugged back into his shirt.

Those who wished to return home were parading out this morning. Bendigo had tried to convince Zachary to stay in Kalon, but they both knew that Whimselon needed a trustworthy leader, and Zach had proven to be so as he led the warriors across the lands to get to Bendigo.

Shutting the balcony doors, he stood in the silence of his room. A prick of awareness struck the back of his neck, and he took his time turning around to face his bed. His blood pulsed. Sitting on the bed, appearing as if dropped from the sky, was The Book. Its cover lay open, revealing a page that had not yet been read.

Bendigo inched forward, gazing at the pages and trying to piece it together. Dagon had said that he was The Book, therefore The Book should have disappeared with his death, but now, here it lay. Perhaps it was here because Dagon was not, in fact, dead but in the afterlife.

The tips of his fingers grazed the opened page. Words. Beautiful words. As he read them, his heartbreak disappeared.

Dear friends,

From evil, light has come. There will never be a victory for death again in the ages to come. Hope has returned, and one day, you will see me again. You are here today and one day will be gone, but I'm here waiting for you. Press on, my warriors, for I am with you in spirit.

— Dagon

Acknowledgements

There are a lot of people to thank, but I must start off with my husband. From the moment I told him I wanted to self-publish, he was all for it. He never once doubted my ability to produce this book into what it has become. And he deserves a medal for supporting me through the numerous breakdowns I had in the process.

Then there is the family that I grew up with. My dad, mom and sister. They have always known that one day I would publish my work. It was never a question. When I was too small to write words, I would draw pictures in story form and my sister would write the words for me. My dad showed me how to use Microsoft Word so I could start typing full length books, and my mom has read everything I've sent her way. It helps to have a supportive family who sees your passions as much as you do. I'm grateful for growing up in a home where books were treasured, discussed and written.

To my little son. Even you had a part to play in this. You remind me that sitting behind a computer all day (even if I'm enjoying it) isn't as rewarding as watching you go down a slide at the playground or going on walks to collect acorns.

To my Instagram writing community: Y'all are the bomb. The highest level of support comes from you. I have made genuine connections with other writers, readers and creators who are on the same publication journey as me and it has made this process that much sweeter.

Elysia, I bet you didn't know you'd be in here! Having found a writing buddy on Instagram who just so happened to live in the same city as me was God's hand. You've been a huge source of encouragement and I can't wait to keep writing books together.

An expansive thanks to Robin LeeAnn for editing my novel and cleaning it up to be crisp, clear and wonderful. Your insight has helped me to grow as a writer and I am incredibly thankful.

To Rena, for creating the cover design that I always dreamed of. You exceeded my expectations. I can't say thank you enough.

And lastly, but not least, I thank God for giving me the passion, gift and drive to write. There are a lot of things in this world that are painful, depressing and difficult. Because God knows me, he knows how deeply I feel all of those things. So, he gave me words. He gave me a way to experience goodness while I'm here on this Earth. I will forever be thankful to Him for allowing me to publish my works. All glory to God and may I never make it about me.

CONNECT WITH ME

Follow me on Instagram: @keira.f.jacobs
Follow me on TikTok: @authorkeira.f.jacobs

Keira F. Jacobs lives in South Carolina with her husband and son. She drinks coffee too much, laughs too loud, and doesn't know if she has a southern twang or a mid-western accent anymore. Perhaps a mix of both.

Follow her social media pages to stay in the loop on future work. Read her poem, "The Sisters in the Attic" in the Exquisite Poison Anthology by Phantom House Press.

Lightning Source UK Ltd.
Milton Keynes UK
UKHW010817121222
413794UK00004B/392